BOUND BY BLOOD

MORECAMBE BAY TRILOGY 2

PAUL J. TEAGUE

ALSO BY PAUL J. TEAGUE

Morecambe Bay Trilogy 1

Book 1 - Left For Dead

Book 2 - Circle of Lies

Book 3 - Truth Be Told

Morecambe Bay Trilogy 2

Book 4 - Trust Me Once

Book 5 - Fall From Grace

Book 6 - Bound By Blood

Morecambe Bay Trilogy 3

Book 7 - First To Die

Book 8 - Nothing To Lose

Book 9 - Last To Tell

Note: The Morecambe Bay trilogies are best read in the order shown above.

Don't Tell Meg Trilogy

Features DCI Kate Summers and Steven Terry.

Book 1 - Don't Tell Meg

Book 2 - The Murder Place

Book 3 - The Forgotten Children

Standalone Thrillers

Dead of Night

One Last Chance

No More Secrets

So Many Lies

Two Years After

Friends Who Lie

Now You See Her

PROLOGUE

7:53 pm December 31st, 1999

Tiffany knew that carrying out their plans would destroy the tattered remnants of her family, but it was too late to go back now, even if she wanted to. She loved Brett, and it was high time she left her brief and miserable marriage. Somehow, she'd got caught in a trap of relationships, money, property and children. Everything was a mess and unpicking it would have a massive impact. She secretly hoped it might also knock the smug smirk off David's face once and for all.

She had to look her best for the event, that much she understood. She would trot out everything David loved about her – or had once loved – like a tired circus act, but she'd deliver her final performance with full show business panache. It was time to play her finest role as a supportive wife, doting mother and pillar of the community. Nobody must know they were about to stitch up her brother and her husband, rendering them impotent in a way that would enrage both of the narcissistic monsters.

They hadn't always been like this. Fabian had been a good brother when they were children, but she'd seen the first signs of his appetites as a young teenager. He'd quickly become entrepreneurial and ambitious, and his greed and determination came to know no bounds.

She'd loved David too once, for a short time, but he and her brother were a dangerous combination. Like Bonnie and Clyde, Fred and Rosemary West or Ian Brady and Myra Hindley, there was something about the pairing that brought out the very worst in both. And David had little time for the kids. It was such a corny mistake to make in their marriage, but Tiffany had made it; she lived for the children, but David didn't. And when Rowan came along... well, David must have suspected something wasn't right.

Brett offered her a way out. But she was no ordinary housewife, making a midnight dash with a new lover. There were three children involved for starters, and a property and land inheritance potentially worth millions. Then there was the issue of the power of attorney granted to her brother while she was suffering from post-natal depression. Tiffany had long cursed the accident of biology which meant a wonderful experience like giving birth had brought her crashing down to the depths of a depression so desperate that she would attempt to take her own life. In a moment of weakness, Fabian struck and had her temporarily committed. He might as well have locked her in a cupboard and thrown away the key. Her existence became one of reliance and appeasement, a cage from which she saw no escape until Brett entered her life.

Tiffany checked her hair in the full-length mirror.

David had always preferred it worn up. He loved her neck, or so he said. Whether he'd even noticed it for the past year was another matter altogether, but he'd desired her once; he would surely notice what she'd done.

That bitch Joanne Taylor was getting her precious children ready. She was another insult Tiffany had been forced to accept. They'd agreed to let the kids sleep as long as they wanted to, in the vague hope they might make it to midnight without tears, tantrums and over-tiredness forcing them to leave before the new millennium showed its face.

David was sleeping with Joanne, she knew it. Their affair had started before he had brought her into their home to care for the children. It was some way of recruiting a new childminder: give the job to someone you're sleeping with. She would have admired the sheer audacity of it if it hadn't been so crushing for her. Tiffany didn't just want to leave; she was desperate to hurt the bastard for everything he'd done.

There was nothing like a tight, black dress showing lots of cleavage to draw the attention of the men. She hated her feminist self for even playing that card, but it was a means to an end, part of a greater plan for that night. She adjusted her bra, which was much less practical than she preferred, checked her lipstick wasn't smudged and made her way downstairs.

The moment she entered the kitchen, she could tell they'd just pulled away from each other. This was what her life was like now, constantly hearing whispers and sensing intimate liaisons in rooms around the house. Damn the woman for living under the same roof as them, masquerading as the nanny. Tiffany had wondered if she was descending into the black hole of madness again, but

Brett reassured her she wasn't. Being with Brett calmed her mind and helped her make sense of her world.

David could barely contain his contempt for her. They were hardly touching each other when she fell pregnant with Rowan; little wonder he had his suspicions.

Joanne had played the same card as she had, with a figure-hugging, sleek dress, an expensive haircut, her cleavage on full display and a make-up job worthy of a professional. She looked spectacular; no wonder David had fallen so hard for her. But the evil, money-grabbing bitch had seen her opportunity, making no attempt to hide her contempt for Tiffany when David wasn't around. It was time for revenge; she and Brett would have the last laugh.

'Good, you're ready,' David said, barely looking at her. 'I've had to change my plans, I'm afraid. I need to leave at ten o'clock to meet a business contact in Morecambe. It can't be helped, but I'll do my bit with the villagers until then.'

Had he seen the look of panic on her face? She tried to conceal it, but it seemed he could read her mind these days. She ran through the implications of this change to the schedule. She would have to warn Brett to take more care. If David was out in the car park early, he might spot him there, waiting for their moment to escape.

'I just need to go upstairs again, I've forgotten to unplug my straighteners,' she lied. Brett had to know about the change of plan; this might be the last chance to call him. She had to put the tickets in her handbag too. It was safest to do that at the last moment. If David or Joanne saw them, it would be game over. Even Brett wasn't aware of that part of her plan.

She did her best to walk calmly up to the bedroom,

trying not to look like she was up to something. Hastily, she texted Brett.

David leaving village hall at 10. *Will get out asap after that. Don't forget passport. Will explain later. Take care, don't let him see you x*

She put her phone in her bag and slid her hand under the mattress. The tickets were still there. Her heart gave a jump; she'd half expected them to be gone. They had to get away tonight. The legal document revoking David's power of attorney over her affairs came into force at one minute past midnight. By then, she'd be away with Brett and they wouldn't be able to touch her any longer. Then Fabian, David and Joanne could all go to hell.

She placed the envelope in the inner compartment of her bag and zipped it shut. It was showtime.

The village hall affair was as she'd imagined. They'd done a wonderful job of making the place look amazing, with helium-filled balloons and streamers all over the place. The village hall committee had made the ordinarily bland chairs and tables look spectacular, thanks to some artfully placed accessories and table decorations. David's contribution took pride of place on the stage: an expensive flat screen TV, on which they would watch the celebrations from around the country. The village DJ was there, filling in between sets from a competent covers band. And all around were fractious, over-excited children who should have been in bed hours ago, and tense parents praying they might make it to see in one of the most important new year events of their lifetime.

David left at ten o'clock, as he'd said he would. He'd spent much of the evening with Joanne, circulating with his lover, confirming the villagers' usual gossip and idle speculation. He let Tiffany know he was leaving with a few scant words. She glanced around to check Joanne's whereabouts, then texted Brett. Her new year and her new life would begin as soon as David had gone. This was the last time she would see him. When the chimes sounded for midnight, they would be well on their way.

She checked around for Joanne again. Where was she? Had she left with David? It was ten past ten and Brett would be waiting out there, expecting her at any moment. Rowan obliged by crying when a particularly loud track burst through the DJ's speakers. It was her cue. She gathered the children together and made her excuses to the villagers she'd been exchanging pleasantries with.

'I'm so sorry, it doesn't look like I'm going to make it; Rowan's had enough now. I'll be with you in spirit.'

It took a good ten minutes to get out of the village hall. She wished she could have told them all to get lost and leave her alone, but she knew they meant well. What a relief it was to step out into the crisp, fresh night air.

Brett flashed his lights at her from the far end of the car park. He'd concealed himself well from David.

Suddenly, Joanne appeared from nowhere and rushed towards her, accompanied by a man she'd seen only once before. She had a vague idea he was a doctor. He raised his arm, and she felt a short, sharp prick in her neck. As Tiffany fell to the ground, she heard David's voice.

After that, it was a mess of fragments: a drive to a remote place, lots of car lights and hushed, hurried conversations, a terrible commotion, Brett shouting, a gun shot... then panic. Tiffany felt herself fading, and everything went black.

When she came round, she was in the driver's seat of the car, in a strange place, with the engine still running. Her head felt as if it was smothered with a thick blanket of fog, and she was only dimly aware of Brett's sister Kate at her side, in a panic, with fear in her voice, dragging her out of the vehicle, laying her on the ground. And the children. The children were gone, and Rowan's teddy bear toy was bobbing about in the sea. Oh God, what had they done?

CHAPTER ONE

Charlotte was shivering uncontrollably. While Vinnie had been on her tail, she'd pushed the bone-chilling coldness to the back of her mind, but now, crouching on the exposed platform at the base of the wind turbine far out at sea, it was all she could think of. It seemed to take the maintenance team an age to make what looked like a short crossing, but having been deceived once already by the scale of the turbines, she decided her eyes must be playing tricks on her. At last her rescuers pulled up their boat beside the ladder, their heavy feet clanking on the steps of the steel rungs.

'Bring up a blanket!' the first man shouted down to one of his colleagues. He pulled himself up onto the platform and rushed over to Charlotte.

'Are you okay? Can you understand me?'

Charlotte's mouth was so numb that she could only manage a few words.

'I'm cold, very cold.'

A woman joined them on the platform, tearing open a packet and pulling out a foil blanket. Charlotte had seen them on TV and had always wondered what use they'd be.

'She doesn't seem too bad,' the woman said. 'Her eyes are alert; we need to get her on the boat and out of those wet clothes.'

'How the hell did you even get out here?' the man asked.

'I took a wrong turn on my jet-ski,' Charlotte answered.

'Well, she's still got a sense of humour, so it can't be too bad,' the woman observed.

'We're going to help you onto the boat. What's your name?' the man asked.

'Charlotte.'

'Okay, Charlotte, let's get you onto the boat so you can change out of those clothes. All we can offer you is a pair of overalls and an oversized T-shirt, but they should help, at least. Is there anybody we need to call?'

Charlotte thought about Lucia; should she let her know what had happened? Yes, she must. Her daughter was on alert to call the police. She needed to speak to the police as well, but she had a plan for that which could wait until later. She didn't want to risk the cops swarming around like a nest of angry ants. To keep Will safe, she'd have to get the police involved at the right time.

'Later,' she replied. 'Will call later. Please don't get the police—'

'I'm not so sure we can promise that,' the man answered. 'You've entered private property and got into trouble at sea. There are rules and regulations—'

The woman glared at him.

'Bill—'

'What?'

'Don't be a prick. She's a middle-aged woman who came a cropper on a jet-ski. I'll put money on her being a professional of some sort.'

'But—'

'No need to be a dick about it. Let's get her warmed up and think this through.'

Bill nodded and offered Charlotte his arm to help her up. She shuffled to the edge of the platform. Although there were barriers around it, the view down to the boat was still daunting, with the waves thundering below. When she'd been climbing up there, fuelled by adrenaline, it hadn't seemed so high. Even with Vinnie out of the way – for now – she was scared to make her descent. Bill and the woman both helped her down to the boat where two other male crew mates were waiting on board.

'Right, give the lady some privacy,' the woman said. 'I'm Tina, by the way. Come through here with me and we'll get you into some dry clothes. How about you get the kettle on, Bill?'

This woman appeared to be in charge, or at least she had the respect of the crew. Charlotte accepted her help to get out of her wet clothing; it was like peeling off a second skin. She dried herself off with a small hand towel and chose some clothes from the mixed array they'd managed to piece together between them. She felt like she was selecting random items from a jumble sale.

'Sorry, I've no knickers to offer you, but I can assure you those shorts are clean. You might find the overalls a bit more forgiving with them on.'

Charlotte mused over how her life had come to this low point. For the third time in a week, she needed emergency underwear.

There was a knock at the door.

'It's safe to come in,' Tina called.

Bill entered cautiously, holding two cups of steaming liquid.

'I made cup-a-soups; it seemed like the best thing to do.'

'Good call, Bill.' Tina smiled at him. 'Why don't you and the guys finish the last checks while I take care of Charlotte here? Give me a shout if you need me.'

'Will do,' Bill replied, leaving them to it.

Charlotte took a seat, grateful to be in dry clothes. Tina encouraged her to wrap the foil blanket around her and as the chicken soup made its way into her belly, she felt much better and ready to talk.

'So how does a woman like you end up stranded at the base of a wind turbine? You're lucky; they're usually locked up, but we left the ladder down to leave some equipment there before heading back to shore.'

'Well, thank God it was,' Charlotte replied. She could feel her mouth now. 'It was only from talking to a chap called Sam Halford about this place that I thought to—'

'You know Sam?'

'Yes. I take it you wind turbine people are all familiar with each other?' Charlotte asked.

'Yes, I know Sam. We work for a different company, but he's up at Walney regularly, so I see him around. He's a good guy, he knows his stuff. How did you come across him?'

'I work for the Morecambe newspaper,' Charlotte replied. 'I did an interview with him. I'm just thankful these turbines are here; I don't know what I'd have done otherwise.'

'Do you mind if I ask how you got out here?' Tina probed.

Charlotte took a chance. Bill sounded like a by-the-book kind of guy, but she sensed Tina wasn't.

'I'm in a spot of trouble—'

'You can say that again,' Tina laughed. 'Most women

just forget their handbag or break off a heel.'

'Yes, well, I don't like to do things by halves.'

Charlotte took another sip of her soup, now it was cooling. The sea was rough, tossing the boat around and making it tricky to keep the cup steady. She hoped she wouldn't throw up; it would add insult to injury.

'Bill was talking about reporting this incident. Is there any way we can avoid that?' she chanced. 'Can you delay things until I sort myself out?'

Tina studied her face.

'Are you running away from somebody?'

'Something like that,' Charlotte replied. 'I've got myself into a scrape and I'm figuring out how to get out of it. I'd rather not get the authorities involved just yet. My husband is in danger too.'

'Jeez, Charlotte, why does it feel like the female James Bond just washed up on my wind turbine? I thought something was up when you didn't have a wetsuit on. Nobody rides a jet-ski at sea without a wetsuit. At least you had flares with you to alert us.'

'The jet-ski wasn't even mine. I stole it.'

Tina looked at Charlotte again, a twinkle of admiration in her eyes.

'I hope I'm still stirring up shit like you when I'm your age. No offence meant. I'm late thirties, but you must be... what, late forties?'

'You've just improved an unbelievably bad day.' Charlotte laughed. 'I'm early fifties. It must be the bedraggled hair that makes it difficult to tell.'

Charlotte was relieved to see Tina seemed to be in charge; Bill might not be so accommodating. However, when he knocked at the door and announced they'd managed to haul the jet-ski out of the water, she felt a gush of gratitude towards him. At least taking the vehicle out of circulation for a few days would let Jed have his peace and quiet.

'Here's what I can do for you,' Tina said after a while. 'I'll need to report this in our logs, but I can hold it back a day or two if that helps. I can see this wasn't an attempt at vandalism or a protest, and we didn't need to call out the rescue services, so I can probably make this go away for you—'

'I'd be so grateful if you could,' Charlotte said. 'Just for a day or two; I'll have this sorted out soon.'

It was easy to promise. It would be much harder to deliver. But Charlotte did have half a plan, at least. And it involved Toni Lawson, the police press officer.

'I know it probably doesn't feel this way, but it's your lucky day. We're heading for Barrow Docks right now, but Dae-Ho lives in Galgate; I'm sure I can sweet-talk him into giving you a lift back to your neck of the woods. How does that sound?'

'Perfect, thank you,' Charlotte replied.

'Can I encourage you to get yourself checked out by a doctor or go to A&E?' Tina suggested. Her tone implied she wasn't hopeful about that happening any time soon.

'I feel much better now, honestly, I do.' Charlotte did her best to sound reassuring. 'I'm so grateful for what you've done; I can't tell you how much it's appreciated. But I must get home as soon as possible.'

'I thought you might say that.' Tina said. 'But at least I can say I tried. Do you want me to tell your husband... partner, or family that you're safe?'

Charlotte shook her head.

'No need to do that. I intend telling my husband in person.'

CHAPTER TWO

Charlotte had never been more grateful for a lift than on the drive back from Barrow Docks to Morecambe. Dae-Ho made easy company and seemed to have been warned by Tina to refrain from asking too many questions. Instead he chatted to Charlotte about foreign travel, his love of science fiction and his penchant for sled racing with his Siberian Huskies. The obscure nature of their conversation would have sat well in a bizarre dream, but it provided a welcome distraction from what she'd just been through.

The only awkward moment had been when Bill and Dae-Ho were lifting the jet-ski onto the trailer Dae-Ho used for transporting his dogs to shows.

'There are some nasty marks on your bodywork. What caused those holes? It looks like someone's been shooting at you.'

Charlotte could only muster an awkward laugh, avoiding giving an answer. Dae-Ho looked at her as if waiting for a reply, but Tina kindly moved them on.

'So, remember, I'll have to write this up, but I'll give you a day or two. It might slip through the net, but it might not.

Either way, you got carried out by the tide, managed to use your last fuel to steer over to the platform at the bottom of the turbine and you're very grateful for the heroic efforts of me and my team saving your life against terrific odds. Okay?'

'You missed out the bit about how you single-handedly leapt from the boat to my rescue, ignoring the ferocious waves and risking your own life to save a fellow seafarer,' Charlotte laughed.

'And that bit too,' Tina continued. 'Stick to the story and it should all go away. Mind if I ask what was going on out there? Off the record, I mean.'

'I doubt you'd believe me if I told you.'

'Try me,' Tina ventured.

'My husband is being held hostage because I possess information which might cause a problem for some powerful people. One of them was chasing me and shooting at my jet-ski. I managed to out-run him because I got lucky and chose the vehicle with the most fuel.'

Tina looked at her, her face completely straight. Then she burst out laughing.

'Okay, don't tell me then. But that's a pretty good tale. I like the way you brought in the bit about the gun after what Bill and Dae-Ho were saying.'

She was pleased she'd found an instant friend in Tina, who reminded her of George when she and Will had met him as teenagers at the holiday camp. He was a helper rather than a hinderer; even though he could have made life difficult for them, he chose not to. Tina was a blessing at the end of a challenging day.

As Dae-Ho explained the finer points of sled racing, Charlotte tuned out for a while, enjoying the views along the long road to the motorway as she took stock of her situation.

What had become clear to her from her conversation with Vinnie Mace was that she now had some leverage. Although her hand was weak, given that they were holding her husband hostage, she knew they needed the documents she'd hidden, and they desperately wanted to locate Kate Summers. She had to believe Vinnie had shot at her to disable the jet-ski rather than to kill her. A man who'd been so accomplished in the military wouldn't miss his prey, even if the waves were a bit wild when he was trying to fire his weapon.

She felt in her pocket for her mobile phone, which she'd transferred to her overalls earlier. It was still there. Now she would see if it was as waterproof as the manufacturer claimed on the box. Charlotte couldn't believe her luck; it was still switched on and the display lit up when she touched it. She'd be leaving a five-star review on the website, for sure.

What a mess she must look, she thought as she ran her hands through her hair, stiff and unforgiving from being drenched with sea water. She pulled down the vanity mirror and took a cautious look. It was as bad as she feared; a gaunt face stared back at her.

Dae-Ho had paused for a moment, concentrating on overtaking a tractor which had created a long tailback along the road. Charlotte took the opportunity to make some calls.

'Excuse me while I check in with some people.'

The first message was a text to Lucia. She couldn't call in person yet, for fear of getting emotional. She had to stay strong and focused; finding Will was her priority.

Next she needed to contact Nigel. She'd left the car unlocked at Sunderland Point and Vinnie was bound to have searched it thoroughly, possibly damaging it in the process. It could also have been caught by the tide in the car park, though she had parked it as high as possible up the concrete ramp. She wouldn't be able to retrieve it until the next day now. She decided to take a chance and tell a white lie.

'Hi Nigel, I'm running late. Is it okay if I keep the car with me overnight?'

There was a pause while Nigel checked the booking system.

'I've booked it out all day for you and me. I'll take it when you get back; I have a couple of jobs tomorrow afternoon.'

She finished the call and decided to take a chance. This was too big for her to handle on her own. Telling Tina the truth had felt cathartic, almost confessional, even though she'd thought Charlotte was joking. Kate Summers had warned her off confiding in the officers at the police station. But she hadn't told her not to speak to the press officer, Toni Lawson, who acted as a go-between for the press, the suits and the rank and file officers. She had access to everybody, yet she wasn't one of the troops on the ground. The two women had got on well enough on the two occasions they'd met; it had to be worth a chance, reaching out and seeking her advice. Toni owed her one for passing her toilet tissue in her moment of need at Morecambe Town Hall.

She dialled but Toni's voicemail was on, so all she could do was leave a message.

'Hi Toni, it's Charlotte. Charlotte Grayson. From the newspaper. Can we speak? Not on the phone, but in person. There's a café by the Winter Gardens, it's called Brucciani's; how about there, just before closing time? It's important. Police business, but something I must discuss with you first. Hope you can make it. Shall we aim for five o'clock? No need to call if you're tied up, just text.'

It was all she could do for now, in her exhausted state. The thought of Will, held hostage and terrified, mortified her, but she could do nothing about it. Vinnie was no amateur Morecambe backstreet hoodlum; they'd keep Will safe until they got what they wanted, and so it was up to her to prevent them getting hold of the documents that she'd taken from Kate's house.

Dae-Ho had managed to pass the tractor at last and was now in full flow about his love of science fiction. He was rattling through a list of authors, most of whom she'd never heard of. When Ray Bradbury's name was mentioned, it was enough for her to grasp onto and sustain a superficial conversation until he pulled up at the rear of the Lakes View Guest House. She'd guided him along the back alleyway, firstly because they had to do something with the jet-ski and secondly because she wanted to go in via the back door, in case the building was being watched. In her current dishevelled state, even her family might not recognise her.

With Dae-Ho's help, she managed to wrestle the jet-ski into a vacant parking place. She removed the key to render it useless should anybody try to steal it, then thanked Dae-Ho for his help.

Charlotte made her way through the back door into the hallway. She stopped dead when she saw who was sitting there. There was no doubt about the birthmark; it was Callie Irwin.

CHAPTER THREE

'Callie Irwin?'

'No, Callie Whitehead. But people keep telling me I'm Callie Irwin. I take it you're Charlotte Grayson?'

Isla stepped out of the kitchen, having heard the voices.

'Oh good, you're back, Charlotte. I see you've met Callie already. Is everything okay? We've been desperately worried about you. There's been no sight of Will, or Lucia come to that. I hope you're not in any trouble.'

There was no fooling Isla; she knew Charlotte well enough by now to sense when something serious was going on. They all had past form.

'Things are a bit fraught at the moment, but I'm on top of it for now. Thanks for asking, Isla. And thank you so much for holding the fort. I promise we'll be back to normal soon.'

Isla didn't look convinced.

'I'll leave you and Callie to talk. If you need me or George, just ask, Charlotte. You only have to ask.'

'I know, Isla, and I appreciate it. Thank you.'

Isla returned to the kitchen, leaving Charlotte thankful for the slight lull in bookings which allowed the staff to get on with it.

There was no mistaking Callie; the birthmark was still prominent on her face, and the police had already done the job of confirming the DNA. Charlotte took the chair opposite and tried to decide where to begin. Callie did her a favour and spoke first.

'I've come to you because I saw your article in the newspaper. I did some online research on you after you phoned me in the hospital—'

'Oh, so it was you who answered that day. I did wonder, as nobody spoke.'

'I need someone I can trust, someone who isn't official. My head's exploding with all this. I just want some straight answers. My life has been turned upside down in the past week.'

'You call yourself Callie Whitehead,' Charlotte began. 'Why, when we all know you as Callie Irwin?'

'One month ago, I got an email out of the blue from someone I've never heard of before. They told me I was adopted and the people I've always regarded as Mum and Dad are not my birth parents. It came as such a shock.'

'Oh my God,' was all Charlotte could say. 'What did you do?'

'I took the train back from university and asked my mum and dad point blank. That night was horrendous. There were tears, denials and a lot of shouting.'

'I'm so sorry,' Charlotte said, trying to race ahead and figure out what had happened. 'It's a lot to take in.'

'You bet your life it is,' Callie continued. 'It ended with them admitting they adopted me at the age of four. They were desperate and found me through a private agency. It cost them every last penny they had. Until we had that conversation, I'd had a wonderful life with two incredible parents.'

'What did the email say? Why did you come to Morecambe?'

She stopped, realising Callie was becoming emotional.

'Can I get you a drink or something to eat?' she asked.

'A drink of water would be great, thank you.'

Charlotte went into the kitchen to fetch it.

'Next time you're serving chips, would you put some extras in a bowl for Callie, please?'

The way Isla glanced at her showed she knew something important was going on. Her mother had given her a similar look the first time she stayed out all night as a teenager. She'd tell Isla everything as soon as she could.

Callie took the water gratefully.

'I heard from the police that you have diabetes. Are you okay? Do you need any medical attention?'

'They issued my prescription in the hospital, so I'm fine for a while, thank you. I made the oldest mistake in the book for diabetics. That day on the seafront, I'd been walking around Morecambe all day, covering miles, and I was exhausted. I'd eaten the wrong food because I was so angry and confused, and I forgot to take my medication with me. You'd think I'd know better, the length of time I've had to get used to this condition.'

'So, you've always known yourself as Callie Whitehead. What did the email tell you?'

'It was anonymous, of course. I didn't even know whether to believe it at first. But they sent another one, telling me my real name was Callie Irwin and my birth mother was still alive. Then a day later, I received a small package with a wedding ring inside, a newspaper cutting and a note. *This belongs to your real mother,* it said. It was post marked from Morecambe. I started doing some research, found the news reports online and after questioning Mum and Dad, I came up here to find out for myself.'

'So how on earth do you know Hollie Wickes?'

'You know Hollie? How? I only just found out about her.'

Callie looked shocked, as if everybody else was ten steps ahead of her.

'My husband knows her; he's a teacher at the university. How did she come into your orbit?'

'I got a third note at the hospital, telling me I should call her. I didn't tell the police. Someone slipped it into my dressing gown pocket while I was in a diabetic coma. And there were those photos in the brown envelope of people I'd never seen before. The police kept those; I had no idea who the people were. The note just had Hollie's name and a number. It said: *You're bound by blood. Call her and see.* What the hell does that mean?'

'Do you have any clues on who sent the emails?'

Callie shook her head.

'It was some nondescript email address. Perhaps it was the mystery person who sneaked into my room to leave the note. The police are as clueless as I am. I thought you might be able to help.'

'You know they've been looking for you since you left the hospital, don't you?'

It suddenly occurred to Charlotte that she was speaking to a fugitive of sorts.

'I'm not a criminal, I'm a victim here. Besides, the police can't protect me. Someone just walked into my room in the ICU, for God's sake. This is my life; it's not something the police can toy with. I want to speak to Hollie myself and find out what's going on. I'll call the police and let them know I'm safe. They can still speak to me; I won't screw up their investigation. But I have to figure out what's going on here. If only Hollie would answer my damned messages.'

Charlotte wondered if her expression was giving her away.

'I'm sorry, I have something to do with that. I have Hollie's phone, or rather I had Hollie's phone. It's a long story, but it's in the glove compartment of the company car, which is parked at Sunderland Point at the moment. I saw your calls and wondered what the hell was going on. Hollie had you recorded in her contacts as *Callie?* so I wonder if she received messages from this mystery person too.'

'Why do you have Hollie's phone?' Callie snapped.

'As I said, it's a long story. But if it's any consolation, I can take you directly to Hollie Wickes. Both you and I need to find some answers from her.'

Isla brought a bowl of chips over on a tray.

'Thanks, Isla, that's great. Are you allowed to eat chips, Callie?'

'Yes, thank you. Remember, I don't know who Callie Irwin is. That's why I'm here. You can help me, so I don't have to get involved with the police.'

She looked away, avoiding Charlotte's gaze.

'And I need somewhere to stay. I was also thinking of contacting that Nigel Davies chap who's also reporting on the news story, but he doesn't have a guest house. I hope it's not too much to ask?'

'It's no problem at all. Of course we can find you a room here.'

'I'll leave these with you,' Isla said, passing over the tray. 'As I said, if George or I can help out, just say.'

Charlotte nodded.

'I hope those chips will keep you going for now. We can cook something more substantial for you later if you'd like. Just tell me what you can and can't eat. We cater for a lot of vegetarians and vegans these days, but I don't have much experience with diabetics.'

Callie tucked into the chips and Charlotte gave her some time to finish the bowlful. They were gone in no time at all.

'So, what are we going to do next?' Charlotte asked.

'I want to understand what happened,' Callie replied. 'I can't get my head around this; it's been so sudden. If I hadn't fallen into a coma and then had the police confirm it through the DNA test, I wouldn't have believed it. Apparently, my birth mother is somewhere in this town, but nobody can tell me where. Or they don't want to tell me. I bet you know, don't you?'

Charlotte thought about Tiffany, held in the care home as if it was a prison, wondering for all those years what had happened to her babies. She couldn't begin to contemplate how painful it must be.

'I do know where your mother is. I've met her and I'm sure there wasn't a day that passed without her thinking about you and your siblings—'

'And that's another thing,' Callie interrupted. 'The news stories reckon I'm supposed to have a brother too. And what the hell happened to my birth dad? Did he survive? My head feels like it's going to explode. It's so hard to deal with it all.' Her voice quivered with emotion.

Charlotte put her arm out to comfort her.

'Where do you want to start?' she asked quietly.

'At the beginning,' Callie replied. 'I want to go to the slipway and hear the full story from you, with nothing left out. I want to understand what happened that night. And then I want to find my birth family.'

CHAPTER FOUR

Christmas 1998

Tiffany placed the final bauble on the Christmas tree and held up the golden star for Callie and Jane to look at in the playpen. She'd put the tree close enough for them to get a good look, but not so close that they could lunge for any of the decorations. Both were at the stage where anything small and capable of choking them invariably ended up in their mouths. And now the baby was kicking away like it wanted to break out and enjoy its first Christmas ahead of schedule.

It was a struggle to stretch up and place the star on the tree, with her stomach being so rounded. She placed it to the side; she'd ask David to do it when – or if – he decided to show his face that night.

'Okay Callie, Jane, are you ready for the lights?'

Excitement burst from the confinement of the playpen. She counted down from three; after all, it was never too soon to start basic number work.

'Ready? Three... two... one... go!'

The lights began to flash, making both girls whoop with delight. Tiffany moved over to the light switch and turned off the main lighting in the living room. The glow from the bulbs cast pretty shadows from the branches across the walls and the blue, yellow, red and green hues created a pyrotechnics display for the two children to wonder at.

Tiffany sat in the armchair by the side of the tree and gave her legs a rest. This baby seemed heavier than the first two; she couldn't recall waddling at six months before.

She heard a car door slam outside. The children jumped in expectation and moments later David Irwin burst through the door. His mood on entering the house was all-important. There was a time, not so long ago, when he would step into the hallway and give the children a cheery welcome. It had been short-lived. The children picked up on his mood immediately and Jane began to cry.

As he came into view in the doorway of the lounge, he tripped over two small pairs of red wellington boots which had been discarded in the hall when they'd come back from a walk in the village. Tiffany had forgotten to line them up tidily, as David preferred.

'Jesus, Tiffany, I've told you before about cleaning up the kids' crap. It's all over the place; their toys are like a creeping rash. Tidy up, for Christ's sake. It's like living in a pigsty.'

Tiffany had learned from experience it was better to say nothing. She'd tried defending herself once, saying she had her hands full and the pregnancy was tiring her out so much that she could barely keep up with her own basic needs, let alone look after the kids, but it hadn't had any effect. David was not the sort of man who mucked in, but he had a strong impulse towards tidiness and order. At least he didn't hit her or the children; he kept things verbal.

She tried to ignore David's huffing as he turned back to the hall to take off his shoes and coat. They'd be put away neatly, for sure. As he walked into the lounge, he changed the mood instantly, like an unwelcome guest at a party. The baby jumped inside her. Ever since she'd felt the movement in her belly, she'd been aware how tense she was around her husband. It was as if the baby was urging her to get rid of this man before it showed its tiny face.

The girls looked expectantly at him, but he didn't respond. Tiffany could have cried as she saw Jane raise her arms to be picked up. If he saw it, he didn't show it.

'I've decided you're not coping well again, Tiffany,' he announced after examining the tree. 'You're struggling, I can tell.'

'I'm fine, really I am—' she began.

'It's not just the boots and the mess. Look at you. It's not even five o'clock and you look like you're ready for bed already.'

'It's just that the girls are tiring, there's a lot to do—'

'Anyhow, I've sorted it. It won't be a problem anymore.'

She looked at him, knowing she had no say in this. All she could do was wait to hear what he'd decided in her absence.

'I'm bringing someone in, a nanny,' he began. 'I'm moving her into the other en suite bedroom at the end of the upstairs hallway. She'll be self-contained over there and close to the children.'

'We don't need any help—'

'Have you got dinner on yet, Tiffany?'

'No, I've been doing the Christmas tree with the girls.'

'Exactly. You can't even stay on top of the basics. You need some help. The sooner we can get you back on your meds, the better—'

'David, I told you, I'm not taking medication while I'm pregnant.'

This was the closest she got to a protest. The kids' welfare forced her to stand up for herself. She tried to be grateful for the smaller things; at least he didn't get violent or shout, but he appeared to have very little interest in any of them.

'Are you advertising for a nanny?' she ventured.

'It's sorted already,' he announced, walking over to the pile of post she'd left for him on a bookshelf. Most of the post had his name on it; the words *Mr & Mrs Irwin* were a rare sight on an envelope these days.

'Sorted? What do you mean? Don't I get a say in who comes into my house?'

'There's really no need,' he continued, as if she was an annoying fly which had dared to buzz into the house. 'She's highly recommended and is exceptionally good with children. She just happened to have an opening, so I snatched her up. She's never done live-in before, but her flat is up at the end of December and she needs somewhere to stay. It makes perfect sense.'

Nothing about the situation made any sense to Tiffany. He'd swept through her life like a tornado, charming and attentive to her and the children at first, but the moment the whirlwind romance was cemented by a marriage certificate, the remoteness began. But after what she'd been through, she was glad for some stability in their lives; love didn't seem to matter so much.

Being off the pills helped. Having Jane so close to Callie had knocked her for six. Her world had spiralled out of control. She'd never known anything like it. She hadn't had any previous problems with mental illness. The medication had helped, and when David came into her life, he'd consulted a doctor friend who had prescribed something stronger. It certainly solved the problem, but she hated being on it. It gave her a sense of not being herself, as if she was existing outside her own body. This pregnancy gave her the ideal excuse to come off the medication and regain some sense of control over her mind.

'Do I get to find out who she is?' Tiffany asked. She knew she had the chance to ask a few questions now, then he'd brush her aside, tired of pretending she even had a say in the matter.

'Her name is Joanne Taylor; she lives in Morecambe and she's the same age as you. She doesn't have kids of her own, but she's had lots of experience working with young children. She's moving in on December 30th, the day before her tenancy ends. I've arranged for her to meet you tomorrow morning. You'll like her, she's great.'

With every move David made, she wondered when she'd dig her heels in and insist enough was enough. But she never found the energy for it. Each little thing didn't seem worth a big bust up in front of the children, but when she looked at the ground she'd lost in her own life, it added up. If only she'd fought harder, but she was always so worn out, constantly postponing the battle for another day.

David was working through his post, all of it typewritten and official. He stopped at one letter and studied it.

'You still haven't signed the paperwork, Tiffany. I thought we discussed this?'

'I've been so busy with the children. I wanted to take a proper look at everything first. It's a big step.'

David moved over to her, kissing her on the forehead and waving his hands playfully at the children. They jumped at his attention like stray dogs being thrown a scrap of meat by a butcher. She loved it on the rare occasions when he was kind and engaged. It was why she'd fallen for him in the first place. But now she'd take any kindness, wherever it came from.

'I'd better start getting dinner on. You must be hungry,' she said.

David helped her out of the armchair. Even that felt like a major operation; soon she'd need a pulley system to hoist her up. Cooking a meal was the last thing she felt like doing. She would have slept for a straight twenty-four hours if she could. But she had to stall him from the paperwork. She would smear some food over the forms, pretending the kids had spoiled them. Then she'd make an excuse about the replacement paperwork going missing in the post.

Once the birth was safely out of the way, she finally had a plan and the hope of a new life. She just had to hang on in there a little longer for the sake of the kids. She'd already made the concession of using David's surname for the children. There was no way she would let David adopt the two girls.

CHAPTER FIVE

'You need to eat and rest,' Charlotte told Callie. 'I know I do, and you've just come out of hospital, so you have even more reason to get a good night's sleep.'

She thought about Will. She had a small advantage over Vinnie Mace for a short time. As far as he knew, she could have drowned at sea after he was forced back to the shoreline. She assumed he would have searched her car and possibly found the document hidden beneath the spare wheel there. However, the other papers were still secure, one set in Jed's boat and the other on its way after she'd posted it to herself earlier that day.

She could risk a night staying in the guest house. The police and RNLI hadn't been involved in her rescue, so there was no official record of what had happened out at sea. It would give her some time to trace Will's last movements, and if her meeting with Toni Lawson went well, she would call in the cavalry and put an end to everything. She had to get Will back safely, without alerting the rogue copper at the police station.

'I'm going to put you in room 10,' Charlotte said as she stood up. 'Eat what you want; there won't be a bill.'

'Thank you.'

Callie stared up at her with exhaustion in her eyes.

'You know, the night before I was found in a coma, I actually slept on the beach,' she said. 'I won't be doing that again. I was in such a rush when I left home, I forgot to take my cash card too.'

'Well, you'd always have been welcome here,' Charlotte said, and she held Callie's gaze, so she knew how sincerely she meant it.

'But please promise me one thing.'

'Of course. What is it?'

'Please promise me you won't contact Hollie Wickes, not just yet, even though you must be desperate to speak to her. Besides, I have her phone, and I intend to return it.'

Callie studied Charlotte's face as if she was trying to work out whether she could trust her.

'Is there a reason for that?'

'Yes, a good one. Hollie reached out to my husband at the university; she's a student there. Doesn't that strike you as a bit odd? Why would she? We're not even involved with—'

'What?' Callie probed.

Of course they were involved with it. If DCI Summers was linked through her brother and had laid her hands on documents which Vinnie Mace and Fabian Armstrong wanted, then Will was a route to Charlotte. Her connection with DCI Summers had been well catalogued in the newspaper coverage of their last escapades together.

They wanted DCI Summers, and Will was just the fall guy for some set-up or blackmail. But why would Hollie Wickes get involved? Charlotte decided to keep her questions to herself for the time being. She also thanked her lucky stars that she hadn't given Will too hard a time over her suspicion that he was having an affair.

'I just remembered I have a meeting along the road just before five o'clock. It's an important one too, with the police press officer. Let me have this meeting, you get a good night's rest, and we'll sort all this out tomorrow. I'm exhausted too, I've had quite a day.'

Charlotte explained to Isla what was going on and asked her to keep a room free for her that night. If she used the rear entrance and didn't enter the family accommodation, she would be safe from Vinnie Mace for the time being. She had the mobile number from which he'd called her earlier that day; she would call him next time, when she was no longer on the back foot.

She looked at the clock in the hallway.

'You know what I'm going to say, don't you?' she grimaced at Isla. 'It'll be over soon; I'll be back here over-cooking the fried eggs before you know it.'

'Go off, do what you have to do and be safe. I'll hold the fort here. Just come back to us in one piece.'

Charlotte yearned for sleep, but once the meeting with Toni was out of the way, she could take to her bed and then devote her energy to finding Will the following day. Poor Will. *Hang on in there one more night*, she told herself. She prayed they wouldn't harm her husband as long as they believed DCI Summers was alive. He was their guarantee that she wouldn't snitch to the police too.

She changed out of the clothing she'd been given by the wind farm team and felt immediately more human. Things were getting so bad that Isla hadn't even commented on her temporary clothing.

When she arrived at Brucciani's, she cursed her bad

luck. It was closed already and they were wiping the tables down as she walked through the door.

'Sorry my darling,' the waitress said as she looked up. 'We've stopped serving.'

Charlotte apologised and looked around for Toni then checked her phone. Damn, Toni hadn't even got back to her yet. She paced up and down outside the café until the waitress started giving her funny looks. As she stood at the kerb, looking up and down the street, Toni frightened the life out of her by approaching from behind.

'Hey, Charlotte, good to see you. Nice to see you've put some decent clothes on since last time.'

She laughed at her own quip and Charlotte joined in. It was a good job Toni hadn't seen her half an hour earlier.

'The café is closed, I'm afraid. Shall we walk over to the Midland Hotel and grab a table there?'

'Yes, why not?' Toni agreed, looking across the road towards the hotel. 'Would you believe it, I've been in my new post almost a month and I still haven't been in there yet.'

They crossed the road, bought soft drinks and found a seat. It wasn't yet six o'clock, so they were in the quiet phase between late afternoon teas and the arrival of the early drinkers.

'Sorry I didn't get your text. I've been in meetings all afternoon, but I saw it as I was getting ready to leave the office and dashed over in the car.'

'I'm relieved you did; I didn't want to wait until tomorrow to speak to you.'

'How can I help you?' Toni began. 'You said it was about a police issue. I might not be the best person to speak to.'

'You're the only person I can speak to at the moment,' Charlotte replied. 'Do you know DCI Kate Summers?'

'Not personally. She's the most wanted police officer in Morecambe at the moment. But I've only exchanged a few words with her, all about press matters rather than personal issues. Why?'

'I have to know I can trust you.'

'Of course you can, Charlotte.'

'There's a bad cop in Morecambe. I don't know who it is, but I can't risk what I'm telling you now getting back to him. Or her.'

Toni seemed surprised.

'There are crooked cops wherever you go, Charlotte. But I promise to keep what you say confidential.'

'I'm in contact with Kate Summers.'

Charlotte noticed the flinch, only short and sharp, but definitely there.

'Do you know where she is?'

'No. But I know how to contact her.'

'You realise she's wanted in connection with a murder investigation? I'll share something with you confidentially now; it's embargoed until midday tomorrow but you'll get a press release about it first thing in the morning. A personal item belonging to DCI Summers was found on the scene of Evan Farrish's murder by police forensics. She's now wanted on suspicion of murder—'

'Kate Summers did not kill Evan Farrish.'

'We don't know that, Charlotte—'

'I do. I don't care what your evidence says. She's being set up. That's why she's gone into hiding. Her life is in danger.'

Toni studied her face.

'We'll have to agree to disagree on that one, Charlotte.

But if you have contact information for DCI Summers, you should consider handing it over. For her own sake, she needs to come in for questioning.'

'She would do it in an instant if she thought it was safe,' Charlotte replied, wondering if she should be speaking to Toni. She was playing it by the book, and it wasn't helpful. It was worth one more try.

'Kate Summers has evidence which will prove her innocence.'

'So why doesn't she just hand it over? She of all people understands how this works.'

'As I said, powerful people want to stop that information getting out. That's why Kate has entrusted it to me.'

For the second time, Toni flinched in her chair. She'd make a useless poker player. Her eyes narrowed.

'Okay, now you've got my attention, Charlotte. So, what you're telling me is that you've become an accomplice to a suspected murder.'

CHAPTER SIX

Callie had been out for the count when Charlotte knocked on her door after returning from the fruitless meeting with Toni. She was so concerned about another relapse after the earlier complications with diabetes that she'd even taken the liberty of using the master key to check in on her. Thankfully Callie was fully dressed and sleeping soundly on top of the bed; she hadn't even bothered to pull back the quilt. It gave Charlotte the opportunity to help clear the tables after the evening shift, check in with Isla and Piper and feel like she was mucking in again after such a long absence.

Her mind had been anywhere but on gammon and pineapple main courses and ice cream sundae desserts. All she could think of was Will, and what she needed to do next to find him, whilst preserving Kate Summers' secrecy. She was relieved in a way that neither of them had a clue where Kate was hiding; she might not withstand being threatened in exchange for Will's freedom.

After a fitful night's sleep, Charlotte still felt no better about her meeting with Toni Lawson. It had left an unpleasant taste in her mouth, but she couldn't put her finger on what was bothering her. She'd expected a more friendly approach, but she'd faced an overzealous press officer who appeared to have unspoken designs on becoming a detective sometime soon.

Having checked in on Callie again first thing in the morning and finding she'd barely moved from her sleeping position, Charlotte showered and helped out with the morning shift. She wouldn't be able to do anything until daylight anyway, and it would at least make Isla and Agnieszka feel like she hadn't disappeared off the face of the earth. As she served fry-ups to guests and cleared more tables, she made her plan for the day.

She had to retrieve the company car, which meant a taxi ride out to Sunderland Point. There was a jet-ski at the back of the guest house which did not belong to her; she'd have to let the two young guys know and make her apologies to them. She could only guess how that would play out.

Next, she would check in with Nigel and make sure she could hang onto the company car a bit longer. She hoped Vinnie hadn't smashed it up; there would be some explaining to do if he had.

Her plan was to go to the university and retrace Will's steps. One of his colleagues must know where he'd gone after the work event. It might give her some clues about where they'd taken him. She wished she'd slept better the night before; exhaustion was already setting in and the day had barely started.

As Charlotte was coming out of the dining room with a pile of stacked plates in each hand, she almost bumped into the postman in the hall.

'Leave it just inside the kitchen, would you?' she asked.

Agnieszka and Isla were taking a few minutes to chat during a lull from guest demands.

'You haven't seen Will in the last couple of days, have you?' Charlotte asked.

'No, he is keeping – how do you say – a lowly profile?' Agnieszka said. 'Is he okay?'

For a moment, the words were on her lips. But Agnieszka and Isla had their own troubles, and she could handle this on her own. Was she crazy thinking that? No, she had some leverage. Hopefully the postman had just delivered a letter which contained some of that leverage.

'Yes, he's just had a funny schedule this week. You haven't shared a bus ride home from the university or anything like that, have you?'

The look on Agnieszka's face told her she hadn't.

She scraped the plates and stacked them in the dishwasher, then walked over to check the pile of post. There it was: the letter she'd posted to herself the previous day. She grabbed it and ran up the stairs two steps at a time, anxious to get it hidden away. Where should she hide it? There was a row of Pot Noodles in one of the kitchen cupboards, stored in case of a visit from Olli, who considered them to be a food group. She carefully tore off one of the foil tops, leaving a small part attached to the plastic body, then shook out the dehydrated contents into the pedal bin and put the envelope into the pot, curling it so it sat snugly inside.

A search under the sink unearthed an abandoned tube of half-squeezed glue which she used to secure the lid before replacing the pot in the cupboard. Unless a diet of Pot Noodles was responsible for Vinnie Mace's athletic physique, which seemed unlikely, no one who broke in would think of looking there for the documents. She just had to remember it was in the Sweet and Sour pot. She wondered if Olli would even notice the difference if he poured hot water on it and ate it.

She scribbled a note to Callie and went to check if she was still sleeping. Seeing she was, Charlotte left the note at Callie's side.

Help yourself to breakfast and to any of the facilities. There won't be a bill for anything. Meet me at the slipway at 11 o'clock. Charlotte.

Having checked the shifts were covered over the weekend, she made a vow to Isla that if things weren't back to normal by next Monday morning, she had her permission to go on strike. If it wasn't sorted by then, she had resolved to go to the police anyway, reporting it to both Lancaster and Morecambe police stations. She would warn them of a rogue officer and seek protection. But first she would do her level best to find Will and help Kate Summers prove her innocence.

By eight o'clock, she'd paid the taxi driver for an expensive run out to Sunderland Point and was back at the car. She was relieved to be doing something again, recognising her restlessness the previous night had been frustration at not being able to get on with things. If only she could sleep for as long as Callie.

Surprisingly, the car was intact: no smashed windows, and no forced doors. It didn't feel right. She'd have expected Vinnie to smash it up, if only out of frustration at her escape. The car was still unlocked, just as she'd left it, and the remote key was still working, despite being soaked in sea water the day before. She checked for the envelope. It was still there in its hiding place.

Charlotte glanced across the shingle to where she'd stolen the jet-ski the day before. Thankfully the two guys weren't out there yet. Jed's boat was there; should she leave the other envelope in it? If he went out to sea, it might get soaked. She decided to leave it, confident she'd tucked it away safely. If she gathered all the documents together, it would make her more vulnerable.

She checked the car over a second time but there was no evidence of tampering. The second jet-ski was pulled up on the shingle, so Vinnie must have made it back to where he'd started. It didn't make sense for him to have left the car untouched. She got into the driver's seat and leaned over to check the glove compartment. Hollie Wickes' phone was still there, but it had no charge left in it now. She would drop it off at the university library when she got there; she needed to wash her hands of it.

The drive to Lancaster was slow, and she cursed as she hit the slow-moving trail of morning rush-hour traffic. Stuck in a queue behind traffic lights, she texted Nigel to get a head of steam on the day.

Okay if I hang onto the car until midday? If this pays off, you'll have your headline for Wednesday's newspaper!

The text went almost immediately, and her phone began to ring moments later. The traffic started to move as it did so, so she tapped the answer button and placed it on speaker so she could watch the road.

'Charlotte, what the hell is going on?'

'Good morning to you too!' she answered.

'Teddy went off on one this morning. We've had the police round here already asking about a member of staff stealing a jet-ski and taking it out to sea. Excuse my language, but what the fuck is going on with you?'

Charlotte hadn't even thought about that. She'd been so intent on the wind farm team not getting the police involved that she'd missed the obvious; the young guys would report it.

'Look, Nigel, I'm getting close to finding out what's going on now, but I can't tell you anything yet. Please will you cover for me and book the car out until midday? Things are heating up for me, but I'm almost there. And if I crack this thing, you'll get yourself one hell of a front-page story.'

'I'm worried about you, Charlotte. Have you been annoying Fabian Armstrong again? You're placing yourself in danger and that's not our job. We report on the news, we don't make it.'

'I promise you I won't put myself in danger. I'm in deeper than I could have imagined, but this Irwin story is bigger than either of us thought. Cover for me, Nigel, please, and I promise I'll tell you everything as soon as I can.'

'Teddy is so annoyed about this police visit, it's a damn good job you wrote such a good article in this week's newspaper. Those chips are cashed in now, Charlotte. Whatever you do next will need to be good. I really don't know how much longer I can cover for you after this.'

CHAPTER SEVEN

Charlotte could tell Nigel's goodwill was running out and resolved to give it one more day before she asked for help. First on her list was to speak to DCI Summers, to make sure she wasn't placing her in any danger.

She climbed into the car and paused a moment, wondering about the document in Jed's boat. Doubts were beginning to set in. Should she take the document with her or not? Would it strengthen her position if they caught her again? If only she had someone to talk to, someone to share the strain of what was going on. Will was her best bet; she had to make finding him her next priority.

All the way back to Lancaster, endless possible outcomes swirled around in her head until they became a whirlwind of confusion. As she reached the turn off to the university campus, she realised with a jolt that she'd made the entire journey on autopilot. She found a visitor parking space and locked the car, trying to remember on which part of the campus Will's department was based.

Standing in front of a large map of the university, on which the words *You are here* were confidently displayed, she did her best to locate some key landmarks so she could figure out which way to walk. In the end, she gave up and changed her strategy. Searching through her email archive, she found a message written by Will and sent from his university account. To her delight, Google Maps obliged by marking his building with a bright red icon on her phone. She set up the app to guide her to her destination, then noticed the library was on the way to Will's office. She ran back to the car to pick up Hollie's phone. She would be relieved to get rid of it and stop feeling like a criminal.

Will's work colleagues would be her first target. Google Maps obliged by depositing her at precisely the right location. Having grown up using AA route maps and A-Z city guides, she loved being able to use her phone instead of her brain at times like this.

'Hi, I'm Charlotte Grayson, Will's wife,' she said to the man in the reception area of the department.

'Oh, hi Charlotte, Will's told us all about you. All good, I should add.'

He was a young guy, probably a student or intern, bright and fresh-faced. The world had barely begun knocking the stuffing out of him.

Charlotte showed him her reporter's ID card. She could have been anybody, as far as they were concerned.

'How can I help you? Is Will feeling better now?'

'What do you mean?'

'We got a call yesterday morning saying he wouldn't be coming in; he was feeling ill after the department's event the night before.'

'Who called?'

This might provide a lead of some sorts. Charlotte willed him to speak faster.

'Some guy. A friend from the guest house, he said.'

'Did you see Will at the event? Were you there?'

'Sure,' the young man answered, his interest piqued by her obvious concern. 'He was meeting you in town afterwards, wasn't he? We finished late, and he missed the last bus. He used the hitching post to get back to the town—'

'The hitching post? What's that?'

'It's by the bus stop at the last roundabout before you leave the campus. Students use it to hitch rides into town. It saves a fortune in bus fares.'

'Did you travel together?'

'No, we saw him off at the underpass. A couple of us offered him a floor for the night on campus, but he said you'd be worried. So we left him to it.'

A part of her was relieved Hollie Wickes' name hadn't been mentioned. But she was no closer to tracking his movements.

'Did anybody hitch with him?'

'Yes, Andrea over there.'

The man pointed to a stunning-looking Afro-Caribbean woman with the most incredible braided hair Charlotte had ever seen.

'Andrea,' the man called over, 'what happened when you and Will hitched the other night?'

'Nothing,' she said, 'I got dropped off at the top of town and Will said he wanted to be dropped off by the Travelodge.'

'Were you picked up by a student?' Charlotte asked.

Andrea stood and walked over to join them.

'Are you Charlotte?' she asked. 'You must be, you look just like Will described. Delighted to meet you.'

They shook hands.

'We got the lift in a very classy car. If it was a student car, they were an extraordinarily rich student. I assumed he was someone senior and important, judging from his manner.'

'Do you know where he was heading after he dropped Will off?' Charlotte asked.

'No, he didn't say. But I did notice he had White Lund Industrial Estate on his satnav. I just assumed he'd been there earlier and hadn't changed the coordinates. Wherever he'd been, it was close to Sparks Auto-Repairs; it was one of those weird things I noticed. Does that help?'

'You bet it does,' Charlotte replied. At last she had a head start on Vinnie Mace. He would never get a car like that serviced at a backstreet garage like Sparks Auto-Repairs. They must have a unit round there, probably an empty one, in which they were keeping Will.

'Is Will alright?' the young man asked.

'He will be now,' Charlotte replied before thanking them and starting the walk back to the car. She was in such a rush, she almost forgot to drop off Hollie's phone. As she walked into the main square around which the campus was built, she saw the library up ahead and toyed with the idea of leaving it until later. She decided to drop it in; it would only take a minute.

Once in the reception area, she caught the attention of a staff member. As she began speaking, she thought she heard a call of 'Excuse me' behind her, but assumed it was meant for someone else. She took out Hollie's phone and handed it over.

'I found this outside the library a couple of days ago. I'm sorry I forgot to drop it in sooner, but I'll bet the owner will be delighted to be reunited with—'

'Excuse me!' came the voice again, closer this time.

'You'd be surprised how many students leave them in the study cubicles. Thank you,' the library assistant replied.

'That's my bloody phone!'

Charlotte turned around to see an angry Hollie Wickes charging at her. Her hand reached out for the mobile phone which Charlotte was in the process of passing across the desk.

Charlotte instinctively snatched the phone back. Half in tears, half in fury, Hollie lunged at Charlotte and tried to seize the phone.

'You bitch, you took that from my room.'

'Oh no, that's not—'

Hollie made a second grab for the phone just as Charlotte was about to hand it over to her. She seemed to believe she was about to be struck, because she pushed Charlotte out of the way, causing her to lose balance and stagger back into a wooden shelf to her rear, packed with recommended reads. She crashed into it, sending the books flying, with gasps of shock flaring up around her. As Charlotte lay on the floor with books all around her and several students and staff members beginning to fuss over her, she saw the library assistant making a call on the phone at her desk. There was only one thing to do. She slid Hollie's mobile phone across the floor to her feet, stood up, and made a run for it before the university's security team arrived.

CHAPTER EIGHT

December 1999

'It's been nine months since Rowan was born. It's not unreasonable to have one night out, is it?'

Tiffany was furious with David. He knew she was going out with the girls that night and he'd promised to get home in time.

'Besides, what's the point of us paying Joanne a salary if she has a better social life than we do?'

She'd learnt since Rowan's birth that this was always the winning argument. They were clearly having an affair, and she was convinced it was the reason he'd moved her in. The kids liked her, sure, but Tiffany had never set eyes on a single piece of paperwork which confirmed Joanne's qualifications or prior work experience.

Tiffany didn't care any more; she'd hatched her plan with Brett, and it was only a matter of time before they could set a date and sort out one final legal matter. Every time David raised the topic of the adoption papers, she deflected him by asking to see Joanne's references.

'Once you show me who's looking after my children every day, I'll sign your bloody paperwork. I'll do it straight away. But it sits in that drawer unsigned until you do.'

She knew she was becoming brazen now, but her contempt of him grew as her escape came closer. His disdain for her had become more proactive too and his interest in Rowan, other than in the opportunities the baby offered to accompany Joanne on pram-walks, was even less than it had been for Callie and Jane. She'd fallen hook, line and sinker for his shallow charms and now she was having to dig herself out of a hole of her own making.

'Right, go out then, why don't you?' David shouted. 'Most new mothers would be delighted to spend the night with their newborn child—'

'Most new mothers would be as desperate as I am for a night to themselves after nine months of sleepless nights and breast-feeding.'

'I told you Joanne could deal with the feeding—'

'And I told you I want him on breast milk for the first months of his life. You know I hate expressing milk; it makes me feel like one of my father's cows.'

David stopped and fussed about with something or other as a distraction. She couldn't understand why he made such a big deal of it; her absence would give him a couple of hours with Joanne. Wasn't that what he wanted?

An hour later she was sitting up in bed at Brett's house, the flush of passionate lovemaking still evident on her face. She had a sense of stillness and contentment that she hadn't known in her own home for some time.

'Surely he must suspect something by now?' Brett asked.

'I honestly don't think he cares any more,' Tiffany replied, laying her head on his chest. She loved the feel of him. He was the first man whose body felt like it was made to hold her and only her.

'Besides, he and Joanne are sleeping together, I'm certain of it. We're stuck in some horrible game of chess. He wants me to sign the adoption papers for Jane and Callie, and I want him and Fabian to get that damn power of attorney rescinded. We're all left staring at each other across the room, none of us wanting to make the first move. But don't worry, I'm on to it. If I can get the power of attorney legally removed on my own with the correct medical paperwork, I'll deny him adoption rights and then we're clear.'

'I want to set a date, Tiff. I want to stop talking about it and I want to make it happen.'

'I know, I want it too. I was thinking New Year—'

'Before then. I've sold the house.'

'Already?'

'Yes, it's sold. If we can leave before New Year, that will save me renting anywhere. The new owners want the house before Christmas, and I can stay in a hotel for two weeks if I have to.'

Tiffany raised her head from Brett's chest, pulled herself up against the headboard and looked into his eyes.

'How about New Year's Eve?' she said.

'New Year's Eve? That's a crazy time to do it, isn't it?'

'It's the perfect time to do it. The entire world is going insane over the new millennium. Why not then?'

Brett took a moment before responding.

'Can you sort your paperwork by then? Can we make a clean break from David?'

'As clean as it's ever going to be. As for the farm, Fabian and I will never agree on it. We have the wind energy firm ready to sign and seal the deal for a twenty-year lease, but he's not interested. He says we should be shooting higher, for nuclear or chemicals, but there's no way I'm doing that to the villagers. I want a wind farm on the land; I won't let it be developed. My mum and dad would be turning in their graves if they knew what Fabian was up to. We can still use the land for grazing with wind turbines on it.'

Brett threw back the sheets and climbed out of bed. Tiffany admired his lithe, athletic body. Not only was he great company, but he also looked amazing too.

'Come on,' he said, heading for the shower.

'What?' she asked.

'Let's get cleaned up and go out.'

'Really?'

'Yes. You've been up to your ears in nappies and washing for far too long. Much as I'd love to spend the evening in bed with you, you told David you'd be back by eleven o'clock at the latest. Let's go into town and have some fun. You deserve it. Besides, I'm meeting my sister Kate later; I said we'd see each other at Crystal T's.'

'Have you told her yet?'

Tiffany threw back the sheets and walked across the room to join Brett. She was still struggling to shed her baby weight, but Brett couldn't care less. She'd waited years to be looked at like that by a man.

'No, not yet.'

Brett had a guilty expression.

'Why not? You said you would.'

This subject had become a tricky area to navigate, much like the adoption papers with David. If only she knew why Brett was putting it off.

Brett drew her in close and she felt a spark of electricity run through her as their naked bodies fused together.

'I owe my sister everything,' Brett began. 'When dad died, I went off the rails for a time.'

'Nobody could blame you, after what happened.'

'I can see that now, but Kate was only young herself then. She took care of everything: the legal paperwork, all the funeral arrangements and everything. She was patient with me and supported me as if she was my own mother.'

'I get that,' Tiffany replied, luxuriating in the warmth of his body against hers. 'So why not tell her?'

'Because it feels like a betrayal, Tiff. She went off to train for the police and she came back to Morecambe whenever she could, to make sure I was okay. When she should have been out on the town with her friends, she prioritised me and my welfare. She's back now, and I'm sure she only returned to a policing job in Morecambe so she could keep an eye on me.'

'But you're an adult now, Brett. I have three kids and I'm only a bit older than you. You're no kid brother anymore.'

'I know that, Tiff, and so does she. It just feels like a betrayal. I will tell her, honestly, but it'll break her heart and I can't bring myself to do it just yet.'

What Brett had said to Tiffany weighed on her mind as they showered, got dressed and headed out into Morecambe for a drink. She envied Brett and his relationship with his sister. As the only daughter of a farmer, she had very much been an afterthought compared to Fabian. Her father was only interested in his son, the man who would keep the farm going after his death. She was always expected to marry some local farmer and perpetuate the cycle. It had caused fierce battles with her father while her mother was still alive.

Fabian had always despised her for that. The moment their father died, he was like a plague of locusts, ready to strip every asset they owned for profit and development.

But she had other plans. Her brother was a scumbag; she'd had to accept that fact a long time ago.

Sitting in the bar of Crystal T's after moving on from a quieter pub, she clung onto her last minutes with Brett, feeling like Cinderella at the ball. But she couldn't stay out as late as midnight; she had to return to her suspicious husband. It wasn't the stuff fairy tales were made of.

The music was loud and pervasive, but the sound of the catchy tunes invigorated her, making her feel less like a new mother and more like the young woman that she was. She loved the children dearly, but she needed a night like this.

'Kate's here. I'm sorry, Tiff, but you need to go. She's early.'

'Where, which one is she? Can't I meet her?'

'Not yet, Tiff, I'm sorry. I have to tell her in my own way, not like this. Please try to understand. It's a big thing we're doing. I know you can't wait to get away from David, but for me, it's mixed with sadness and guilt.'

Tiffany looked at him. She loved this man, and she wanted to be with him. With a brief touch of his arm, she headed off, not wanting to land him in a difficult situation. Like Cinderella, she slipped off into the night. She only hoped they'd get their happy ever after.

CHAPTER NINE

Charlotte couldn't afford to get caught up in a scrape with the university security guards. It would cause complications, and she'd had enough of those to last a lifetime already. She put her head down and strode out, ignoring the crowd which had gathered, some to help, others to find out what had sent the display flying in the entrance of the library. She returned to the car at a half-walk, half-jog, expecting to be pursued, but she blended easily into the crowds of students moving between lectures and made her escape.

It had been bad luck running into Hollie, but it was no surprise that she was in the library; she should have timed it better.

Charlotte checked the clock on the car dashboard as she climbed into the vehicle. She was tight for time to meet Callie as arranged, but she couldn't resist swinging into the White Lund Industrial Estate and checking out the units around Sparks Auto-Repairs; it was her best lead.

As she left the university campus, she drove a little faster than she should have, slowing again as she reached the city boundaries. Not only was the liveried car an easy target for complaints from the public, but she also needed to avoid any run-ins with the police until she was ready to face them on her own terms. She cursed Toni Lawson once again for not being more helpful. Toni's attitude had made her feel more isolated than before; she'd hoped to find in her the sort of good counsel Kate Summers had once offered.

The early morning traffic had cleared, allowing her to make good progress towards the industrial estate. She had a rough idea where Sparks Auto-Repairs was, due to their regular trips to the cash and carry. The irony of being able to stock up with produce for the guest house whilst simultaneously trying to rescue her husband from his kidnappers was not lost on her. She had to remember that Vinnie would not know what had happened to her yet. He was as capable as any relative or journalist of ringing around the hospitals along the coastline and asking if she'd been brought in. Until they found a body or casualty, or a police report was filed, Vinnie Mace was running blind, and that suited her.

She parked the car a short distance from Sparks Auto-Repairs, not wanting to make the presence of the newspaper vehicle too obvious in case Vinnie was holed up there. She walked a circuit of the area and only found one vacant industrial unit. It looked like it had been lying empty for some time. The agent was offering leasing incentives according to a weather-beaten board which was hanging on to the wall for dear life.

This looked like a problem unit, the ideal place from which a man like Vinnie would operate. She scanned the area for security cameras but couldn't spot any. There had once been a camera on the side of the building, but now all that remained was a rusted frame and a dilapidated warning sign claiming 24/7 surveillance.

As she drew nearer to the unit, she was able to read the faded sign which announced it had been *Cath's Craft Supplies* prior to its closure. The words hung there like ghostly reminders of a former occupant. The door and the windows at the front were boarded up with chipboard, but a large new black padlock was attached to the front door.

Someone had entered this place recently. She shook the padlock, not really knowing why; it held firm, as she knew it would. The rear of the unit was reached via a securely locked side gate with another new padlock. It would be foolish to climb over the fence at that time of day, with so much activity on the industrial estate. Besides, there was nothing to suggest this was anything but a dead end.

But she refused to accept it. If Vinnie Mace had this place marked as a destination on his satnav, there was something important here. She would meet up with Callie then return later for a proper snoop under cover of darkness. If Will was in there, she would find him.

Charlotte returned to the car, frustrated and impatient, and drove back to Morecambe, her mind occupied with ways to move things forward. She was still fine for time with the company vehicle, but the lack of a car was beginning to be frustrating. She had effectively helped herself to one of three office pool vehicles as her personal taxi, and she'd need to keep it overnight.

As she pulled into a vacant parking space at the roadside, she considered asking Nigel to cover for her one last time. Would he go for it? He'd sounded impatient when they'd last spoken, and she didn't want to push him too far. Instead, she grabbed her mobile and dialled the newspaper switchboard.

'Bay View Weekly, 'ow can I 'elp you?' came Reagan's voice.

'Hello Reagan, it's Charlotte. Are you feeling better now?'

'Yeah, 'allo Charlotte, it was just like you said. Teddy was okay about it, I just 'ave to do that 'ealth and safety thingy. Thanks for being so nice.'

'I'm pleased to hear that, Reagan; I was sure it would all be okay. Would you mind putting me through to Teddy's office, please? I'm in a spot of trouble myself.'

'Oh, bloody 'ell, good luck, I hope it's okay.'

Charlotte heard Reagan transferring the call.

'Teddy here. I hope you've got a good explanation about that jet-ski, Charlotte.'

Charlotte took a breath and summoned what was left of her confidence.

'Listen, Teddy, remember what you said about great journalism at the morning meeting?'

'Yes, of course.'

'If you want the best bit of investigative journalism your newspaper has seen for a long time, then please trust me. If I don't deliver, you have my permission to send me packing with my tail between my legs.'

'But when the police get involved—'

'I need two favours from you, Teddy. Tell the police the jet-ski is safely stored at the rear of the Lakes View Guest House. They'll find a few bullet holes in it; you'll have to send my apologies.'

'Dammit, Charlotte, what the hell have you been up to?'

'The second favour is that I need to use the company car overnight. If it's not back by midday tomorrow, I'll either be dead or your front-page story will have become bigger than you ever expected. If I do bring it back, I promise you you'll have your biggest story since—'

'Since last time you were on the front pages after Edward Callow's death?'

'Exactly. You know I can deliver when it comes to shifting newspapers. I need you to trust me for 24 hours. That's all. If I'm still alive then, you can call the police yourself.'

There was silence on the end of the line. She heard Teddy begin to talk, then he stopped and was silent again. At last he answered.

'All right, Charlotte. I saw something rare and amazing in that feature you wrote for me. I'm going to take a chance on you. Just promise me you won't do anything stupid, okay?'

'Now, Teddy, would I do anything stupid?'

She couldn't believe she was talking to the head of the newspaper like this, but she had to brazen it out to get the car.

Fortunately Teddy changed the subject. 'By the way, Reagan told me what you'd said to her after the fire. There are a lot of people in the office who'd love to throw that girl to the lions. I know she's not the most perfect receptionist, but the kid deserves a break. Thank you for being a friend to her. Did you realise her entire family was killed in a car accident when she was twelve years old?'

'Oh my god, poor Reagan. No, she never mentioned it.'

'She never does. She grew up in the care system after that and vowed to rebuild her life when she left at eighteen years old. This was the first job she came for. Better people were in for the job, but I saw something in her and decided to take a chance on her. We haven't been taken over by one of the big newspaper chains yet, so I can still make crazy decisions. I'm making one of those decisions now, Charlotte. Be safe and don't let me down. Become the incredible journalist I believe you are, and make sure you stay alive while you're doing it.'

Charlotte was so pleased she hadn't dismissed Reagan. The first time she'd ever walked into the office, she'd been put off by the way she spoke and her obvious lack of education. But the girl had guts and determination, and she knew only too well how hard it could be to summon those qualities in the face of overwhelming adversity. Good for Reagan.

'You promise me you won't take any risks, Charlotte?' came Teddy's voice.

'I can't promise you that, but I can assure you this is going to be one hell of a front-page news story.'

'How did you sleep?' Charlotte asked, thinking Callie looked so much better than when they'd first met in the hallway of the guest house the previous night. They'd met in a café and ordered small coffees, since they weren't staying long. Callie was wearing a beanie hat which she'd pulled down over her forehead to conceal most of the birthmark.

'I feel so much better,' Callie replied. 'It was so difficult to get any rest in hospital when I came out of the coma. I just drifted in and out of sleep all day and all night; it's such a weird environment when you're trying to recover.'

Charlotte remembered her brief hospital stays when the children were born. Callie was right; the interruptions were endless.

'You were out for the count when I came into your room this morning. I figured I should just leave you to sleep.'

'Well, it was a good call, thank you. And that lady, Isla, who works for you in the kitchens, she's brilliant. She looked after me so well this morning. I met her husband

George and their dog, Una, when he came to pick her up after work. They're such a lovely couple.'

'Right, we need to get things straight here,' Charlotte began. 'I'm sure I can help you piece together what happened in the past, but I can't give you every answer. That's where we can help each other, I hope. Between us, we can work this thing out.'

'What do you know about my birth mother?' Callie asked.

Charlotte wished she'd started with an easier question. For a moment, she considered sugar-coating her answer. Then she changed her mind. Callie was an adult and had every right to know. The police would have to observe data protection and privacy rules, seek consent and all the other red tape that hindered their job, but she had more of a free rein.

Callie drained her coffee and sat in silence as Charlotte explained everything she'd learned about the case since Nigel had first received the tip-off in the office. She looked ready to absorb everything, listening and waiting until Charlotte had finished before asking her first question. By the time she'd finished, Callie even knew about the Kate Summers connection.

'I can't believe I never knew anything about this,' Callie said at last. 'I've been living my life in oblivion; my mum and dad never told me any of it.'

'I have no experience of these things,' Charlotte said, wondering how her adoptive parents must be feeling, 'but you should always remember your mum and dad were doing what they thought was right. Whatever happened in your past, they were all you'd ever known until recently, and you loved them for it.'

'But there's so much deception involved, Charlotte. It's difficult to take it all in.'

'I'm far from a model parent, Callie, but I can assure you everything I do as a mother is with my children's best interests at heart. I don't always get it right, but I would do anything for my kids. Any parent would.'

Callie considered that for a while.

'Why wouldn't the police let me meet my birth mother?' she asked. 'They did the DNA test; they know who I am. Why can't I see her?'

'Things are complicated where your mother is concerned,' Charlotte replied, choosing her words carefully. 'Did they tell you she's in a care home?'

'No. What type of care home? She can't be that old—'

'It's not that type of care home. She's experienced some mental health difficulties. It's a private home, not so far from here.'

'Where?'

'You should wait a while before you see her.'

'Where is it, Charlotte? I want to meet her.'

'It's in Torrisholme. They're not very friendly there.'

'You've seen her? You've met my mum?'

'Callie, it's dangerous for you. You'll never get in there without alerting the police—'

'How did you get in? Because that's how we'll get in this time.'

Charlotte took a good look at Callie and recognised in her the resolve of a woman who knew what had to be done.

'I sneaked in. And I got chased off. You can't just walk in there.'

'Well, you did. How would you feel if you'd just found out the woman you thought was your birth mother has been lying to you all your life and your real mother is just a couple of miles up the road? Screw the police and their procedures, I want to see her. I don't care how ill she is. I'll bet she wants to see me too.'

Everything in Charlotte's head screamed the need for care and caution, but if she were in Callie's shoes, she'd want the same thing.

'We'll have to crawl through a hole in a hedge to get in,' Charlotte warned. 'And even then, we've got to get your mum's attention through the window. It might not work, and we could land ourselves in trouble.'

'It's only a matter of time until the police catch up with me anyway. The more information I can get my hands on, the better. It's why I sought you out, Charlotte. You strike me as a person who doesn't stick to the rules. I need someone like you right now.'

They finished their coffees in silence.

'I want to go to the slipway,' Callie said, without warning. 'That's why we came. I want you to walk me through what happened before I meet my birth mother.'

They walked over to the slipway in silence, as if they were about to visit the grave of a loved one.

'What happened here?' Callie asked. 'Not the sanitised police version. I want to know what went on that night. I find it unbelievable that I was here. I have no memory of it. I must have been three or four years old at the time, so why don't I remember any of it?'

'I reckon DCI Summers can help fill in some of the blanks,' Charlotte ventured. 'I'm not sure how much she knows, but she was involved in this back in 1999. She's in danger now and there's a reason you were contacted by a stranger after all these years. There are forces at work and I can't figure out how it all fits together. But it does all slot together, Callie, and I'm sure we can work it out.'

She left Callie on her own for several minutes until she was ready to leave. Charlotte was struck by how much her behaviour mirrored Steven Terry's, pacing the area, seeking ghosts from her past who refused to show their faces.

Eventually she was ready to continue their journey to the Briar Bank Care Home. Charlotte left the car parked nearby so they could walk up the road towards the building. She pulled her hair tight in a band to prevent it getting caught in the hedge, should they be forced to make a hasty retreat once again.

The two women hovered furtively about fifty metres from the care home before moving in close to squeeze through the hedge. Charlotte was delighted to see there were no flashy cars in the car park; the management team obviously wasn't around.

'I'll go first,' Charlotte said. It made sense when she already knew the basic layout of the building. She lowered herself to the ground and pulled herself through the small gap in the hedge. Callie followed her through, making it look much easier, then they moved to the side of the building to check for signs of activity in the grounds.

Charlotte peered around the corner. The gardens were quiet.

'Okay, we're clear.'

They moved around the side of the building and came face to face with a member of staff who'd just stepped out from one of the rooms via the patio door. Charlotte and the woman stared at each other for a moment before recognising each other. It was the lady who'd confided in Charlotte on the sea front, an ally.

'Are you here for Tiff, love?' the woman whispered.

'Yes. This is her daughter.'

The woman gasped.

'Come this way,' she said, turning back into the room.

'Do you know her?' Callie whispered.

'It's a long story... another long story,' Charlotte replied. 'But yes, she's a friend. She'll help us. She loves your mum, don't worry.'

Callie and Charlotte followed her. Nobody else was in the room; the bed was stripped ready to be cleaned.

'Josie died last night,' the woman said quietly. 'She was a good age. I'm just cleaning out her things.'

She guided them through the room and peered around the door.

'Tiff's room is three doors along. Be quick, here's the key. She's up and about, I saw her earlier. She's sitting in her chair.'

Charlotte took the key and led the way along the corridor. As she reached the door, she gave a gentle tap then opened it with the key. Once they were inside, Callie closed the door quietly behind them.

Tiffany looked up from her chair and studied Charlotte's face. Then she looked across at Callie who'd stepped out to Charlotte's side. Tiffany looked at Callie for a moment then a single tear rolled down her cheek.

'Callie, my darling, beautiful girl. I always knew you had to be alive.'

CHAPTER ELEVEN

Charlotte watched Callie's face as Tiffany identified her without hesitation. If there had been any hint of doubt in her mind that the DNA report had got it wrong, or that it was all some intricate hoax, it had now been put to rest.

Charlotte wondered if she would recognise her own children after 20 years. There were occasions when Olli had crawled out of bed after a long sleep in, so tired and dishevelled that she'd barely recognised him after one night.

'Callie Irwin, my daughter. Come closer, my beautiful Callie.'

'I'm called Callie Whitehead now; I've never been Callie Irwin in my living memory.'

She seemed prickly about the name, but then it was her entire history. Charlotte couldn't even imagine what it would be like to discover you had a completely different identity. Callie walked over and Tiffany stood up and hugged her. Although Callie didn't reciprocate, she didn't push her away either.

Tiffany moved her hand up to Callie's beanie hat and pushed it up slightly.

'Your birthmark never faded. I used to worry so much about it when you were younger. Did you ever notice it's the shape of a—'

'A daffodil.' Callie completed the sentence. She began to sob.

'It's all going to be fine, Callie, don't worry. I always used to see the shape of a daffodil and think how fitting it was. You always lit up a room when you were in it, just like a yellow flower. I've missed you so much, my darling.'

Callie hugged Tiffany and they cried together.

'I recognise your voice,' Callie said. 'You used to sing Lavender's Blue to me to help me sleep. I thought I'd imagined or dreamed it, but it was you.'

Tiffany laughed through her tears.

'It would send you to sleep every time you had nightmares or when you were scared of the dark. We used to love singing that song together.'

Charlotte felt her eyes brimming with tears, overwhelmed with the poignancy of the moment. But they couldn't relax; this had to be a fleeting visit. It wasn't over yet.

'What happened to us?' Callie asked. 'Why were we separated?'

'We lost you darling. We tried to save you, but they were just too powerful for us—'

'Who's we?' Callie asked.

'Brett and me. And Brett's sister. We had a plan to give you a beautiful life. But it all went wrong. David beat me. He was ahead of me all the time. I didn't even see him coming.'

'Callie,' Charlotte interrupted, 'we can't stay around. I know you want to, but you're still on the run and I've got pressing matters to attend to. We need to finish here and be on our way.'

Tiffany and Callie were standing close now, each touching the other like they feared they might slip away again.

'Tiffany, we're going to get you out of here,' Charlotte said, drying her eyes and recovering her resolve. 'I know what they're doing to you, what they're up to—'

'Find Brett's storage unit,' she said. She spoke more clearly than when Charlotte had seen her previously. 'I have no idea where it is, but you'll find the paperwork in there. If you find that, you'll be able to shake off David and Fabian once and for all. I wasn't strong enough. Brett and I couldn't manage it together. See if you can beat them. My Callie, you're strong enough to do it. You were strong-willed as a baby; I can still see it in your eyes now.'

The woman who was helping them entered the room, a worried look on her face.

'They're doing the drug rounds, love; you'd best get out of here. I'll let you out of Tiffany's patio doors.'

'We're getting Tiffany out of here,' Charlotte said, 'We'll be back, we're not leaving her here any longer than we have to. Look after her please... You never told me your name.'

'You might as well know it now. It's Fiona.'

She rushed to the patio doors at the far end of Tiffany's room and opened them, ushering Callie and Charlotte outside.

'Thank you for doing this for Tiff,' she said. 'It's about time someone started looking out for that poor woman. I couldn't do anything on my own.'

Charlotte reached out and touched Fiona's arm.

'You've done plenty already, Fiona. Thank you.'

Callie gave Tiffany a final hug and followed Charlotte

through the doors. Fiona swiftly locked up behind them, and the two women made their way back to the hedge. They pulled themselves through the small gap in silence, then walked away from the care home as fast as they could. When they were a safe distance away from it, Callie broke down in tears. Charlotte put her arm around her shoulders.

'It's too much to cope with,' she sobbed. 'It's so overwhelming, Charlotte. What do I do? My whole life is being turned upside down, and I just don't know how to cope.'

'It's a lot to deal with,' Charlotte said gently. 'You need to give yourself some time to get used to it.'

'What happened to us?' Callie asked, her voice rising in anger. 'How can three children just disappear like that without anyone asking any questions?'

'That's what I've been trying to find out,' Charlotte replied. 'It's a big mess, Callie, but I'm close to the truth now.'

'Who is this Brett she was talking about? And who is my father? I feel like we're no further forward than we were. It's a huge mess. Maybe I should go back to the police now and let them solve it—'

'You can't do that.'

Charlotte could see her abrupt change in tone had given Callie a jolt.

'I beg your pardon?'

'I suspect there's something going on over land rights, Callie. It dates back two decades – to when you were a toddler living with Tiffany – and I reckon it's why you disappeared. I also believe there's a reason why you were asked to connect with Hollie Wickes after all this time. If you can trust me, Callie, I think we can do this without the police. Besides, not everybody at the police station is on our side.'

'Are you telling me we can't trust the police?'

'No, we can't, Callie, I'm sorry. This is bigger than either of us. It concerns a lot of money and a dispute which seems to go a long way back. My friend DCI Kate Summers can help, but she's been framed by somebody and she's in hiding at the moment. I'm sure she was on to something, and that's why they're trying to find her. They're making her life impossible by implicating her in a murder case. Kate Summers is our answer, and I'm working on that.'

Callie studied her face, as if she was making her final choice of an ally.

'I want to speak to Hollie Wickes. If she's connected with all this, I want to hear what she has to say.'

'I'd very much like you to speak to Hollie too,' Charlotte replied, recalling their altercation earlier that day. 'In fact, I'd like to speak to Hollie Wickes myself, but she might not be so eager to speak to me. She has her phone now, so why don't you call her? I'll drive you there, but you mustn't mention me.'

The two women walked over to a nearby bench and sat down. Callie found her mobile phone in her pocket and located Hollie's number in the missed calls. She dialled and put it on speaker phone. They looked at each other, waiting to see if the call was answered.

'Callie Irwin?'

It was Hollie Wickes' voice. Charlotte could tell Callie was about to correct her over the name.

'Go with it,' she whispered, 'that's how she knows you. It's how we all know you.'

'Yes, it's me. Why did you want me to call you?'

'I was told to call you. Somebody contacted me out of the blue a couple of weeks back. They scared me. They told me I'm not who I think I am. They asked me to do some things to find out the truth about my past. They gave me your number, but I couldn't summon up the courage to get in touch. Then my phone was stolen, and I couldn't call you back.'

'I'm here now. Where do you live?'

'I'm a student at the university now, but my real home is in Merseyside. I've lived there as long as I can remember. Who are you?'

'You know me as Callie Irwin, but I've been called Callie Whitehead all my life. I live in Kent; I didn't know anything about this area until I received an anonymous email, the same as yours. And I've just met the woman who's supposed... who is my birth mother. I'm not sure what to do.'

There was silence on the end of the line. This was a Hollie Wickes Charlotte was not familiar with. She'd seen her as a predator at first then, in the library; she'd been angry, really angry. And now she was claiming to be scared and confused, the same as Callie. And they'd both been contacted via a mysterious email.

'The email told me the same thing,' Hollie continued after a short pause. 'I don't believe what it told me. All my life, I've been sure who my mum and dad are—'

'What else did it tell you?' Callie pushed.

'It said my name is Jane. Apparently, my real name is Jane Irwin.'

CHAPTER TWELVE

December 1999

Before Tiffany had children, she imagined playgroups were all about the babies. She'd use words like personal development and social interaction which she learnt whilst reading numerous parenting books before everything fell apart. But once the post-natal depression had set in, she discovered playgroups were more about the mums than the children. It had become unpaid therapy for her, a place where she could be sure she wasn't going crazy.

When Callie screamed all night with colic, she'd assumed it meant she was failing as a mother, that she had to be doing something wrong. When Callie refused her breast milk and the midwife scolded her for considering formula, the only conclusion she could draw – because all the other mothers seemed to manage it – was that she was deficient in some way.

It was only after a chance encounter in the doctor's surgery one day and a suggestion that she might like to try the village playgroup that Tiffany finally found out the truth: parenting is, by-and-large, a shitstorm of trial and error and no new parent on earth has a clue what they're doing. In making the discovery, Tiffany had unlocked a wonderful, free therapy where she could laugh and cry at the terrible things her children did and finally realise it wasn't her fault.

She looked forward to Thursdays, the day Georgina didn't have to go to her part-time job and could come to playgroup with her three children. Tiffany had liked Georgina ever since she'd likened the pair of them to two suckling sows, overwhelmed by youngsters and just wanting to lay on the floor and close their eyes while their piglets drained all life and energy from them.

Georgina had become a trusted friend as they'd progressed through the playgroup, each adding a child every 13 months or so until they both finally drew the line at three. Georgina was fortunate that the children still had the same father, unlike Tiffany. She could relax with her friend because Georgina knew all about her demons: the post-natal depression, the difficult birth which led to a caesarean, and the psychological bullying David subjected her to.

'I'd put a laxative in Joanne's cornflakes if I were you,' Georgina said, laughing. 'He won't fancy her so much if she's stuck in the bathroom all day.'

Tiffany almost spat out her mouthful of tea at the idea. She loved Georgina for helping her to see the funny side of what was going on, even though it was deadly serious.

'How are you coping with Rowan now? He seems such a sweet little thing.'

She leaned over to look at the baby who was fast asleep in his car seat at Tiffany's side. They were surrounded by a post-apocalyptic array of toys on a carpet which would have kept a police DNA team employed for months analysing the various body fluids which the toddlers had left on it. Tiffany had once had to stop Jane from sucking on the corner of the carpet. Her only hope was that it would give her child immunity to any global pandemic which may or may not arise in future years.

'Surely David's settled, now the baby has arrived? I mean, no man's ever completely happy because of the interruption to normal service in the bedroom—'

Tiffany almost lost another mouthful of tea.

'But at least it means we can brush them away for a few months and get some respite from their constant demands. But Rowan must have had some positive impact, surely?'

Tiffany leaned in.

'Can you keep a secret, Georgie?'

Georgina leaned in closely, mirroring her friend's posture.

'This is why I love my Thursdays, Tiff,' she whispered. 'You've always got some decent gossip for me. I don't know what I expected from motherhood, but it turns out endless shitty nappies and monosyllabic conversations aren't enough for me. The monosyllabic conversation is referring to my hubby, by the way, I can have a good chat with the kids.'

'Rowan isn't David's.'

Georgina took a melodramatic intake of breath and her eyes looked like they were about to pop out of their sockets.

'You're teasing me?'

'I can't prove it yet, but I'm certain of it. Unless David could make me pregnant through the power of thought, it wasn't him.'

Georgina gave Tiffany a soft and playful tap on her arm.

'Good for you,' she said. 'That dick of a husband of yours has had it coming for a long time. You should have left him ages ago. At least my marriage is just a dull march towards a relationship lobotomy. David is horrible to you; I don't know how you've put up with it for so long.'

'You know why it is, Georgie. It's not quite as simple as walking away. But I will, once I've secured the children's future.'

'So, who's the father? And does David suspect?'

'I love you, Georgie, but there's no way I'm telling you who the father is. I can't risk that just yet—'

'How long?'

'Since last summer.'

Georgie gave her a second playful tap.

'You little devil, good for you.'

'It's as good as over between David and me now. He can barely conceal his contempt of me. Now he's got Joanne in the house, he's all for me getting some personal space. It suits me because I can see Br—'

'Nearly slipped up there!' Georgina ribbed her.

'When I missed my period, I seduced David one night. You've never seen a man so scared in his life. But I had to make sure we'd slept together to cover my trail. I can't risk having to leave the marriage with no voice in what happens to the land and the money.'

'Golly, that means none of the kids are his—'

'Golly?'

It was Tiffany's turn to tease now.

'You've been around small children for too long. I think you mean to say, *fuck me!*'

'That's exactly what I mean,' Georgina said with a laugh. 'That's lovely dear,' she continued, speaking to her middle child who had just presented her with an Action Man onto which a Barbie head had been transplanted.

'So, if I'm right about Rowan, none of the children are

his. David keeps pushing this adoption thing, but he only wants it for control. He's not interested in the children; it's the money and land he wants. I'm not giving him that power. Not now I've resolved to leave him—'

'My God, you're actually going to do it?'

'Yes, I've got a plan. I must get this power of attorney rescinded first though, then I can walk away. It's important to protect the interests of the children.'

'I can get you a paternity test done on the quiet if you want one.'

Tiffany looked at Georgina. She had a straight face.

'How?'

'I have an old school friend at the university. Let's just say he's helped me before.'

It was Tiffany's eyes which almost burst out of their sockets this time.

'You didn't?'

'While we're having this confessional, I may as well get it off my chest. At least it gives you some ammunition if I ever blurt out your story. I'm not proud of it, but I had a quickie at the back of a restaurant with a waiter in between Toby and Anne. It was on a girl's night out. I'd drunk too much and was overjoyed at being able to go out for the night.'

'What was the result?'

'Have you not noticed Anne likes setting up pretend tables with the plastic crockery set?'

'No? You're kidding?'

Georgina burst out laughing.

'I'm teasing you,' she laughed, 'All I got from that waiter was a rash which soon cleared up after a course of antibiotics. My kids are from the same father, but I learnt my lesson. No more asking the waiter what's on the list of specials.'

Tiffany reached out and hugged Georgina.

'What was that for?' her friend asked.

'I love you, Georgie; you keep me sane. Whenever I feel like I'm going crazy, I spend a Thursday morning here with you and I realise we're the sane ones... it's everybody else who's mad.'

'I mean it though,' Georgina said seriously, 'we can do it on the quiet and at least you'll know. It will help secure your parental rights over Rowan and put a lid on David's control over you. What do you think?'

Tiffany looked into her friend's face and saw she meant it.

'Let's do it,' she replied at last. 'When I leave David, I need to make sure everything is watertight. If I don't take care of all the loose ends, I'll never get away from him. And I simply can't bring myself to contemplate how awful that life would be.'

CHAPTER THIRTEEN

Charlotte grasped the meaning of what Hollie had just said a second or two before Callie did. She gasped out loud. Hollie was Jane Irwin?

'Are you there with someone? This isn't some kind of joke is it?' Hollie asked.

Her voice was suddenly defensive.

'Don't tell her it's me,' Charlotte warned Callie in a gentle whisper.

'I'm just here with a friend,' Callie bluffed. 'It's okay, I can trust her. You're telling me we're sisters?'

Charlotte wanted to shout out the entire family tree. The two women didn't grasp the significance of what had just been said. They had been so young when they were taken to their new parents that they were completely oblivious to their former life. But Charlotte understood.

'That's what the email said,' Hollie confirmed. 'It said we're bound by blood, even though I don't know it.'

'But you have two parents and can't remember any other life before them?' Callie asked.

'No, I can't. Sometimes I remember snippets, but I just

put them down to not remembering things correctly because I was so young. For instance, I have a recurring memory about me and a friend playing in a woodland area with stairs that went up a slope. My mum and dad told me I must have imagined it—'

'Was it walled?' Callie asked.

'Yes, how did you know?'

'Because I have the same memory. I assumed I was with a friend too. But was that you? How can it have been you?'

Charlotte could see Callie was getting upset again, and Hollie's voice was faltering on the end of the line.

'Did your parents ever tell you that you were adopted?' Callie asked.

'No,' Hollie replied. 'I'm an only child and it's all I've ever known. I love my mum and dad, they've been so good to me—'

'Have you challenged them about being adopted yet?'

'No, not yet. How can I do that to them? They'd be heartbroken if I was wrong. I wanted to find out more first. Do you think it's real? Do you believe we're really sisters?'

Charlotte waved at Callie to get her attention.

'Mute the call,' she mouthed.

'One minute, Hollie, I just need to mute you. I won't be long—'

Callie pressed the button and nodded to Charlotte.

'We have to meet her,' Charlotte began.

'We?' Callie asked.

'Well, you at first. I want to talk to Hollie, but we need to tread carefully. Don't tell her I'm coming, please, or it'll all get difficult—'

'What's been going on between you?'

'I'll tell you later,' Charlotte promised, 'but let's just say I reckon we're all being played here. Ask Hollie if she'll meet us at The Old Bell in Lancaster. It's nice and central there; I don't know if she has a car. We'd better not join her on the campus, I'd prefer to meet on neutral ground.'

'I feel like there's something you're not telling me, Charlotte.'

'I'll tell you after you finish your call. Don't keep Hollie on hold too long. The Old Bell is in a place called Bashful Alley. I used to go there with my husband when we were students. It's a tea shop.'

Callie unmuted the call and made the arrangements. Once she'd ended the conversation, she sat there staring at Charlotte for a while, then burst into tears again.

Charlotte put an arm around her. 'It's a lot to deal with in one day. Don't worry about it; it's understandable if you're overwhelmed by it all.'

It was like speaking to one of her own children; there wasn't that much of an age difference. If Olli and Lucia had been adopted, would she have told them? She probably would, but only when the children were older and able to decide whether they wanted to search for their birth parents. She'd always imagined how painful it would be for an adoptive parent to reveal the truth to their child. It was an impossible situation all round.

There was also a thorny issue which she couldn't bear to think about: if the children had disappeared beneath the police radar in 2000, had their adoption even been legal? Charlotte had no intention of opening that can of worms. There would be plenty of time for somebody else to raise those questions later.

'Surely your parents are the people who brought you up and loved you?' Lucia had suggested when they'd discussed the subject at the kitchen table one day. Charlotte knew it wasn't as simple as that.

Callie pushed her once again to explain why there were bad feelings between her and Hollie. Charlotte told her everything except that her husband was being held captive. She hadn't even told her own children, so she wasn't about to share it with Callie.

'Why would she have tried to contact your husband?' Callie asked.

'Well, I'm not sure Hollie was acting on her own. When we had our little tussle in the library, she was angry with me. As I told you earlier, I suspect something is amiss here, it doesn't feel right.'

Callie started scrolling through her phone apps, opening her emails and searching through them.

'The email address they used could be anybody's. Look.'

She held up the device and Charlotte peered at it. She was right. It was easy enough; Lucia had recently taught her how to create disposable emails to sign up for free gifts from a website. The email address disappeared after 24 hours and she avoided all the follow-up marketing afterwards. Charlotte didn't even know about it until Lucia showed her how it worked. It was highly probable that the email to Callie was untraceable.

Callie shook her head.

'How come you've found out all this information about me, Charlotte, when the police seem clueless?'

'Well, we couldn't have got the DNA confirmation without the police. The other information came in snippets from a variety of sources. At some point I'm guessing Hollie needs to do a DNA test, just to be certain. I wonder what happened to your brother, Rowan?'

'The email didn't say anything about a brother,' Callie replied. 'It's weird enough to discover I have a sister. I believed I was an only child, just as Hollie did.'

'I wonder if that's why your parents adopted you,' Charlotte mused. 'If they were unable to conceive, it would make sense. They must have been desperate for you, so it's no wonder you were loved so much.'

'I feel like everything we're doing here is betraying my mum and dad.' Callie began to cry again. 'I love them both, and I don't ever want to lose them. But I have to know who I am. Tiffany recognised me straight away, and even Hollie remembers playing in the wooded area.'

'You're not betraying your mum and dad,' Charlotte replied. 'It doesn't mean you love them any less. Tiffany is your birth mother, and it looks like Hollie may be your sister. You all have a right to find out about your past. And poor Tiffany... I can't even begin to imagine what she's endured since you disappeared.'

Charlotte's phone rang and Nigel's name appeared on the screen.

'I need to get this,' she said.

'Hi Charlotte, where are you?'

'Do you really want to know?' she replied.

'Yes, and I want to apologise for not having your back earlier. Teddy told me about what you did for Reagan and I just wanted to give you my support in whatever you're doing. I'm just so worried about you; you seem to attract trouble wherever you go. It's hard to keep track of you—'

'Nigel, it's fine, I get it.'

Charlotte was pleased for the apology; she'd been surprised at Nigel's response earlier.

'I'm so close now, Nigel. This is going to be an amazing news story. I can't tell you any of it yet, but I'll share it with you as soon as I can. We've been together on this all along.'

'Okay, thank you. I've been feeling bad all morning about what I said.'

'Do you think DI Comfort is trustworthy?' Charlotte asked.

'Why?' Nigel asked. 'He's been around for years, and he seems like a nice guy. I only have a professional relationship with him, but I'd say he's respected locally, yes. Why, what do you want to know?'

'Because I need to know who I can trust,' she replied.

'Well contrary to my earlier flakiness, you can rely on me,' Nigel said. 'I'm not so daft as to expect you to keep out of trouble, but if you need me, just call. I'll be ready and waiting whenever you need me, Charlotte.'

CHAPTER FOURTEEN

Charlotte wanted to go back to the industrial unit where she suspected Will was being held, but the telephone conversation with Hollie Wickes had lit another fire in her and she was desperate to find out more about Hollie's experiences with the mystery sender of the emails. Besides, it wasn't dark yet, she had to wait until nightfall before returning to the industrial estate.

She decided to prioritise Hollie first, while she still had an advantage over Vinnie Mace. He wouldn't yet know how she'd fared after the jet-ski incident. But his ignorance wouldn't last forever; Fabian Armstrong seemed to have considerable resources at his fingertips.

'We should get going,' Charlotte said to Callie, who'd been in a world of her own while she was making her call to Nigel. 'It won't take Hollie long to hop on a bus and get to the town centre; we mustn't miss her. Are you okay?'

'I'm stunned by all of this, Charlotte. I just met my birth mother, and only five minutes ago I finished speaking to a woman who claims to be my birth sister. I've been completely oblivious to all of this for the past twenty years.

It just seems... unbelievable, it's the only word for it. I assume if I was born as Callie Irwin and none of us drowned in the bay as they suspected, there must be two more people from the past wandering around out there.'

By Charlotte's reckoning, there were potentially more than that, but she couldn't risk overwhelming Callie. Besides, she had a big request for the arranged meeting in Lancaster and she needed her new companion to keep a steady mind.

'Let's walk back to the car,' she said. 'We can chat on the journey.'

As they returned to the parked vehicle, Charlotte remembered there was a pay phone in the square where she'd caught the bus on her previous impromptu visit. She clicked open the central locking and asked Callie to wait for her while she made a call. She had some change in her pocket, and it was high time she checked in with Kate Summers while she had the opportunity to make an untraceable call.

Thankfully the telephone box was much more pleasant than the first one had been in Lancaster. She found Kate's number, put plenty of change in the slot and held her breath as the call connected.

'Kate, it's me. Are you all right?'

'Thank God, Charlotte, I wondered if I was going to hear from you. Did you get the papers?'

'Yes, I had to hand one over, but three are safe. There was a number scribbled down on the envelope; is it important?'

'Yes, yes, it's vitally important. Please keep everything safe. Once you've got everything collected together, I want you to pick me up and we'll go to the police station together.

I'll also tip off the press beforehand to make sure nobody gets to me. It's the only way to manage this now.'

Charlotte thought of Nigel. If the newspaper received an exclusive tip-off, it would be amazing. She hoped Nigel had been serious when he'd promised to be on standby; he would have some fast typing to do if they ever got this situation under control.

The sound Charlotte had noticed on the previous call was in the background again. She still couldn't place it.

'Where are you, Kate? What's that sound I can hear?'

'You know I can't tell you yet, Charlotte. I need you to do one last thing for me, then we'll be clear. The number on the envelope, it's for a storage unit on Heysham Business Park. I need you to go there and look for a navy blue cardboard folder. It's wrapped in a plastic bag to keep it dry. Once you've got hold of it, we have everything we need—'

'Who owns the storage unit, Kate? Is it yours? Will I run into any trouble?'

'You might have to do a bit of explaining. It's my brother's storage unit. His stuff has been there for twenty years—'

'Twenty years? And they didn't throw it all out?'

'That's just it, Charlotte. Somebody has been paying the rental on the unit for two decades. The direct debit was changed shortly after Brett disappeared. I only discovered this recently and then... look, I don't want to tell you more than absolutely necessary, just in case they get to you. The less you know, the less you can tell them.'

'They've got Will, Kate—'

'What do you mean?'

'They're holding him somewhere. They know I picked up something important at your house and they want it. They're threatening us.'

'Oh no, Charlotte, I'm so sorry you got dragged into this. Have they hurt him? Is he okay?'

'I don't suppose they'll hurt him as long as they know I have what they want. I'm still figuring that bit out.'

Charlotte heard Kate's hand moving over the mouthpiece of her phone, and through it she heard Kate screaming out in frustration. She knew the feeling. Sometimes it felt like they were completely out of options.

'You must put Will's safety over mine,' Kate said, 'You'll have to risk it with the police—'

'I spoke to them, Kate. I had to.'

'Who did you speak to?'

'Toni Lawson, the press lady. I figured she's not an officer as such, so I was hoping she might advise me.'

'I don't know her well enough,' Kate sighed. 'She may be safe, she may not; I'm not sure. If you want to call in my colleagues to help Will, don't hesitate to do it, Charlotte. I'll have to figure out the rest, but do not put his life at risk.'

They'd already passed that stage as far as Charlotte was concerned, but she kept the thought to herself.

'Are you safe, Kate? Have you got food?'

'It's not the best accommodation I've had, let's put it that way, but there's no way my police colleagues or anybody else will find me here. And if they do, I'll see them coming in plenty of time.'

'Okay. Look, I'll get to the storage unit as soon as I can. But I need to sort out a couple of other things first. Can you hang on that long?'

Charlotte explained what had been happening with the Irwin children. Kate was as astonished by the developments as she had been.

'We're so close now, Charlotte, I can almost touch it with my fingers. Everybody is coming out of the woodwork at once. We must get the timing right; we can't allow Fabian Armstrong to strike ahead of us. If he does, every scrap of evidence will disappear, and we'll never put this case to bed. Hang on in there if you can, Charlotte, but promise me you won't put Will or yourself at risk.'

Charlotte laughed; she heard Kate do the same on the other end of the line.

'Now, you know as well as I do that's probably not going to happen. I won't do anything crazy, I promise, but you know how this all plays out.'

'I do, Charlotte, unfortunately I do. Let's meet up for lunch when all this is over, and we can have a good catch up. We've got a lot to talk about.'

'Believe me, I haven't told you the half of it,' Charlotte said with a laugh. It felt good to be having a regular conversation with someone who understood, without some bully boy waving his gun at her.

'We might need a weekend away, rather than a lunch. There are a few things I haven't told you yet.'

The distinctive noise in the background was still there; she wished she could work out what was causing it. She said goodbye to Kate, after promising to check in more regularly.

Callie was waiting back in the car, anxious to get going again.

'There's something I want you to do,' Charlotte said as she buckled up in her seat and started the engine. 'Hollie isn't going to be happy to see me, so I need you to prepare the way for me. But we will need to clear the air. Hollie has to see me as a friend, not an enemy, and you can help.'

'What do you want me to do?' Callie asked.

'You're not going to like it, but I want you to have an open phone line to my mobile phone while you're chatting to her. I want to listen in—'

'That's a bit much, Charlotte. Is it even legal?'

'Probably not, but I can't risk her flaring up when she sees me again. And I need to hear from her own lips what was going on with my husband. Hollie might be your sister by birth, but neither of us knows that yet, not without some DNA evidence. It might just be some clever ploy to bring everybody out into the open.'

'You're so suspicious, Charlotte. How else would she have remembered the time in the woods?'

'I'm guessing your birth mother will have mentioned the occasion to somebody. You only need a few choice snippets of personal information and you can convince people of most things. For your sake and mine, Callie, please do this. I'd never forgive myself if she was deceiving you and I'd just delivered you into the hands of somebody who might do you some harm.'

'Of course I'll help, Charlotte. You've already done more than the police ever have. But I still think you're over-reacting.'

'I know I sound like some conspiracy theorist at times,' Charlotte replied, 'but I wouldn't put anything past the people we're dealing with.'

CHAPTER FIFTEEN

From her table at the far end of the tearoom, Charlotte watched the first meeting of the two women. She felt mildly ridiculous, having taken Callie's hat as a disguise and borrowed her ear buds to listen into the conversation. If the stakes hadn't been so high, she'd have burst out laughing at her ridiculous take on a police surveillance operation. It was poorly conceived and cheaply delivered, but it was all she'd got.

A wave of nostalgia washed over her as she recalled the times she and Will had spent at The Old Bell as students in the eighties, new lovers forging the framework of a relationship that would endure for years. Her desire to see him was urgent. She pictured them both as students, sharing a toasted tea cake to make their grants go further and squeezing the last drops out of a pot of tea, but caring very little about anything except being together and enjoying each other's company. It was good that the tearoom had still survived after all those years when so much around it had changed.

Callie and Hollie's first meeting was awkward; they

weren't sure whether to shake hands or give each other a stand-offish embrace. What happened was a combination of both, but it broke the ice, and the sound of their uncomfortable laughter came over loud and clear in Charlotte's ear.

'Are you ready to order?' the waitress asked.

Charlotte placed a simple order for a cold, soft drink and tuned back into the conversation.

'I'm trying to work out if you even look like me,' Callie said.

'Me too,' Hollie replied. 'It's mad, isn't it?'

'I love your piercing,' Callie ventured, sounding awkward in her attempts to get the conversation going.

Charlotte had every sympathy. What do you say to the woman who you discover is probably your sister after twenty years of not knowing she even exists?

Hollie smiled. 'Thanks. My mum and dad... God, it sounds so weird saying that now. What does this make them, my adoptive mum and dad?'

Charlotte wanted to shout out across the room; *They're still your mum and dad, Hollie, and they always will be.*

'They didn't want me to get it done, because they thought it might stop me getting jobs when I left uni. I just told them I'll take it out if it's a problem. They told me they don't understand where I get my stubborn streak from; well, now we know.'

'Did you ever feel like you didn't belong?' Callie asked. 'I honestly had no idea I might be adopted. The lack of baby pictures gave it away, now I think about it. They used to make some excuse about not owning a camera back then. But you'd still have baby pictures, however hard-up you were, wouldn't you?'

Callie's voice was louder than Hollie's, the mobile phone being closer to her on the table. However, despite the hubbub of chatter in the tearoom, Charlotte could hear both of them clearly.

'I'm younger than you, aren't I? I do have baby pictures, but only a handful. My mum and dad said people didn't photograph every moment of their waking life back in those days. It was probably a dig about how much I use my phone.'

Charlotte willed Callie to bring her into the conversation. This was the ideal opportunity.

'You said you lost your phone. What happened? I've been trying to reach you.'

Charlotte almost jumped up and cheered. The sooner Callie cleared the way for her to join the conversation, the better.

'Oh, I got caught up in something I regret now. I thought I was helping, but it's turned into a bit of a nightmare. Some crazy woman ended up stealing my phone because she reckoned I was jumping into bed with her husband.'

Charlotte felt her face reddening, desperate to leap to her own defence.

'Were you?' Callie asked.

'No, of course not, if you knew the age of the guy—'

The sooner Charlotte represented herself in this conversation, the better. She'd never realised how awkward it was listening in to people speaking about her.

Hollie leaned in towards Callie. 'I'll be honest with you; I was relieved when you finally contacted me. I thought I'd been caught in some massive con trick. After this person contacted me to tell me I had a sibling, they asked me to reach out to this guy and get to know him. They told me he was key to finding you and the rest of my family. He also said this chap's wife was involved, so I contacted her at a local run too.'

Charlotte recalled the parkrun where Hollie had tagged along with her and Daisy for a few minutes, making small talk. It was fascinating to hear the other side of the story.

'Turns out she's a psycho. She stole my phone and did the whole bunny boiler thing on me.'

'Why did she think you were sleeping with her husband?'

Charlotte was grateful to Callie for attempting some form of fair hearing for her. Her cold drink arrived, and she thanked the waitress.

'Well, that's where it all gets nasty. Somebody's spooked this guy, I don't know how. He challenged me about some photograph of me he found in his pocket. I didn't put it there; I reckon it was his crazy wife.'

Charlotte had the upper hand and Callie needed to move this on. If Hollie didn't slip that photograph into Will's pocket, and she didn't, it must have been somebody else. So, who was it?

'Are you aware the police want to speak to me?' Callie changed the subject. 'I met our mum this morning too—'

'You know who she is? You've seen her? So, they weren't lying?'

'No, I've had the DNA tests to confirm I am Callie Irwin by birth. It feels so weird that I'm supposed to be a different person. How does that even happen?'

'I need to get a DNA test done,' Hollie said. 'How does it work? I've seen cheap kits in the chemist; you can do it yourself these days, can't you?'

'I don't know much about it,' Callie admitted. 'Mine was taken in the hospital. But we do need to get you tested. It's the only way you can be sure.'

'What if it's some elaborate hoax?' Hollie continued. 'I don't know how I'd cope if it was a set-up. It would be so cruel; why would anybody want to do that?'

'I need to visit the rest rooms,' Callie said. 'I've got something else I want to share with you when I come back.'

Charlotte attempted to make herself less conspicuous. This was their cue; they'd agreed to exchange notes in the ladies' toilets. She continued to face away from their table and moved as discreetly as possible. Callie joined her in the toilets.

'It's not a good idea to introduce yourself; she thinks you're crazy,' Callie told her.

'I need to. She has to realise I'm not the enemy. If she wants to get her birth mother out of the care home – and we have to assume she is Jane Irwin until she gets her DNA tested – she has to work with me, not against me. We must bite the bullet, Callie. Please.'

Callie nodded and the two women returned to their places in the tearoom.

'I need you to trust me,' Callie began, as Charlotte replaced the ear bud to monitor the conversation. 'The woman who you said is crazy... well, I know her.'

'You know the crazy woman? How? Is she the one who's been screwing about with my life?'

'No, steady, let me explain. This woman's name is Charlotte—'

'I know that already.'

Charlotte sensed Hollie's prickly reaction even over the phone line.

'She's the one who helped me meet my – our – birth mother, Tiffany. Mum recognised me as soon as I walked into her room. She's being kept in a mental health facility. Charlotte works for the local newspaper and has been investigating our disappearance. She believes there's some sort of malicious activity going on and Tiffany is the victim.'

'Like I said, she's a crazy woman—'

'Hollie, please, just listen.'

Charlotte smiled. The DNA would need to confirm it, but it sounded like Callie was the elder sister alright.

'I want you to meet Charlotte.'

'I'd rather punch her in the face.'

'Hollie! If you want to find out the truth about the past, who do you trust most? Some anonymous source who won't make themselves known to you, or the woman who's in this tearoom at this very moment and desperately wants to speak to you?'

Charlotte gulped. This was it. They were either about to have a stand-up row in a cosy tearoom or Hollie would take a chance and trust her.

'She's here now?' Hollie said, standing up. 'Where? Where is that crazy bitch?'

It was time to come face to face with Hollie. Charlotte stood up, removed her hat, picked up her drink and walked over to the table. She understood why Hollie was angry with her, and she wasn't intending to defend her actions, but they needed to speak.

'Hello, Hollie, I'm Charlotte. I'm sorry we got off to a bad start. But please, just give me ten minutes to explain everything. If you don't want to believe me, that's fine. I'll give you my home address and you can report me to the police. I promise. I want to help you, Hollie. I want to help you both.'

Callie had her hand on Hollie's arm as if she half expected her to leap up and attack Charlotte. By the look on Hollie's face, even she hadn't fully decided what was going to happen next. Charlotte pressed on.

'I know you're angry with me, Hollie, and I don't blame you. I did take your phone, but I thought you were the one causing trouble for me. I see it clearly now. Whoever contacted you and Callie out of the blue, they're the ones causing all this trouble. That's who has been making us both go crazy. We've both been played, Hollie. And it's time we seized back the initiative and started flushing out these damn cowards.'

CHAPTER SIXTEEN

December 1999

Tiffany always looked forward to the walk up to St Peter's Church. She could imagine that part of the village as it might have looked when her mother and father were newly married. She liked to lay a seasonal wreath on their graves as soon as one was available in the shops. It only took one winter gale blowing in from the sea to scatter flowers at that time of year.

Walking up the narrow lane was an exercise in child management in itself. As soon as she sorted out one child, another demanded her attention. She released the catch on Rowan's car seat and bent over to extract him from the car safely.

She was grateful for the combined pram and pushchair, which provided the protection of a pram for Rowan, a forward-facing pushchair for Jane, and – should it be required – a clip-on wheeled board, not unlike a skateboard, which allowed Callie to stand on it and hitch a ride. Callie's reins were fastened to the handle, since she was at an age where it was best to be firmly tethered in case she made an impromptu dash for freedom.

Tiffany looked at the birth mark on Callie's face. She'd often wished it was somewhere else less visible. She had seen the marks referred to as stork bites, and they were supposed to fade over time. But Callie's showed no signs of fading, and she feared the inevitable teasing when her daughter entered primary school then graduated to the bear pit of secondary education. She ran her hands through Callie's soft hair and wished she could take the blemish away for her.

Once she'd got Rowan out of his car seat, she laid him gently in the pram, making sure his tiny knitted hat was on securely and his white scratch mittens were tucked into his cardigan. She arranged the sheets and blankets around him to keep him warm. His features gave no indication of who the father might be, even though she knew it was Brett. He couldn't possibly be David's child; the marriage had moved to coldness too quickly. She couldn't wait for Georgina to get the test results from her friend at the university; the paperwork would confirm everything.

The more she thought about it, the more she was convinced David had been after her money and the land from the start. She'd been vulnerable, reeling from her failed relationship with Callie and Jane's father, a man who was there for the good times but struggled to cope with the bad times. The caesarean had needed a long physical recovery and she was still reeling from a debilitating bout of post-natal depression.

David had seemed like a knight in shining armour, fulfilling her desperate need for adult company and physical closeness. But the moment the ring was on her finger, the drawbridge came up and he no longer seemed to care. In her less trusting moments, she wondered if the whole thing had been a set-up. Had she been manoeuvred into loving David Irwin? She was like a stray dog, accepting love from anyone; had he preyed on her in a moment of weakness?

Having organised all three children, she led them up the main street and took the turn towards the church. They would grow fractious if she spent too long at the graves, so they would conclude events by going to the walled, wooded area which led up to the ruined chapel at the top of the cliffs. This was always a highlight of their visits. She would release Jane from the pushchair and the two girls would be happy toddling and crawling among the trees, counting their way up and down the steps built into the gentle slope. It would provide a brief period of respite for her too, knowing the girls were safe from any harm; she could sit on one of the benches.

The sight of the fierce grey sea and the crashing waves beyond the church never ceased to take her breath away. Perched on the cliff tops against the backdrop of the bay, the structure stood proud and defiant against the ravages of the weather, as it had done for years. She wondered if she would be buried here, like generations of the Armstrong family, or if events would drive her away from the place she called home.

Her mother and father's burial plots were at the back of the graveyard, and whenever she visited them, she knew there wasn't a better place for the two of them to lay at rest. They'd met in this part of the world, married and died here. But as much as she loved the area, it was beginning to feel like she didn't belong.

At least she hadn't married Callie and Jane's father. The moment life had become tricky, he'd disappeared. He wasn't interested in staying in touch with the children, nor did he make any demands on Tiffany. Now, with her hasty and ill-judged marriage to David, it had all gone wrong again.

But with Brett, she could put it right. It felt like they were being cast aside from this part of the world, steered into living somewhere else. She hoped it would be a fresh start; Brett was different, so good with the children. She would tell him he was Rowan's father just as soon as the paperwork was all sorted. It would be the icing on the cake when they left with the children, her thank-you gift to him for the faith he'd shown in her.

Her mother's grave was weather-beaten now, the name *Lilian Armstrong* worn and faded, but her father's was still new, the granite bright, the gilded lettering clear and distinct. She wished she could have cried more when her father died. Theirs had been a difficult relationship; she'd always felt second best to Fabian, as if she wasn't up to taking over the farm and running it just as capably as her brother. Her mother had always believed in her though, whatever mistakes she had made. She missed her mum.

Tiffany reached under the pram section of the buggy and pulled out the wreaths. Jane started to push forward, tugging on the reins which kept her safe in the pushchair. Tiffany handed a wreath to Callie, guiding her little gloved hands away from the prickles of the holly, and asked her to place it on Granddad's grave. She unclipped Jane and repeated the action, her heart ready to explode as she watched her beautiful tiny children laying the wreaths as if it were the most important job in the world.

With the wreaths laid, Tiffany let Callie and Jane toddle at their own pace towards the wooded area. They knew where they were going so didn't hang around long. After a run around among the trees, Tiffany was often lucky enough for all three of them to fall asleep in the car at the same time. If they did, she would park on the drive outside the house and sleep in the car with them. Joanne was supposed to be helping more, but it didn't seem to be making much difference to how tired Tiffany felt.

As she let the girls run ahead beyond the old stone wall, she spotted Aida Bryn sitting alone on one of the benches by the entrance. She pulled up the buggy at the side, put on the brake and took a seat next to her.

'Hello, Aida, I haven't seen you around here in ages. I'd heard you were ill; is everything all right now?'

Aida looked like her body was all but worn out. She was in her late nineties, still taking care of herself, a widow since her husband lost his life at sea forty years previously.

'Hello Tiffany, my darling. The child has been born, I see, a boy too.'

Tiffany brought Aida up to date with what had been happening since she'd last seen her. People like Aida were her last remaining link to her mother and father. They'd all lived in a time that seemed better, one without computers and even televisions for many people, an era when this place was dedicated to fishing and a life based around the sea.

'You've been to see your Ma and Pa?' Aida asked.

'Yes, and the girls love the wood so much.'

As if on cue, Callie shouted in the distance.

'Mum, look, Jane can walk up the steps!'

'That's lovely,' Tiffany shouted. She turned to Aida. 'I do like it here; they can't fall and hurt themselves and the walls make a natural boundary so I don't lose sight of them.'

'They've got your temperament,' Aida continued, smiling at the sight of the girls absorbed in their play. 'I'm pleased they didn't get your brother's traits; he was a rascal, that one.'

Tiffany loved hearing Aida's stories from their family's past. It was like travelling back in time to revisit her childhood.

'Your mother saw the devil in that boy. She asked me once what she should do about it. She'd caught him shooting robins with his air rifle in one of the fields. "What kind of child shoots robins, Aida?" she said to me. "Children love robins; they shouldn't want to kill them." She was worried, all right.'

'I never knew that,' Tiffany replied. She knew Fabian could be a bully, but she'd never seen that spiteful side to him. Or had she? An image came to mind of him kicking a cow in calf once when she was younger. Maybe the cruel streak had been there all the time.

'What did you say to her?' Tiffany asked, sensing Aida was going somewhere with this.

'I told her to watch that one. I said evil shows itself early in children, and it never goes away once it shows its face.'

'What did she do? Did she take notice of you?'

'She did, though she was angry with me at first for suggesting it. But we met in the village two weeks later and she apologised to me. She said, "Aida, you were right. I never saw it before. There's something about Fabian which isn't quite right." Don't get me wrong, she loved your brother; he was her child after all. But she knew she'd have to watch him. Because if he wasn't shooting robins, she knew he'd be hurting something else.'

CHAPTER SEVENTEEN

It was growing dark outside and the staff in the tearoom were beginning to clear the tables, wipe them down and neaten the chairs. Charlotte knew the signs. Although you'd never read it in a brochure or hear a proprietor admit it, this was catering code for *buzz off, we want to go home, we're tired.* There was a definite point in the evening at the guest house when diners were overstaying their welcome, and most took the hint as the staff began clearing up around them.

Charlotte and her two young companions had been engaged in lively conversation for some time, and each had an empty glass or cup in front of them. They hadn't even been spending money while they'd been taking up a full table.

'It's time we made a move,' Charlotte prompted. 'Are you happy to declare a truce, Hollie? For now, at least?'

'Yeah, I'm still furious with you for taking my phone, but I'll take your word for it, for now. It makes more sense that we're all being played than it does you taking a page out of the Fatal Attraction handbook.'

'Good, I'm pleased about that. If we can agree to work together for a little while, you have my permission to steal my phone and send rude messages on my social media accounts. You might want to warn people first though. Any dodgy pictures you send wouldn't be a pretty sight.'

Callie laughed, but Hollie gave a look of distaste that was typical of a young person barely out of their teenage years, born out of a firm disbelief that anybody over the age of thirty could have anything remotely attractive about them.

She'll soon learn, Charlotte thought.

'Hollie and I are probably going to go into town to make an evening of it,' Callie said. 'There's so much to talk about that neither of us is ready to go our separate ways yet. Are you joining us, Charlotte?'

'No, I have something I need to do,' she replied, mindful that she wanted to return to the industrial unit as soon as possible. If Will was inside, there would be a light on, a car parked nearby or at least some clue. She handed Callie the hat she'd been using as a disguise.

'You'd better take this,' Charlotte suggested. 'Remember, the police are still looking for you. Thank your lucky stars the only photograph of you they've published is from twenty years ago. There's not much chance of the general public spotting you for now. But promise me you'll take care.'

Callie touched Charlotte's arm.

'I will. Thank you Charlotte, you've already helped me more than the police. I'll walk into the police station when I'm ready, but I can't work at their pace; I have to understand what's going on. This is my life – our lives – after all.'

Charlotte handed Callie a ten-pound note from her pocket.

'Take this, and at the risk of sounding like your mother, make sure you hold back enough for your bus fare or a taxi. If you need to draw any money to lend to Callie, I'll pay you back, Hollie.'

Callie nodded and Charlotte picked up the bill which had been deposited on the table. She settled it by payment card and left a good tip, apologising to the waitress for delaying the staff.

'We'll be expecting you at the guest house,' Charlotte said, returning to Callie and Hollie. If she hadn't known beforehand, she'd have placed them as sisters if they'd been random customers in her own restaurant area. They seemed in tune with each other already; it was uncanny how quickly the two had bonded.

As she made her way back to the car park in the town centre, a wave of resentment swept over her, then passed as quickly as it arrived. For a moment, she felt a pang of jealousy that Hollie and Callie had some form of resolution already, while she was still a castaway at sea, with only a hunch about where her husband might be. Moreover, she still faced danger from Vinnie Mace, who would use his military skills to find her sooner or later. The conversation in the tearoom had distracted her, but now she was apprehensive about the task ahead.

Equally frustrating was the slow-moving line of traffic out of Lancaster. It seemed to take forever to crawl through the city, but eventually she was on her way to the White Lund Industrial Estate, where she hoped she would find Will. She pulled up some distance away from the unit, deciding to use the welcome cover of their regular cash and carry, which was a short distance away. Did fictional tough guys like Jack Reacher ever consider topping up with supplies at the cash and carry before embarking on what might turn out to be a hazardous operation? Probably not, she decided.

It had grown dusky, and the streetlights were coming on. She wanted to see if there was any life at all at the former craft store. If she felt out of her depth, she made a promise to herself that she would involve the police. But she refused to give up Kate Summers. Kate was everybody's way out of this. But she had to get to that industrial unit first.

The unit was straight ahead. Her heart jumped as she saw a car parked outside: a Tesla, just like the one owned by Doctor Maxwell Henderson. The excitement turned to raging panic when she realised why he might be there. Had they hurt Will? She tried to calm down, telling herself there were all sorts of reasons why the doctor might be in their dingy hideout. Vinnie and his mate had been involved in a minor accident on the motorway, and if one of them had been hurt, the doctor was probably patching them up. She couldn't see any other cars though, which suggested he was there alone.

She walked to the front of the building and set off a security light. Cursing, she stepped back into a shadowy area and waited a while. All seemed quiet.

She didn't want to enter the building from the front. The security light would give the game away every time. There was only one thing for it: she'd have to get over the gate and sneak round the back. On closer examination she realised that wouldn't work either; there were deadly spikes on top.

On a whim, she checked the padlock, not expecting it to be unlocked for one moment, but she was in luck. Someone had arranged the lock to give the appearance of being secured, but they hadn't pushed it in fully. Working quietly, she unhooked the chain from the lock, unwrapped it and slipped through the gap. She took care to replace the restraint as she'd found it. At least she could make a fast escape if someone spotted her.

The side of the industrial unit was in darkness, with no security lights. At the sound of voices, she stopped at a barred window to listen, straining to hear. It was no good; the sound was too muffled. Yet this had to be the place. Will was inside, she was certain of it.

Once she reached the end of the building, Charlotte peered around the corner. There was Vinnie's car, the front wing crunched by the impact from the earlier motorway chase. She was delighted to see his vehicle had fared worse than the company car, but it also meant he was probably in there, gun and all. She had to do everything possible to find Will without Vinnie realising she was back in circulation. If he had his gun, she was in above her head and would have to alert DI Comfort or Toni Lawson to get the gun squad in there. She had no desire to stare down the barrel of a deadly weapon again.

Alert for more security lights, she moved to the rear side of the unit, hugging the wall. There was a window ahead, a clear one which would finally give her a view of what was going on inside. She edged towards it, alert for the voices which didn't seem to be coming from the room. It was worth risking a look; she was desperate to see Will. If they'd hurt him, what would she do?

She stooped below the window, listening for sounds of life inside, but there was nothing. Slowly, she pushed herself up to see over the window ledge. Doctor Henderson had his back to her, and he was sorting through his medical bag.

As she raised herself up a little higher, she heard the

crunch of a footstep on gravel to her side and felt a sharp jab in her neck. Her legs gave way beneath her and she felt herself dropping to the ground.

CHAPTER EIGHTEEN

The first thing Charlotte recognised was Will's voice. She'd never heard him like this before: nervy, on edge, fearful. Then there were footsteps, on a hard, concrete surface, echoing along the floor. Aside from the woozy sensation in her head, a persistent sting in her neck suggested she'd been injected, no doubt with some drug from Dr Henderson's medicine bag. Her head was covered too, with something like a pillowcase. She tried to move her hands, but they were tied to her front. Of course they were. Her ankles were secured too.

'Will?' she ventured.

'I'm here, Charlotte—'

The dull thud of a fist on flesh was followed by a guttural sound from Will.

'You bastards,' she shouted. 'This is nothing to do with my husband. If you want information, you'll have to get it from me.'

There was relaxed laughter, from familiar voices. Vinnie and Fabian's doctor friend sounded calm and in control. She struggled against her restraints, but they were tight and there was little she could do to loosen them.

'So, you've come round at last. You can't beat a drop of Propofol to stop someone dead in their tracks. It took virtually nothing to knock you out.'

'Just tell me what you want, Vinnie. What's all this about? Why are you so desperate to get your hands on those documents?'

'This doesn't work like the films, Charlotte. I don't confess all our plans to you so you can make some death-defying escape. What happens here is that I get to showcase some tricks I learnt in Afghanistan. If you're sensible about things, your husband walks away with all his fingers intact and you get to retain your knee caps.'

Charlotte had always wondered why people in films who found themselves in a similar situation to herself continued to struggle despite being tightly bound. She'd got her answer. It was a natural instinct when your entire body was overcome with a cocktail of hate, anger, frustration and helplessness. It seemed to be the only way to express herself, however futile.

She heard a rip of tape and a scuffle to the rear of her. Will called out.

'Just do what you have to, Charlotte. Kate can take care of—'

Will was silenced by the application of the tape. She heard him struggling to call to her, but was unable to make out his words.

Charlotte felt her entire body trembling. Whatever had made her think she was able to steal a lead on these men? They seemed unassailable, doing whatever they wanted, whenever they wanted, and she was swiftly running out of options to protect herself, Will and Kate. How could Kate take care of herself, when she'd been set up for a murder she didn't commit and was on the run from Vinnie? Her family had already been forced to flee to France for safety.

'I want to see my husband,' she said, as defiantly as she could, given that the effects of the drug were still lingering. 'I want to see him for myself. Then maybe I'll talk.'

'Let's be very clear about this, Charlotte. You have no control here.'

Without warning, a terrifying sawing sound began close to the side of her head. Her body convulsed with shock.

The sound stopped as quickly as it began. She felt two hands grasp her from under her armpits and haul her up onto a chair.

'I need your finger, Charlotte—'

'For Christ's sake, what the hell are you going to do?'

The sawing sound began again. She flinched and struggled, even though she knew it was pointless.

'Your finger please,' Vinnie repeated.

'You've tied my hands. I can barely move, you moron,' she seethed.

Charlotte half expected a fist to come slamming into the face covering. Instead, Vinnie moved her roughly, then pulled out her hands so that they were in front of her. She closed her eyes, determined to retain as much dignity as possible in the face of this terrifying intimidation.

'Finger out,' Vinnie demanded. She did as she was told, struggling to sit upright, her legs now so weak from fear that she wouldn't have been able to stand on them even if she'd wanted to. She waited for the sound of the saw, bracing herself for unbearable pain. Instead, a hand grasped her finger and placed it against a flat, plastic surface.

'Thanks,' Vinnie said, 'I just wanted to unlock your phone.'

'You bastard!' Charlotte shouted. 'Do you get off on all this? You're a sociopath, whatever that psychological report told you. Who compiled the report, the good doctor over there? Why is he even here? Isn't he supposed to be curing patients, not hurting them?'

'Oh, by the way, now you mention it, we know you were snooping around Doctor Henderson's house. You've heard of CCTV, I take it? Well, it's all over the doctor's house and we've got footage of you creeping all over the place. And yes, we'll be using that if we need to report the theft of certain valuable items which have gone missing from the doctor's house. To help focus your mind, those valuable items were concealed in the loft space of the house where your son lives with his girlfriend, just waiting for a police tip-off. How much do you reckon a conviction of theft will damage his fledgling career?'

'Okay, you win the "how high can I pee" contest. Now, how about we get down to business? Why am I here? Why is Will here? What do you want?'

'You know what I want, Charlotte. I want the paper-work you retrieved from Kate Summers' house and the loca-tion of her brother's storage unit and the key or passcode if you have it. And I want Kate Summers, or at least, I want to find out where she's hiding.'

'What will happen to Kate when you find her?'

'That all depends. There's a little matter we have to clear up over her brother. She's been a naughty girl, has your friend DCI Summers. Did you know she concealed evidence when he disappeared twenty years ago? A newly recruited police constable, with the safety wheels only just removed, and corrupt from the start.'

'If Kate Summers broke any rules, she did it for a

damned good reason. She must have been protecting some-body. I'd trust that woman with my life—'

'But would you give up your life for her, Charlotte?'

Charlotte had no intention of anybody having to give up their life. If there was a way to keep them all alive with all their fingers intact, she would do what it took.

'What's it going to take to do this the civilised way, Vinnie?'

'Unfortunately, Charlotte, we're beyond that now. When Kate Summers went into hiding, she drew a line in the sand. She made it a race. Either she gets there first or we do. And we have more resources, more incentives and more motivation to sort this out. You and Kate, alas, have a lot to lose. Doctor Henderson, it's time to get started.'

Charlotte heard a movement across the room, then Will let out some desperate, muffled cries. If only she could see. It was completely disorienting not to have a sense of the room and what was going on.

'You asked me what the Doctor is doing here, Charlotte. He has a particularly important job. He's going to keep your husband conscious while I ask you some very simple ques-tions. Will doesn't play guitar, does he? Only he might have a little difficulty if he wants to try, after our little chat tonight.'

The sound of the electronic saw started again at the far side of the room and Charlotte flinched as she heard Will's stifled cry through his taped-up mouth.

CHAPTER NINETEEN

Will's muffled cries were short-lived. Charlotte struggled to loosen her ties, but the hard plastic dug into her skin. There was no wriggling her way out of these restraints. She would need to be cut out, and there didn't seem much prospect of that in the immediate future.

'Will? Will? What have you done to him, you dickheads?'

A silence settled over the room. Had Will passed out with the pain? She imagined his bloody finger lying on the ground and fought to hold down a scream. She wouldn't give them the satisfaction.

What were her options? She had to get them out of this alive, and preferably unharmed. She could give up the documents. Vinnie had mentioned Brett's storage unit too, so there was no hiding that either. If she gave them Kate's telephone number, might they locate her? They'd be able to pinpoint her mobile phone to a mast, but only with the correct equipment and access. Was Fabian Armstrong powerful enough to do that?

Charlotte considered Kate's warning about a rogue police officer. A copper on the payroll might organise a signal trace to a mast. If she could warn Kate in time, at least her friend could find a new hiding place.

Her spirits sank further when she realised she probably wouldn't get out of this unharmed. Why would they let her and Will go? Vinnie wouldn't torture the two of them then allow them to go running to the police. Their only value to Vinnie was in the information he wanted. Once he had it, they'd be no further use to him. She had to delay him as long as possible in the hope that Lucia, Olli or Isla – or perhaps even Callie – would alert the police and the cavalry would come charging in before Vinnie got what he wanted.

She jumped in fright as the noise of the saw sounded directly at the side of her head. Vinnie laughed.

'You should have seen your reaction, you nearly jumped as high as the roof just then.'

The doctor was laughing too. Didn't these men have hobbies? Was this all they could do to occupy their time, frightening innocent people out of their wits?

'What have you done to Will? I want to see my husband. You'll get nothing from me until I see he's okay.'

Vinnie's hand clasped the back of whatever they'd placed over her head and pulled it tight around her neck. He pulled it tighter and tighter; her breathing was becoming more constricted by the second.

'I – can't – breathe…' she pleaded.

'Yeah, that's the general idea,' Vinnie replied calmly. 'Don't worry, I've done this many times before. The Afghans last longer because the air is thinner up in the mountains and they're used to it. There's about another minute until you pass out, but it's never an exact science.'

Charlotte had never experienced a sensation like it. When the water had been sloshing around her on the causeway, she'd at least been able to grab breaths in between the ebb and flow of the waves. What Vinnie was doing constricted her airway, a crushing feeling which stopped her from gasping for air. The worst thing was not being able to move her arms and legs; she could only struggle, trying to wriggle out of Vinnie's vice-like grasp. Just as she felt herself losing consciousness, he released her. She gulped, frantically drawing the air into her lungs.

'Hey, I might try a bit of water-boarding later,' Vinnie said, close by her ear. 'I miss doing that. I held the record in Afghanistan, you know. I could extract a confession, real or fictional, within three hours from even the toughest rebel and leave them a mental wreck afterwards. If only they gave out medals for skills like that, I'd be covered in them.'

'You're psychotic,' Charlotte gasped at him, her voice faltering and painful. 'There's something wrong with you. No sane person does this to another—'

Vinnie grabbed the bottom of her hood and pulled it tighter. She flinched again, taking a deep breath before he cut off her air supply. His grip relaxed.

'Only kidding,' he laughed, 'But do stop the insults, Charlotte. I know you don't like this – it's not a spa day – but I really don't care. We keep doing this until I get what I want. If I get a one-star rating at the end, I've done a great job.'

'What happens to us if I give you the information? Will you let us go?'

'That depends,' Vinnie replied.

'On what?'

'On whether you have everything we need. You see, Kate is the icing on the cake. We need to tie this up swiftly when we make our move. Let's just say everything is a little precarious right now. But yes, if we get what we're after, you and your husband walk free.'

'But you've hurt him already. Why should I give you anything?'

'Oh, Will's fine,' Vinnie began.

'You chopped off his finger.'

'No, Charlotte, I didn't. I didn't have to. He fainted at the mere suggestion of it. I'll give those Afghan rebels one thing, they had a lot more staying power than your husband.'

'Why should I believe a rat like you?'

If she ever got out of those ties, she'd charge at Vinnie like an angry rhinoceros and attack him until he died.

'Listen, Charlotte, for a man like me, this is just another day in the office. What we've been doing so far is my equivalent of gentle stretching exercises. We haven't even made a proper start yet. So, believe me when I tell you I'm just warming Will up on the stove, and we're nowhere near boiling point yet.'

'I want to see him. Then I'll start to talk.'

'No, you start to talk, then you see him.'

'There's a document hidden in the spare wheel area in the company car, which is parked at the cash and carry. You can go and get it now if you want, to prove I'm telling the truth.'

'If you're wasting my time, Charlotte—'

'I'm not, I promise.'

'There's no riding off into the sunset on some kid's jet-ski this time. By the way, you were impressive. It takes some guts to pull a move like that. It's why your ties are so tight; I need to watch you. You're less predictable than the rebels.'

'Let me see Will. Then you get the document. It'll only

take you five minutes to collect it. If I'm lying to you, you can remove one of my fingers. You'll see, I'm not lying.'

'Okay, maybe we won't have to do this the hard way. I'm going to remove your hood—'

'For the count of ten,' Charlotte chanced. 'I need a proper look at him. I'll count to ten, then I'll cooperate, if you're not lying about hurting him.'

'Okay then, maybe the water-boarding will wait. Shame. I had a bet with the doctor that I'd break your husband within thirty minutes. You, I reckon, might be pig-headed enough to hold out for an hour. But no longer, I wagered fifty pounds on it.'

Charlotte felt Vinnie's hand at the back of the hood, and she jumped, believing he was going to pull it tight again. Her neck still felt like it had been crushed, but she had to forget the discomfort and focus on survival.

'I'm going to pull the hood up, and I'll do the counting.'

Everything with these guys was about control. They were a psychologist's dream. The hood came off, and Vinnie began to count.

'One...'

Her eyes adjusted to the dim light. Vinnie was right by her side.

'Two...'

Will was ahead of her, slumped in an old office chair. His wrists were securely taped to the armrests of the chair and his feet were taped too.

'Three...'

Will's fingers were intact and there was no sign of any blood, though he was out cold. He looked exhausted and dirty, but they did not appear to have harmed him physically.

'Four...'

The doctor was standing at the side. On the old, battered table was a selection of sinister looking surgical implements. He looked like a runner on the start line, waiting for the pistol to trigger the beginning of a race.

'Five...'

There were two mobile phones, hers and Will's, placed on top of an upside-down packing box to her left. Nearby, a circular saw had been casually discarded, as if Vinnie had been in the middle of some DIY task.

'Six...'

She'd almost ignored it, how screwed up was that? Both she and Will were positioned on a large, plastic decorating sheet laid out on the ground. It would keep any blood off the floor and allow these vile men to clear up their mess.

'Seven...'

She was right; they'd used nylon ties on her hands and feet. She'd used them herself once, as a teacher, to secure an event banner to the school gates. They were almost impossible to release, even if you had your hands free.

'Eight...'

Will was beginning to stir. Charlotte looked to her side and saw the syringe they'd used to knock her out had been carelessly left on another box just to her side. It was not completely empty. Vinnie had said it didn't take much to knock her out.

'Nine, and that's enough now. I lied about counting to ten. You've had a good look at your husband; you can see we haven't hurt him – yet – and it's all you're getting.'

As he spoke, he replaced the hood, and she was plunged back into total darkness. But it didn't matter, she'd had enough time. She had a plan. There were enough items in the room for them to get out of there with all their fingers intact. If Will could rouse himself quickly, it was time to show Vinnie Mace that a married couple fighting for their lives could cause him much more trouble than any Afghan rebel he'd ever encountered.

CHAPTER TWENTY

December 1999

Tiffany didn't have much to thank Joanne Taylor for, but she was useful to have around when she wanted to sneak off to attend to legal matters. She was sitting outside the offices of Hetherington, Charles and Bickerstock, a Lancaster solicitor which, to her knowledge, had no connection whatsoever with her family, David, Fabian or anybody else she'd ever known.

The name of the company reminded her of something from a Charles Dickens novel; she wouldn't have been surprised if Bob Cratchit had shown her into the office that day. The legal experts whose names were behind the company must have retired or died many years ago, because her appointment at ten o'clock was with Eric Winder.

She'd almost burst out laughing when she saw the look on Joanne's face as she told her she had to take care of the children for the entire morning. They were sitting at the breakfast table; David hadn't even made a pretence of returning to their bedroom the night before.

'I need you to watch the children today; I have a post-natal check-up at the hospital.'

If dropping faces made a sound, she'd have heard an almighty crash.

'I wish you'd told me; I was hoping to get my hair done today.'

She looked over at David, no doubt seeking his support.

He crumpled his eyebrows slightly as a warning. Tiffany understood it, even if Joanne did not.

Don't let's push our luck. You are supposed to be the nanny.

They were a couple of rats and she was trapped in their filthy nest. She'd soon teach the smug scumbags a lesson.

Joanne gave a melodramatic sigh.

'I suppose I can get it done later. My roots are terrible, I can't let them go any longer.'

'They look fine,' David said. It was the most effusive compliment Tiffany had heard in months. What a pity he'd directed it at Joanne.

Tiffany had secured her free pass for the morning and planned to see the solicitors then share a lunch with Brett at the Maritime Museum before heading back. They were so close she could almost reach out and touch her new freedom.

'So, how are you today, Mrs Irwin?' Eric Winder said as he pulled out a chair for her and took his position behind his desk. This was her fourth visit, and he was still so formal and old-fashioned. She hoped it meant he was up to the job.

'I'm good, thank you. Where are we up to with the power of attorney?'

'We're almost there,' he smiled. It was not an unreserved smile though; she sensed a *but* coming.

'Is there some kind of hitch?' she asked, sensing trouble.

'No, not a hitch,' he replied, 'but as I informed you at our first meeting last month, I need to contact the office where the original power of attorney was drawn up.'

'Yes, so?'

'Well, I met my colleague Sebastian Tillotson at a local networking event last week and I had an informal and confidential word about it.'

Davies, Tillotson and Walker were the family solicitors. They'd handled her father's estate and Fabian and David had used them to snatch away her rights when she'd had her post-natal depression. They sounded more like a sixties pop band, but they'd been aligned with the Armstrong family for almost one century, albeit not in its present form. Like any pop band, the line-up had changed.

'What did he have to say?' Tiffany asked. If Eric Winder was about to drop a bombshell on her, she would scream.

'Well, clearly, if this power of attorney is to be revoked, it's necessary to make a formal request through Davies, Tillotson and Walker for the original paperwork.'

'And?' Tiffany said, losing patience now. The man's delivery was so slow; she'd seen paint dry quicker.

'They'll make your husband and your brother aware of your move. At that point, I can't conceal what you're doing any longer.'

'Oh,' was all she could say. She'd hoped it was possible without their knowledge.

'Can't it be set up like a house sale?' she ventured. 'Once you press the button, doesn't everything go through at a set time on a set day?'

'It won't quite work like that, because you're taking this action against your brother's will.'

'We have the doctor's letters and the psychological

report. They both confirm I'm completely recovered and fully capable of exercising my own best judgement. Surely they can't challenge them now?'

'They might. And from what you've told me about your relationship with your brother and your husband, they may well do so.'

'How would they do that?'

'They could challenge a deed of revocation through the courts. I'd have to say, it would be a spiteful thing to do and I'm not sure how my legal colleagues would view it. It would be a bit like holding you a legal hostage, and it would be a very unsavoury matter. We have proved your mental capacity, so from the point of view of the Office of the Public Guardian it won't be an issue. But I felt I should warn you before we take the final steps on this. I want your permission before I formally notify Davies, Tillotson and Walker of your intent. Are you happy to give it?'

Every time she made a move, Tiffany felt trapped. She'd had one bout of bad depression, just one, yet it had given those bastards control over her life. She wasn't going to hurt Callie and she never would; it pained her to even think of it. But they'd said she was about to smother her child with a pillow, in order to force her into hospital for a month. If she hadn't signed the power of attorney documents, she'd never have got out.

They'd set her up and lied, telling her she would never see her children again if she didn't sign. What other choice did she have? She hated both of them. She and Fabian had never been particularly close as older children, but this was the final straw. Their father's death had forced them together again out of necessity, to sort out his estate.

Tiffany wanted to hurt those men, really hurt them for

what they'd done to her. They'd stripped her of any self-respect and dignity, and she would never forgive them for it.

'How finely can you time it?' she asked Mr Winder. 'How late can we leave it before we have to show them our hand?'

'I'll do everything I can to set it up for a swift confirmation, to minimise any delay and limit the opportunity to challenge. It's always tricky where diminished responsibility is concerned. We have medical proof that the factors which led to the original deed no longer apply, but they might attempt to challenge that. Your husband, for instance, could make further allegations about you hurting the children again—'

'I never touched Jane. That was a complete lie—'

'I know, I believe you Mrs Irwin; but you have a track record of mental health issues. It's exceedingly difficult to shake off, however unfair it may seem. I might add this is a particularly nasty case. We often see spiteful acts like this between spouses, but seldom anything as vindictive as this between siblings. It's all very unsettling.'

He could say that again.

'It must be done by New Year,' she told him. There was no way around it, but if they left it until the dead zone between Christmas and New Year, it would be difficult for them to challenge her. With any luck she'd be gone by then.

'I don't normally express an opinion on my clients' affairs, but I really do wish you the best of luck in this, Mrs Irwin. And if you need legal representation after the revocation, my firm would be delighted to represent you.'

I bet you would, Tiffany thought. They shook hands and Tiffany left the office. So, it was done. The power of attorney would resolve the property and land issues, then she was clear to tell David to get stuffed. She'd wait out the prescribed periods for formal separation, then divorce, and she'd be shot of him as soon as possible. Tiffany checked her watch. She still had a good hour before Brett would be free for his lunch break. Her heart beat faster with excitement at the prospect of spending some more time with him.

Soon they would be together, and Fabian and David would be fading shadows from a former life. But there was one more part of the plan which she hadn't even shared with Brett yet. She hadn't plucked up the courage yet; it was still a fledgling thought in her own mind, and she could barely believe she'd even considered it.

Tiffany turned around and headed for the nearest travel agent. She had five tickets to buy: all of them one-way, open tickets to Australia.

CHAPTER TWENTY-ONE

'Please don't fraternise with the guests,' Vinnie said.

Charlotte assumed he was talking to Doctor Henderson, who she hadn't heard speaking yet. He'd chuckled along with Vinnie at the appropriate sadistic moments, like they were a pair of sinister Beavis and Butthead cartoon characters laughing at the misfortune of others, but she'd heard none of the relaxed voice he'd used when chatting to Fabian Armstrong at his house off Heysham Road. Was the doctor scared of Vinnie Mace?

'Okay, Charlotte, I'm giving you one chance, then we get this party started. If I don't find this document in the car, I'll remove the first of Will's fingers before I even utter a word to you. You know I searched the car at Sunderland Point, don't you? I couldn't find anything then.'

'It's well hidden. I tucked it up into a gap in the hub. Give it a proper search this time, it's there, I promise.'

'Clever. I didn't think you would have had the sense to put it somewhere really safe. Where did Kate Summers hide those documents, by the way? We've searched that property once already, and there was no sign of them.'

'In the Monopoly game. It seems like you're not so hot when it comes to us women, Vinnie. Maybe it's because we don't think like a psychotic monster, so it's easy to deceive you—'

Vinnie pulled the base of the hood tight and clenched it firmly for a couple of seconds. He'd caught her by surprise whilst exhaling; she wouldn't be able to withstand much of this. As soon as he released his grip, she took in a breath, just in case he was coming back for more, but he started to push his hand deep into her pocket. She closed her eyes, fearful of what he might do. So far, he'd only indulged in threats of physical violence, but if it turned to sexual violence, that was another thing entirely. These men knew exactly what to do to make their victims compliant.

Vinnie located her car keys and pulled them out of her pocket.

'Did you think you were getting lucky there?' he asked.

Charlotte felt so repulsed and terrified that she couldn't speak.

'If I can offer you any reassurance about this evening's entertainment, I can tell you it won't involve anything like that. What kind of weirdo do you think I am?'

'I wouldn't put anything past you, Vinnie—'

'Shut up, Charlotte. I'm sick of your voice already. You have five minutes, doctor, so get your tools ready. Let's go for the teeth first. I always loved that scene in the film Marathon Man. When did you last have a check-up, Charlotte? It doesn't matter, you're getting a free one tonight.'

Charlotte had found the torture scene excruciating to watch when they'd watched the movie on video as students. She and Will only had one chance at this, and they had to get it right.

The only indication that Vinnie had left the building was the slam of the door at the rear. She waited until she was confident he'd gone.

'So, you know I was in your house, Doctor Henderson. I saw your certificates. What happened to you?'

There was silence.

'You must have had the medical world at your feet at one time. Why does a professional like you take up with men like this? You're not one of them, are you?'

'Shut up,' came the reply. It carried a lot less conviction than Vinnie's voice.

'Are you all right, Will?'

'Be quiet!' Henderson barked, like a teacher not quite in control of the class.

Will mumbled.

'Hey, Will, remember that time at my college when we got in trouble at the library? I'll tell you when—'

'I want you to shut up,' Henderson tried again.

'Or what?' Charlotte challenged. She'd seen the tools at the doctor's disposal. But she was taking a gamble that he was the wing-man, the weedy kid who got a social boost by sniggering whenever the school bully picked on some inno-cent victim in the playground, relieved at not being on the receiving end of the beating.

'Or else,' came the reply, as the doctor jangled some instrumentation to her side.

'You hear that, Will?'

A mumbled reply came, through a taped mouth. She hoped like hell it was a *yes*.

'So why did you leave the medical profession, doctor? If you're going to torture us, we may as well get to know each other better beforehand.'

She was playing with fire, but she couldn't have risked it with Vinnie in the room.

'Oh, just some prick who decided to investigate a couple of simple errors on the operating table, that's all.'

She'd drawn out a key piece of information; the pain must still be burning within him. Why else would a highly skilled man like this end up working with people like Vinnie Mace? It must be the only possible source of income with his given skill set. She hoped she'd been right in believing the doctor was no psychopath. If she'd got it wrong, she and Will would both die.

'It's going to take Vinnie ten minutes to walk to my car and back. Can I at least ask you to take this hood off my head so I can catch my breath? The minute you hear Vinnie, put it back. He doesn't need to know.'

'Don't talk to me,' the doctor answered. He was a man out of his depth.

'Do you get any pleasure out of hurting people like us?' Charlotte asked. 'You don't strike me as a bad man; you have a lovely house, a nice car and a fabulous life. You can't want to do this. You're a doctor, for God's sake—'

She hadn't heard him moving towards her. Without warning, he pulled the hood off and brandished a scalpel at her.

'I'll give you one minute with it off,' he said, 'but if you make a wrong move, I'll cut you.'

'Not without Vinnie's say-so you won't,' Charlotte challenged him. She looked at Will. He nodded and began to move his feet so his chair shuffled around. The doctor hadn't seen yet.

'Now!' Charlotte shouted.

As she felt the doctor jump behind her, she rocked her body forward then backwards, tipping the chair into the doctor. He yelled as he lost his balance and the scalpel clattered to the floor. She could hear Will scooting his wheeled chair across the ground as she lay on top of the doctor, holding him down. Each time he struggled, she thrust her weight backwards. She heard the top of the chair crack against his jaw and he quietened. Then she realised he was reaching for the scalpel to his side; without the use of her hands or feet, she could only keep him pinned down until Will got there. The scalpel lay just beyond his fingertips.

Will's chair appeared at her side, one wheel rolling over the doctor's fingers. She felt Henderson's body convulse as his bones crunched under the force of her husband's weight. Then Will tipped his chair and fell to the ground. With his foot, he kicked the scalpel over to her and pivoted around on the floor to reach out with his taped hands. She knew exactly what she needed to do.

Move fast. Cut the tape. Vinnie will be back soon.

She picked up the scalpel with her two bound hands and started to work at the tape around his wrists. Her first attempts were clumsy, cutting his skin and drawing blood.

'Oh God, I'm so sorry Will,' she apologised. It wasn't bad; it would heal, but she hated herself for harming him.

She moved more carefully this time, and before she knew it, the tape was cut. Will parted his hands and tore the tape off his mouth.

'You're bloody amazing, Charlotte. Here, let me cut those ties.'

The doctor, who'd been yelling in pain, attempted to move again, but Charlotte gave another thrust backwards, making his head strike the concrete floor. He stopped struggling, evidently accepting they had the upper hand. Will cut the ties and released Charlotte, helping her to her feet. They hugged briefly, clutching each other tight. Then Will moved over to the table where the circular saw was sitting. Charlotte looked at him.

'No, Will, no. We're not like them.'

'He's got this coming to him.'

Will pulled the trigger on the saw and the deadly blade began to spin.

CHAPTER TWENTY-TWO

'Will, no!' Charlotte shouted.

She watched the circular blade spinning, its jagged blade perilously close to the doctor's head. Henderson was cowering on the ground, whimpering.

'I want some answers from this dick. He's a sadistic piece of crap—'

'Will, no. He's not our problem, Vinnie is. We'll be no further forward if Vinnie marches in here and overpowers the two of us. He's got my car keys and we're not going anywhere without those, stuck on an industrial estate. He has a gun too.'

Will released the trigger on the circular saw and the doctor ceased his pleading.

'What's this about, Henderson? Why did you pick me up at the hitching post that night and drive me here? And why are you threatening my wife?'

He flicked the switch on the saw momentarily and the doctor flinched.

'It's nothing to do with me, honestly. I'm just a hired hand.'

'A well paid one at that,' Charlotte added, retrieving their mobile phones from where Vinnie had left them.

'Here, Will,' she said, passing his over. 'It looks like they kept yours charged. You've got about a million messages from me and the kids. That's some backlog.'

'What does that madman want with us?'

She'd never seen Will as furious as this in all the time they'd been married, not even when the kids had been at their most exasperating.

Will turned back to the doctor, waiting to hear why he was involved.

'They pay me. I got struck off several years ago because I had a couple of accidents in the operating theatre after my wife died. They removed me from the register. You don't recover from something like that; it was my livelihood. My life came tumbling down in a matter of a year. I just help these people; I don't know what they're doing. I don't get involved—'

'Just following orders. Where have I heard that one before?'

'Will, steady.'

'This man's the worst kind of coward, Charlotte. He lets psychopaths like Vinnie do all the dangerous work, and he stands by like some sadist who gets off on this stuff.'

'I've never been involved in something like this before, I swear; I usually just patch up people who need to stay away from hospital. Vinnie works alone—'

'The anaesthetic; that's how we overpower Vinnie,' Charlotte said. It had just occurred to her while the doctor was doing his best to justify himself. She walked over to the partially filled syringe which had been left on the storage box.

'Is this enough to knock him out?' she asked the doctor, but he didn't respond.

Will started the circular saw once again.

'The only thing stopping me from hurting you is my respect for my wife. If she wasn't here, you'd resemble a butcher's shop display by now. So get talking.'

Charlotte looked at him and saw the gleam in his eye. He was hamming it up and doing a good job of it. Even she believed what he'd just said.

'It won't put him to sleep, he's too big and sturdy. But it will incapacitate him. You need to get it in a vein, it'll work quicker—'

'Hush, I heard a noise. It must be Vinnie.'

'I want out of this too. I didn't sign up for this intimidation business. I was fine doing the patching up, because I only had to keep my mouth shut, and I was keeping to my Hippocratic Oath to save lives. But you get caught by these people, and you can't get out—'

'Enough now,' Will said. He placed the saw to his side and took a photo of the doctor's face close up on his phone. Charlotte watched at his side as he swiftly texted it to Olli and Lucia with a short message.

I'm okay. I'm with Mum. If you don't hear from me in 1 hour, call the police. Tell them to find this man. He's called Doctor Henderson. We're at White Lund Industrial Estate. Dad x

'Right, Doctor,' Will began, 'my kids have your photo and if we don't get out of here, they'll call the police. They know who you are. All you have to do is go back to where you were when Vinnie left and keep your mouth shut. We'll do the rest.'

The doctor nodded in acquiescence and returned to where he'd been standing.

'Right, back as we were. Who's going for Vinnie?' Will asked.

'I will,' Charlotte replied. 'I'm going to play the female card, it's the last thing he'll expect from me.'

A door slammed shut in one of the back-office rooms.

'It was a great idea, mentioning the library,' Will said, squeezing Charlotte's hand. As students they'd been banned from using the college library for one week because they were playing on the wheeled chairs, competing to see who could travel the furthest distance with a single kick of the feet. The shame of being suspended from library use had chastened them. It had been silly, puerile and immature; but great fun. Besides, they were young and in love.

That moment of silliness all those years ago had been the shared experience that got them out of a hole. If she could incapacitate Vinnie in the next few minutes, it would have been worth not being able to use the library for a week all those years back.

They got back into their previous positions. Charlotte replaced the hood, then placed her hands so they were resting on her legs, the syringe concealed and ready to deploy. She kicked the cut nylon tie out of the way, but was delighted to discover that the cut tie from around her feet would still sit loosely around her ankles, even though it was no longer restraining her. She saw Will had done the same, doing his best to reassemble his restraints in a way that would hopefully fool Vinnie.

They slumped their heads forward, as if awaiting the next round of intimidation. She hated being unable to watch the doctor to be sure he wasn't tipping off Vinnie with a nod of the head or a motioning of his eyes.

'Well, that's a good start, Charlotte. You told the truth.

If you carry on like this, we might all be home in time to watch the ten o'clock news.'

She listened as he tossed the car remote onto the box on which the phones had been placed.

She sensed Vinnie's pause even through the hood.

'Where have the phones gone?'

Silence.

'What happened to the phones, doctor?'

'Oh, I... I moved them over here to keep them safe. They're with my medical implements if you want them—'

A distraction was needed and fast. They'd been careless with the phones.

Charlotte cleared her throat. 'So, what happens now, Vinnie? I've given you something, so what do I get in return?'

He laughed out loud.

'You don't seem to have read the rules yet, Charlotte. I have all the power here, and you have none. I hope you'll be sensible and tell me where everything else is now. That way, this all ends quickly. Your husband gets to keep at least half of his handsome face and you hang on to most, if not all your fingers. That's what I call a win-win situation, wouldn't you agree?'

'We're not getting out of here alive are we, Vinnie?'

'Charlotte, Charlotte, you malign me. I can't tell you how much it hurts. We're in the business of scaring people; killing is not really part of our repertoire, unless a big land deal is involved. We wouldn't normally go through such trouble for someone like you. Bodies are extremely difficult to dispose of, and our friend Kyle, who takes care of these things for us, well... he's very expensive. I'm not sure you're important enough to justify the expenditure.'

Charlotte followed his voice. Now she'd seen the layout

of the room, she could work out where he was. When he came close enough, she'd strike.

'No, I've already taken care of discrediting you both when this is over. The moment we're done, the police will get an anonymous tip-off and you'll be at the centre of a shitstorm. Let's just say it involves a computer hack and some rather unpleasant and highly illegal pornography placed in some very embarrassing places. Good luck explaining that away.'

'Did you give the pictures of Hollie Wickes to Will?'

'Hollie Wickes? Who the hell is she? No, they must be for real. That's not my work. When I hack a computer, I do it like the military. No trace and nothing for digital forensics teams to find. It looks like the real thing.'

Charlotte recalled her conversation with Hollie, more convinced than ever that there were two forces at work here. Vinnie and Fabian made up just one of them, so who gave Will the photo that she'd found in his pocket? And was Hollie even telling the truth?

Will began to mumble something through the tape across his mouth.

'What's that?' Vinnie asked, over-acting like he was in a TV children's programme. 'I reckon your husband is protesting that he'd never download illegal pornography onto his PC. Too late Will, it's there already. In fact, it wouldn't surprise me if your university department hasn't found it already. These damned perverts, they deserve what they get.'

It was now or never. She could sense that Vinnie had his back turned to her. She tore off the hood, kicked the severed tie away from her ankles and charged at Vinnie from behind. Her initial adrenaline-fuelled launch was stopped short as she discovered she was still unsteady from the anaesthetic she'd been injected with earlier.

Her legs weakened slightly, and it messed up her rear assault of Vinnie. He sensed her rushing at him from behind and turned to face her. Will got to his feet and jumped onto Vinnie's back, causing him to drop the paperwork he'd just retrieved from the car. Charlotte raised the syringe, but Vinnie brushed her away with his right arm, sending the syringe flying, and she crashed to the floor some way from where Doctor Henderson was standing. The syringe was close to Henderson's feet.

Vinnie bent forward and flipped Will off his back.

'Charlotte, the syringe, get the syringe—'

'He has a gun, Will. Be careful—'

Will had recovered and was making for the circular saw. He picked it up and pressed the trigger, the blade turning instantly. He held it up towards Vinnie. Vinnie circled around so his back was to the doctor, and stood facing Will and Charlotte, although the two of them were some distance apart. He put his hand into his jacket and drew out his gun; the same one he'd used to shoot at her on the jet-ski.

'So, who fancies playing a game of rock, paper, scissors?' he smirked. 'Only this is gun, saw and… oh, bare hands. Charlotte?'

He paused to let her defenceless state sink in.

'Okay, change of plan. The world's worst impersonator of the Texas Chainsaw Massacre gets a bullet and Charlotte, you're going to spend the evening enjoying some of my greatest torture hits from Afghanistan. That's enough now. It's time to stop all this messing around.'

He raised his gun and Will dropped the saw, his face white. As Vinnie moved his finger to the trigger, Doctor Henderson – who'd looked petrified throughout the entire exchange – bent down, grabbed the syringe from the floor and planted it in Vinnie's neck. Vinnie plunged to the ground before he could pull the trigger.

'Get out of here,' the doctor shouted. 'It's too late for me, but you can escape. You've got about ten minutes head start on him.'

CHAPTER TWENTY-THREE

'He'll kill you,' Charlotte said.

'No he won't. I'll tell him it was you who injected him in the confusion,' the doctor replied. He looked scared out of his wits, like the puny kid who'd just punched the school bully and was waiting to see what he'd do next.

'Just go. I injected him in a main vein, but it won't keep him down for long. He won't remember much about it when he comes round.'

'Thank you,' Charlotte said. She turned and followed Will, who was already picking up the car keys and heading for the exit.

'Shall I call the police?' he asked as they moved back into the cool night air, emerging into the parking area behind the industrial unit.

'No, not yet,' Charlotte replied. 'Let's find out where Brett's storage unit is and retrieve whatever is in there. Then we can recover the document I left hidden in Jed's boat. I'll telephone Kate Summers when we've gathered it all together and see what she advises. But not yet. Let's press this advantage home.'

They pushed open the gate Charlotte had left unlocked and didn't bother closing it again. That horse had already bolted.

'Damn! The document Vinnie took... I left in there—'

Charlotte had been so concerned about the doctor's fate that she'd forgotten to clear the area before fleeing.

'I got it while you were chatting to Henderson,' Will reassured her, indicating the paperwork he had stuffed into his back pocket. 'He had another document there too, so we have them both back now—'

'Fantastic; it's the one I had to give to Vinnie at Sunderland Point. He's going to be so pissed off with us. We'd best not mess this up now. He won't let us get away again.'

Will passed the car keys to Charlotte, and they hurried over to the cash and carry. It was almost closing time and the security guard was hovering by the barrier, ready to lower it the moment the final customer had left. They made their way over to the vehicle and got inside.

'What did the doctor do to you?' Charlotte asked.

'Best get driving. I'm still alive. It was Vinnie who hurt me; the doctor didn't make any attempt to help, the snivelling rat. In his favour, he did whisper an apology after Vinnie hit me. It still hurts like hell. To be fair, he didn't have much choice. He seems to be in over his head.'

Charlotte waved at the security guard as they left the car park. They were last out; they'd cut it fine. At least she wouldn't be forced to crash the company car through the barrier to make good her escape. It was a minor but welcome blessing, bearing in mind their current predicament.

'I agree. You've seen how all this happens. You get caught up in it bit by bit. I started investigating an interesting news story, and look where we've ended up. It's almost unbelievable.'

She took her hand off the gear stick and squeezed Will's arm.

'God, I'm pleased you're safe. I didn't know what had happened to you. By the way, Hollie Wickes was set up. She's one of the Irwin children.'

'What?'

'It's true. Only a DNA test will prove it, but she's Jane Irwin. I left her speaking to her estranged sister.'

Will placed his head in his hands and sighed.

'What about the photograph?'

'A set-up, or so it seems.'

'Is there nothing these people can't do to bypass the rules?'

Will looked exhausted. She hadn't noticed it so much when they were in the industrial unit, but even in the semi-lit street, she could see it in his face. She squeezed his arm again.

'Not long now; it'll soon be over. Why don't you call the kids and tell them we're fine? Ask them to stay in the Travelodge tonight, just to be sure. Tell them we'll pay. Better to be safe than sorry.'

Charlotte started travelling towards Heysham. Heysham Business Park, Kate had said. That was easy enough to find, but the first storage units she came across weren't open 24/7. For a moment she panicked, fearing they might have to wait until morning to make any progress. Then she found a much larger premises, lit up outside, with signage boasting 24/7 access.

'This must be it,' she said as she pulled up in the car park. At the far side was a sturdy, industrial-looking gate. They got out of the car, the code details from Kate's envelope in Charlotte's hand. As they neared the gate, she saw it had been secured with a heavy padlock operated by a security code. Consulting the information on the piece of paper, she read the numbers to Will as he twisted the numbered dials.

'Bingo!' he said as the padlock snapped open. He pushed open the gate.

'Best take the car inside the compound,' Charlotte suggested. 'I don't trust Vinnie; he seems to have a sixth sense for where we are.'

'How will he find us?' Will asked.

'I don't know, but they tracked you down at the university easily enough. Let's not take any chances.'

They left the gate open and drove into the compound, which was full of containers of various sizes. These were not the battered, gnarled and rusted variety she had seen at Heysham Docks. They were much newer, mounted on blocks to keep them off the ground. They looked like they were mainly used by domestic customers, as the banners had suggested on the approach road.

'That's the one,' Will said, suddenly alert in the car seat beside her as they slowly drove through the compound, trying to figure out how they were numbered.

'How do you know?' Charlotte asked.

'Because it's more weather-beaten than the rest. If it's been sitting there for twenty years, I'm guessing they decided not to replace it. There's a number 24 painted on the side.'

'Yes, you're right, that's the number written on the flap of the envelope from among Kate's papers. There's one more three-digit code on here. I hope it opens another padlock. If it does, we're in.'

Charlotte pulled up the car, and they walked to the front of the storage unit. Will examined the padlock.

'Yes, it's a three-digit number. Read it out to me, please. It's a good job this is a quality lock, or it would have rusted a long time ago.'

As he held the lock, Charlotte noticed for the first time some markings under his fingernails, like small bruises in the soft skin below them. She touched his hand.

'Is that what Vinnie did?'

'Yes. It hurt - a lot. I'm pleased you came along when you did. They were just about to get started on the doctor's surgical toolkit. I'm not sure I could have stood up to that.'

Charlotte wrapped her arms around him and pulled him in close from behind.

'I'm sorry, Will. I'm so sorry they did that to you—'

He touched her hands and pulled them a little tighter around his waist.

'It's not your fault. We can't do anything to stop the monsters around us. They would carry on regardless. We're just collateral damage; they don't care about us.'

They stood together for several moments, enjoying the closeness and calm. At last Will pulled away.

'Much as I'd love to stand like this all night, we'd best get moving.'

He fumbled with the padlock.

'Just read me those numbers again,' he said.

Charlotte repeated them, making sure she hadn't misread a digit.

'It's rusted,' Will cursed. 'That's the right code; I felt it click. But it's rusted into the socket... where are you going?'

'One moment,' Charlotte said, heading to the car and opening the boot. Vinnie hadn't returned the spare tyre to the recess after his search for the document, so she quickly found the wheel wrench, marched over to the container and struck it twice with the tool. The padlock fell to the ground.

'There,' she said, smiling at Will. 'I'm pretty certain Kate Summers won't mind.'

It took both of them to pull open the mechanism which secured the container. It was heavily weathered, but not rusted. The hinges protested at being woken up after over twenty years, but these units were built to last at sea, and they eventually succeeded in prising open the door.

The lighting surrounding the compound wasn't perfect, but it provided enough brightness to see inside. The unit was piled high with boxes, furniture, electrical appliances and even a bicycle. This was what remained of a man's life. Not just any man; Kate Summer's brother. Inside this unit was hidden the reason for Kate's disappearance, and perhaps an explanation of the mystery surrounding the Irwin family.

CHAPTER TWENTY-FOUR

December 1999

The Arndale Centre was Tiffany's favourite place to meet at this time of year. It was warm, dry and flat, perfect for life with three children and a double buggy. As she walked through the automatic doors, a blast of warm air engulfed her, thawing the ice from her face. She was meeting Brett later, in a snatched liaison which had come as an unexpected bonus. He was starting his shift later so he could stay late at work for a special event.

David had business meetings all day, so it was as safe as it could be. Besides, although she'd told David she was in town to change the children's library books, her meeting with Georgina was the main driving force of the day.

Christmas music was playing throughout the covered shopping area. For the first time in ages, Tiffany felt a sense of joy and positivity; it finally felt as if her plan with Brett might happen. At last, she could put her bad relationship choices behind her and start a new life with a good and decent man.

Callie tugged on her reins and Tiffany followed her gaze to see what was proving so exciting. She had spotted the Christmas tree in the centre, surrounded by elves and Santa models. Tiffany followed Callie's tugging and allowed the children to get close to the display. The shops had made a great effort between them, with sparkling baubles, flashing lights, silver and gold stars and an array of miniature wrapped presents adorning the massive tree at the centre of it all.

Behind the tree a small, pop-up play area had been created; this would be perfect for when Georgina arrived. She often wondered if mothers had a sixth sense, as moments later her friend arrived with her own children and buggy. They hugged and greeted each other. The kids didn't care; they were more excited about the Christmas decorations. Callie had already figured out there was a play area at the rear and was busy communicating her excitement to any other child in the group who could understand her.

'Blimey, it's freezing out there,' Georgina said, 'my nose feels like it's about to drop off.'

'Me too, that wind off the sea really catches you when you get out of the car,' Tiffany replied.

'How about we let the kids loose in the play area so we can chat?' Georgina continued.

Rowan was asleep in his pram, so it sounded like the best plan. The toddlers were unleashed in the small play area, which was still quiet, and the two friends took a seat at one of the small tables which had been set up nearby.

'Give me five minutes,' Georgina said, leaping up from her chair. She came back soon afterwards with a cup of tea and a mince pie for them both.

'This is as close as it gets to paradise when you've got

young kids,' Georgina said with a smile. 'Make the most of it. Small pleasures like this keep us sane.'

They exchanged pleasantries, asking after each other's children, but both knew why they were there; it wasn't for a morning of idle chit-chat.

'Did you get the test results?' Tiffany asked at last, unable to sustain the superficial topics of conversation any longer. 'I'm bursting to see what they are.'

'You know I haven't read them, right?' Georgina asked.

'I didn't even think about it, Georgie. I realise it's unofficial, so I assumed you might just tell me verbally. Is there a letter or something?'

'Before I give it to you, my friend made me swear you to secrecy. The university lab is not there to run private test results. It's also expensive to do, so you must never tell anybody where you got the results. Do you promise? My friend could lose his job for this, it's important.'

Tiffany seldom saw Georgina in a serious mood, so she reassured her of her discretion.

'I'd pay if I could, but I'm guessing there's no way to do it without raising red flags. You have my word though; if I ever needed this information in court, I'd pay to have it done elsewhere to generate the official paperwork.'

'Okay, good.'

Georgina reached into her bag which had been flung into the storage pouch underneath her buggy.

'Here, I hope it says what you want it to say.'

Tiffany examined the envelope on both sides. It was completely plain, with not even her name on it. She hadn't felt this sense of anticipation since receiving her school examination results.

'Well, go on, open it,' Georgina urged. 'Remember, I've done this before, so I know what it's like. I wanted to stay with my husband; there was a lot riding on my result when it came.'

Tiffany began to ease the lip of the envelope with her finger, gently pulling it open.

'We use a letter opener at home. I don't like to tear the envelopes open in case I damage the contents.'

'I'm going to rip it open with my teeth if you don't hurry up. Come on Tiff, it's taken all my willpower not to steam open that letter and sneak a look at the results. Get on with it!'

Tiffany laughed, pushed her small finger into the gap she'd made and tore across the top of the envelope. Inside was a folded piece of paper, with some data printed on it via a dot matrix printer. Tiffany scanned it, but it made no sense to her. It was just a row of numbers for the child and one for the alleged father. There was also a row for the mother's data, but it was blank.

'I hate the way they call it *Alleged Father*. What a horrible phrase to use; it makes him sound like some criminal.'

'What does it say?' Georgina prompted.

'I can't work it out,' Tiffany replied, turning over the sheet of paper to see if there was any more information.

'Give it here,' Georgina sighed.

'Whose DNA did you get tested, was it David's?'

'No, it wasn't his DNA. Can you imagine the questions David would have asked?'

'Phew, you had me worried for a moment. I thought you'd used David's DNA. Look, here's the bit you need to study, those numbers are just the scientific stuff, not for the likes of you and I.'

Georgina pointed at one digit, well hidden among the tabulated data.

Tiffany read it three times.

Probability of paternity: 99.9998%

'Oh, thank God,' she said. 'I don't know what I'd have done if he was David's. That would have turned everything on its head.'

'Will you be telling the father?'

Tiffany paused for a moment. 'I'm meeting him here in a half an hour. I will definitely tell him, but I have to pick my time.'

'He must suspect it, surely?'

'I haven't spoken to him about everything that happens in my marriage to David. He's aware the relationship is stagnant, and that David is horrible to me, but we don't dwell on the sexual aspects of our life together. I mean, David is like the iceman of emotional expression, but I have had to lie back and think of England a couple of times since I started my affair. I guess even David feels the need to show willing every now and then, even if it is just a facade.'

'How do you feel about the result? Happy? Scared? Guilty? I felt like a tramp and vowed never to sleep with a handsome waiter ever again. I reckon I escaped with my life when it happened to me.'

Tiffany examined the results again. The precisely written percentage was like getting a grade A in a maths examination. It wasn't just a pass mark or a decent grade. It was exceptional, a clear pass, no doubt about it.

'Part of me feels pure relief that I haven't had a child with David. My first partner was a farmer; can you believe it?'

'Really?' Georgina asked. 'I thought you hated farming. It's *all shit and tractors,* you once said.'

'Yes, exactly. He wanted to keep me in calf all the time, much like the animals on his farm. He was more interested in finding a wife who'd be happy to get up at the crack of dawn every morning to help with the milking. He had no interest in the children; they were just a means of locking me down. And he didn't care about my post-natal depression.'

'The deniers are the worst sort.'

Georgina had a look of sympathy on her face.

'Do you know, he once shouted at me *Cows don't make all this fuss about depression, they just get on with it.* His entire knowledge of the female state was based upon what went on in his barn. That was when I left him. He's never bothered about seeing the children, which suits me. He has his stereotypical farmer's wife now; I reckon he was glad to see the back of me. As for David... well, I really don't know why we married in the first place.'

'But your new man is different, right? You must trust him?'

'I do, completely. He'll be delighted to discover Rowan is his child.'

'So, what's worrying you?' Georgia asked. 'You feel to me like you're not quite sure.'

'It's not my new partner I'm worried about, Georgie. It's me. After two messed up relationships, a nervous breakdown, and David constantly eroding my confidence, I don't trust myself, Georgie. I hope I'm not jumping out of the frying pan and into the fire. And if I was, would I even know it?'

'Where do we begin?' Will said. 'I don't want to start sorting through private things, even if the man hasn't been here for the past twenty years. It feels like it's an intrusion.'

'I doubt Kate will care about the mess we make; she just needs that documentation. She didn't tell me where to look, only that it's in a folder somewhere.'

She scanned the boxes. Each was labelled in a thick, black marker pen with an indication of the contents inside: *Educational certificates*, *Dad memories*, *Family photographs*, *Old school books* and so on. There was a small table, a bicycle, a wardrobe, and even an old-fashioned telephone left on a pile of miscellaneous items. It didn't seem that long since they'd organised their own move to Morecambe from Bristol. She recognised that pile as the last bits and pieces that were almost forgotten at the end of a relocation, items which even the removal team overlooked.

'We may as well start by checking the surfaces,' Charlotte suggested, 'then, if we have to, we'll turn out the boxes.'

Charlotte led the way and Will followed.

'How are your hands?' she asked as they began the task

of shuffling boxes from one pile to the next, not entirely sure they'd recognise what they were looking for even if it was directly in front of them. Will stopped and wiped his eyes, evidently holding back tears. She stopped and walked over to him, pulling him in close.

'I honestly thought they were going to cause me serious harm,' he sobbed. 'I've never been so terrified in my life. How do you deal with what you've been through?'

She pulled him in more tightly.

'Just like you did,' she answered gently. 'Don't ever think this comes easy to me; it doesn't. I'm just like you; I want to cry, scream and hide away. But you saw it: when it's happening, you just have to deal with it. You get through it as best you can. When it's over, you do what you're doing now, you go to bed and shake with fear at what might have happened, then you thank the heavens you got out alive and that your family weren't harmed. You don't get used to this stuff, Will. You just learn to deal with it.'

'I'm so angry with those men. I feel a level of aggression and a desire for violence I've never experienced in my life before. I want to hurt them; I want to destroy them. When I was holding that circular saw near the doctor, I was in such a rage I honestly could have set about him with it, to make him experience the same fear as I did. I wanted to hurt him, Charlotte. That's not me. It's not who I am.'

She kissed him on the cheek and wiped his eyes.

'There's not a violent bone in your body, Will, I know that. I've seen you in situations where you would have had every right to lose your temper or stamp and swear. But in our entire life together, I've never felt at risk or worried that you would ever be violent towards me or the kids. There's a line people cross when they hurt someone, and it's a very definite line. You're incapable of crossing it and so am I. But if we're forced to, if these psychopaths make us, I truly believe we'll do whatever it takes to defend ourselves. It's that fight or flight thing; I would do whatever it takes to protect my friends and family.'

Will was silent for a while. He pulled her in closely, and they stood together for several moments.

Charlotte realised she hadn't felt such an intimate connection for some time. So much of her life had been dominated by the need to recover from her previous injuries that their relationship had become more functional of late. She would put it right. They needed to talk this out, or it would fester. But first, they had to protect Kate Summers.

'I admire you, you know,' Will said, out of the blue. 'It's amazing how you've turned things around since your breakdown in the classroom back in Bristol. I thought we were in trouble for a while as a family, but ever since we returned to Morecambe, you've become this formidable force. What happened in your last job could have broken you, but you've risen up. The change in you is remarkable, and I'm proud of you. The kids are in awe of you, too. You make us all proud.'

Charlotte felt tears welling up. She gave Will a last squeeze then they both resumed their search, working quietly for several minutes. Will stopped and held up a faded folder.

'Could this be it?' he asked.

'Where did you find it?'

'Underneath this box of family photographs. I only looked because this photo was on top of it. It looks like it fell out of the box.'

'Hand it over, would you?' Charlotte asked. She took the image from Will and tilted it towards the open door of the container in order to make the most of the available light.

'Look at this, it's Kate and her brother. They can't be much older than Lucia and Olli. That must be her dad, too. If only we could step back in time and warn them about what was going to happen. Do you think it would do any good?'

'Now you're getting all philosophical on me,' Will teased. She handed him the photo. 'I wonder what happened to her brother?' he said as he studied it. 'Do you really think he died?'

'With everything that's gone on in the past week or so, it wouldn't surprise me if he walked through the door to this container in the next five minutes and asked us what we're doing here. Honestly, I'd believe anything right now. Let's see what's inside this folder.'

Charlotte lifted the flap and took out the contents, which were wrapped in a plastic bag. She opened the bag and peered inside.

'It's a contract of some sort,' she said. 'It's old too; incredibly old. The signatures are spindly and old-fashioned; I'd say this is over twenty years old.'

'Any idea what it is?' Will asked.

Charlotte scanned it.

'It's typewritten, and it's got the name of some firm at the top of it. Hetherington, Charles and Bickerstock. It's property paperwork of some sort; there are land boundaries drawn on it, map references and so on. It's all legal speak as far as I can tell. And I don't recognise the name; Lilian Armstrong (née Matterson); does that mean anything to you?'

'None of this means anything to me,' Will replied, as he handed over the other documents that were still in his pocket. 'Is that what Kate wanted us to find?'

'It must be,' Charlotte answered, continuing to thumb

through the sheets. 'There's something else in here too, more modern. It's printed out on that old dot matrix printer paper. It looks like test results. I've never seen anything like it before. This has to be it—'

She stopped dead. Will had raised his hand to alert her to something.

'What?' she asked.

'Car headlights just swept over the top of the containers over there. Somebody just came in with a car.'

Charlotte stepped outside the container onto the gravel surface to look.

'It's a 24/7 facility; people will be in and out of here at all times of night.'

'What if it's them?' Will asked. The look in his eyes told her he was scared.

'You're being paranoid,' Charlotte answered, scanning ahead to get a glimpse of the vehicle that had entered the compound. To the side of the units was an old van. It looked like it had once been used as a small removal van; lettering had been removed from the sides and the wheel arches were rusting. It was the only vehicle she could see besides their own, but the sound of a purring engine was coming from the far side of a cluster of containers.

'Let's push the door closed on the container and duck into the shadows. Once we see it's safe, we should be on our way.'

Will nodded in agreement. As he pushed the door, the rusting hinge gave a pained creak which rang out in the silence of the night. The heavy door clanged as he pushed it to, but without the padlock to hold it in place, it wouldn't shut firm, so the door remained slightly ajar.

'Quick, let's hide over here, out of the way. We'll get a better view of the area from behind that unit.'

Charlotte moved into the shadows, treading gently so as not to crunch the gravel, and Will joined her. They peered out from behind the unit, waiting for signs of movement. It was so quiet in the stillness of the night that even their breathing sounded loud.

Above the containers at the end of the compound, they saw the light change as the car's headlamps were turned off.

'If it is them, they'll know we're here from seeing the car,' Will whispered. 'Look, your car door is still open. Have you got the keys?'

Charlotte felt in her pocket.

'No, I left them inside it. It's as secure as it's going to get here, so I didn't think we needed to lock it.'

She cursed quietly to herself.

'How can it be them? We got a great lead on Vinnie; he was out cold when we ran. It's probably some contractor locking up his tools for the night or something like that.'

They watched and waited, barely breathing as they heard the crunch of footsteps on gravel. A shadow appeared in the distance, the light casting an elongated form across the ground, a single shadow. She started to move, but Will restrained her.

'Wait a moment,' he whispered. 'Let's just make sure.'

'We'll scare him or her witless if we step out of the shadows,' she said softly, 'they'll think we're mugging them.'

'Please, Charlotte, wait,' Will cautioned.

She returned to her position behind the container. The crunch of footsteps continued. The movement sounded cautious. The shadow grew longer, then a solitary figure stepped out from the side of a storage container. He was holding a gun. Vinnie Mace had found them.

CHAPTER TWENTY-SIX

'How the hell did he know we were here?' Will cursed, his voice trembling. Charlotte shared his exasperation.

'Can he track the car?' she asked.

'I wouldn't put anything past him. What are we going to do?'

Charlotte thought quickly.

'He doesn't know which unit is Brett's,' she said. 'We have that advantage at least—'

Two shots rang out: short, sharp, powerful bursts, not like the gunfire she'd seen on television. He had just shot at the two front tyres of the company vehicle.

Charlotte was worried about Will. Whereas her mind was racing with strategies for getting them out of there, he looked like he was about to crumble.

'Will, we've got to focus. He'll kill us both if he finds us. We need a plan.'

'Hello Charlotte and Will,' Vinnie called out. 'Did you really think I'd be so easy to shake off? Now, I know you're still here because I just disabled your car. Oh, by the way, just to be certain, I'm getting rid of the keys too—'

They heard metal on metal; Vinnie had just thrown the keys onto the roof of one of the containers.

'So, you can either make this easy for yourself and you can walk out of here, or I'll lock up your dead bodies in Brett's unit and you can rot in there for another twenty years. You have worked out that Brett Allan is still alive, I take it?'

Charlotte and Will looked at each other. It was too dark in their hiding place to make out expressions, but Charlotte could sense Will thinking the same as her: *what the hell?*

'Now, let's put an end to this and we can all go home and call it a day.'

'What do we do?' Will whispered.

'We can't use the car,' Charlotte replied, figuring out their options as she spoke. 'We could take Vinnie's—'

'He won't have left the keys in the car.'

'Okay, rub it in, why don't you?' Charlotte said. 'What about that old van? Do you reckon they still use it?'

'That old thing?'

'Well some old things still manage to keep going,' she teased. She figured if she could make him laugh, or at least smile, it might distract him from his obvious state of panic. She'd used the same technique on the children when they were young, albeit she was only trying to wash their hair at the time.

'What about the keys?' he asked.

'Well, that's the risk we take. We have two options as far as I can tell. Well, three, but the third one isn't happening any time soon.'

'What is it?'

'You and I overpower Vinnie—'

Will let out a snort of laughter, immediately placing his hand over his mouth to stifle the sound.

'Sorry,' he mouthed. 'What are the realistic options?'

'Try the van, see if they left the key inside. The other option is to sneak out of the gate and lock Vinnie inside. I like that one least, because he can still shoot at us. He can also shoot the padlock open. We have to try the van.'

'How?' Will asked. The short infusion of humour had dissipated already and the look of fear had returned.

'I want you to distract Vinnie,' Charlotte told him. 'Throw gravel in the opposite direction to the van and steer him away from it. I'll creep around the perimeter and get into the van as quietly as I can. Just keep Vinnie away from me until I can see if there's a key inside—'

'What about me?'

She hadn't thought about that.

'Look, Will, if I get the van started, I'll drive it forwards between the two containers directly ahead of it... numbers five and six. Look, they're clearly marked. Get in the van and I'll keep driving forwards, between the containers. We'll emerge on the exit road—'

'What if Vinnie's closed the gate?'

It hadn't even occurred to her.

'Then we drive through it if we can. But I didn't hear it clanging when he closed it, so I reckon we're safe. Are you up for this?'

Will nodded, but he didn't seem certain.

'I need to know you've got my back, Will. Have you?'

'I've always got your back, Charlotte. I'm just scared.'

'You and me both, but we have to do this, Will. He will kill us if we don't get out of here.'

Will crouched down and sifted some larger stones from the gravel at his feet.

'I'll give you a signal from the container over there to

our left. Watch Vinnie like a hawk; don't let him creep up behind you.'

Charlotte checked the folder was properly secured before giving Will a kiss, then began to step cautiously around the rear of the units. It was almost impossible to stop her shoes crunching on the gravel. She waited until she heard the creak of the door to Brett's container, a sign that Vinnie had found the unit.

'Thank you for finding Brett's container for me, Charlotte,' Vinnie shouted. The more he insisted on giving a running commentary, the more easily she could move behind the units.

'Did you have enough time to find the paperwork or did I get here too soon? There's a pile of junk in there. Come to think of it, once I've shot you and found the paperwork, I might burn out the contents. That'll delay identification for a while. Unless of course you show yourselves now. You can't get out of here. We might as well talk it over.'

She reached the container to the side of the van. It was perilously close to Vinnie, but Will would take care of that. She peered out from the side; Vinnie was inside Brett's container, no doubt trying to figure out if they'd taken the documents. She waved at Will and he held up his hand to confirm he'd seen her. Moments later, a piercing clang rang out as a large stone struck the roof of one of the containers positioned far away from her. Vinnie was out of Brett's container in an instant, gun at the ready. Will followed it up with a second stone. Vinnie stormed away from where Charlotte was hiding, directly towards the container which Will had struck. As Vinnie moved away from her towards the sound, the gravel crunching under his feet, she ran across to the van, keeping low and coming to rest at the side of the passenger door. She waited for Vinnie to move again, then clicked the door handle, praying it wasn't alarmed. The possibility hadn't even occurred to her until the last moment. She opened the door, staying low, waiting for it to creak. It made a scraping sound of metal on metal, but Will timed another stone perfectly, providing a distraction at precisely the right moment. She climbed into the foot well and pulled the door closed behind her, then leaned across to the driver's side, fumbling for the ignition, hoping to find a key. She was out of luck. A wave of panic swept over her. What if she'd made the wrong call? This was a crazy idea.

Keeping low, she placed the paperwork underneath the loose offcut of carpet on the driver's side. She was relieved they'd collected it together in the one folder, it made it easier to conceal. If Vinnie caught them, at least he might not find the documents. As she lifted the carpet, she spotted the edge of a car key tucked away in the far corner. She waited for Will to throw another stone. Vinnie would soon figure out he was being distracted.

Charlotte climbed across to sit in the driver's seat and pushed the key into the ignition area, realising she only had one shot at this. If the van stalled or spluttered, it would take Vinnie a matter of seconds to get to her. And he had a gun, that damn gun. She pushed her body forward as far as she could and placed her fingers firmly on the key as she waited for Will to throw another stone. The metallic clang was followed by more crunches of footsteps in gravel.

She turned the key.

CHAPTER TWENTY-SEVEN

From her crouched position in the van, she saw the glow from the dashboard lights. At least it was connected to the battery; that was a start. She made the second turn. The moment the engine made a sound, she needed to drive. It would have to be smooth and fast; Vinnie would be on her in a moment.

As soon as the engine turned, she released the hand brake and her hand moved to the gear stick, her foot searching for the clutch. There were only two pedals. The engine hadn't fired. She looked around, her senses heightened now by the fear that the van might not run. She tried again; the engine turned but did not catch. Vinnie emerged from behind a container, gun drawn and ready to fire. He stormed towards her as she tried the engine again. Nothing. Vinnie was almost upon her.

Charlotte was bracing herself for the door to open, when Vinnie stopped dead and fell to his knees. Will stood behind him, a table lamp in his hand. He darted to the passenger side of the vehicle while she tried the engine again, her eyes on Vinnie all the time. He was shocked and hurt, but not out cold. She recalled how hard it had been for her to steady herself after the anaesthetic wore off. Vinnie had injected her, but the doctor had injected Vinnie; Vinnie's had probably been more expertly deployed.

At last, the engine fired. She almost screamed with joy as it chugged then finally found its momentum.

'Drive!' Will said.

'It's an automatic; what do I do?'

Will pushed the gear stick into drive and she felt the vehicle lurch forward.

'Floor it!' he said. 'It's like a bumper car, just use the accelerator and the brake. Now go!'

She obeyed, and the van lunged forward. Easing off, she steered between two containers. The van was blacked out at the back, and the rear-view mirror was missing. In her side mirror, she saw Vinnie raising his weapon. Two bullets struck the back of the van, puncturing the metal, but the rear doors absorbed the shots. Charlotte was thankful for the steel panel directly behind the seats.

'Where to?' she asked Will.

'Who knows? The police station?'

'No, not yet. We need a call box. I have to speak to Kate. We have everything she wanted now; it must be time for her to come out of hiding.'

'Go rural,' Will suggested, 'in case he tracks us.'

'He can't track us; we're not in the company car now.'

'Do it anyway. Go via Overton, there's a phone box where you can call Kate and ask her what to do. If he did put a tracker on us, there's no signal on some of these country roads. At least it'll take him off the scent.'

Charlotte was getting the hang of the automatic, though by instinct her hand kept feeling for the gear stick and her left foot constantly searched for the clutch. She took as many side roads as she could, in an erratic course, trying to work out how to throw Vinnie off their tail if he was tracking them in some way. Her mind started working in overdrive; might there have been something in the injection? She offered the theory to Will.

'You've been watching too many spy films,' he replied. 'I'm fairly sure even the British Army can't inject you with trackers yet, let alone Vinnie Mace.'

They soon arrived at Overton. The village was quiet, with just the occasional, late-night dog walker around. The village call box wasn't being used.

'Move the lever to the P position,' Will advised. 'Keep it running; I don't trust that man not to be following us.'

Charlotte got out and opened the door to the call box. She felt in her pockets for change; she had a few coins, sufficient to make a quick call. She still had the scrunched-up piece of paper with Kate's number on it deep in her pocket. She smiled to herself as she remembered Vinnie had put his hand in those pockets when he was searching for her car keys. He hadn't looked for anything else. It was all well and good setting up a torture room, but he could have saved himself a lot of trouble if he'd frisked her first. She wondered if the Afghan rebels ever used elite tricks like that.

She dialled Kate's number.

'Please pick up, Kate,' she urged as the call connection was made.

'Charlotte?'

'Yes. I've got everything.'

'Oh, thank God, Charlotte. The time passes so slowly hidden up here.'

She could hear the distinctive sound again in the background.

'Are you still safe? We need to know what to do next.'

'We?'

'Will and I. Don't ask; it's a long story. I don't believe it myself.'

'You're sure you have everything, Charlotte? Did you find Brett's storage unit?'

'Yes, Will got the folder. It's got some legal contract and something I don't understand; like a Chemistry exam paper or something. Is it what you expected?'

'Yes, yes, it's perfect. And you have the other papers?'

'Not in my hands, but they're safe where nobody can find them. I have them all, Kate. Can you come out of hiding now?'

'There's one more thing, Charlotte. I'm sorry, we're almost there now. I've had a lot of time to think, to work out what they might try to do. I'm sorry to ask you to do this. You need to break Tiffany Irwin out of the care home.'

'Break her out? As in take her without permission?'

'Yes. I only realised it this afternoon. Once they realise we have the paperwork, their only remaining option is to kill Tiffany—'

'Fabian wouldn't do that to his own sister, surely?'

'There's so much money involved here, Charlotte. And not just money. They've every reason to want her dead. And they can do it in an instant. They've kept her cooped up in that care home for years. It only takes a mis-administered drug or a staged suicide bid and they can render the documents useless. We've come so far now; we must close off all the escape routes. Can you do this one last thing for me? I'm sorry to ask you. If I step outside, they'll come for me. Now they know what I know, if they get me, it's all over. For everybody.'

'Kate, it's okay, I'll do it. What should I do with Tiffany when I've got her?'

'Hide her. Somewhere safe. Somewhere where they'll never find her. Oh, and I've been working things out. When it's time to come out of hiding, call DI Comfort. I'm as sure as I can be that he's safe—'

There was a beeping on the line; Charlotte was out of money.

'Stay safe, Kate. I'll get Tiffany. I have a contact inside the home. If she's still on shift, she'll help me. Then I'll call you again and we'll get it sorted out.'

The call was terminated abruptly. Her credit had run out. There was no mercy when it came to ending a call in a pay phone: no money, no call.

'What did she say?' Will asked.

'We have one more thing to do. I'm going to have to find Hollie Wickes again to help us. We need to break Tiffany out of the care home. I'm going to hide her with Hollie. It looks like we're getting a mother and child reunion—'

'What are we going to do, just walk in there and take her out?'

'Something like that,' Charlotte answered. 'But I need to call Hollie first.'

She fumbled for her phone and checked the display.

'No signal. I'll drive back towards civilisation so I can call Hollie. Watch the display, will you? Tell me when I have a signal.'

Charlotte pushed the lever into drive, the car lurched forward, and she pressed down on the accelerator. She turned the car around and headed back to Middleton. As they entered the village, Will confirmed he'd got a mobile signal. She pulled over, parked the car and dialled Hollie, who answered after five rings. She was somewhere busy, a bar or something similar.

'Hollie? It's Charlotte.'

'Hey, Charlotte. I'm still with Callie. We're back at the university, having a drink in the bar. We both feel the same. We don't need a DNA test; somehow we know we're sisters. It just feels right.'

Charlotte didn't challenge her. She understood the two young women were euphoric about being reunited, but the fireworks needed to wait until science had done its work and confirmed the truth via a DNA test.

'You're going to meet your mother tonight, Hollie.'

'Really? When?'

'In about thirty minutes from now. Can you afford a taxi to Torrisholme? I'll pay you back.'

'Yes, why?'

'Tell Callie to meet me at the bench where we stopped this morning. She knows where it is. Half an hour, okay?'

Hollie confirmed the arrangements. She sounded as excited as if somebody had just brought Christmas Day forward by twenty-four hours.

Charlotte ended the call and looked at Will.

'I've just figured something out,' she said, looking across at him.

'What?' he asked.

'The penny dropped finally when I was speaking to Hollie just then. I have no idea why it took me so long to work it out. I know where DCI Summers is hiding.'

CHAPTER TWENTY-EIGHT

December 1999

Tiffany watched as Georgina coaxed her children away from the play area. It was only the promise of gingerbread snowmen at the bakery that intercepted the tantrums. She would have similar problems with Callie and Jane, but she knew the lure of the library would distract them. She hated chasing Georgina off, but Brett would arrive soon, and she couldn't afford to get him embroiled in her life here. They weren't sticking around in Morecambe, after all.

Georgina finally managed to manoeuvre her children so they were ready to head for the bakery. Tiffany hugged her friend while Georgina's reined child tapped at her leg, asking when they were going to the baker's.

'I love you, Georgie,' Tiffany said. 'Thank you so much for organising the test for me. You'll never know how much you've helped me.'

Georgina gently pulled away from Tiffany and looked her directly in the eyes.

'You'd think we were never going to see each other again,' she said.

Tiffany felt a pang of guilt and regret.

'I'll see you at the village hall on New Year's Eve. Have a lovely Christmas. Take care, Georgie.'

She gave them a wave as they walked towards the bakery then did a double take at a passing police officer. The WPC looked familiar, but she couldn't place her.

The library book bribe worked as planned, without any of the tantrums displayed by Georgina's children on leaving the play area. Before long, Callie was toddling towards her with a library book from the pram tray in her hand and she was in time to meet Brett.

He moved in to give her a peck on the cheek, but she brushed him away.

'Not here, not yet, Brett. I want it too, but we can't be too obvious out in the open. I'm happy to be seen together, because nobody knows who you are. But we can't alert anybody to our relationship. If David hears about it, it will mess up everything.'

Tiffany couldn't wait to be with Brett. He lifted her confidence whenever they were together, making her feel everything was going to be okay. She was desperate to hold him, but they'd soon have the rest of their lives together. As they walked along, she drew her hand up into her coat sleeve a little, then reached out to take Brett's hand. They were dressed up for the cold day; nobody would look twice at them.

As they walked and chatted, she considered telling him about Rowan. He was so good with the baby, gazing at him in the pram, marvelling at his tiny, gloved hands, and making Callie and Jane laugh with his funny faces and silly voices. This was the family life she'd wanted.

She decided not to share Rowan's paternity, not just yet. That would be her gift to him. Once they were safely away, she'd tell him; he would be delighted to hear it. There would be none of David's coldness, none of the indifference towards her children. Brett was already a better friend to the children, even though he barely knew them. He would make a wonderful father.

'How long do you have?' Tiffany asked.

'Not long,' Brett replied. 'I'll need to leave you soon. The house is all packed up and ready to go.'

'We should move towards the library then,' Tiffany replied. 'The girls will get restless if they think we're not going. Let's take the longer way round and make the most of what time we have left.'

They walked towards the sliding doors and stepped out into the winter chill, the heaters above the Arndale Centre's entrance forming a protective force field against the biting wind. They took a left turn, towards the rear of the postal delivery depot, talking about their plans for the future. Tiffany looked ahead. A man was walking towards them with a familiar gait; it was David.

'Oh no, it's David. You need to make yourself scarce—'

'Where?'

'Up ahead, he's seen us. Go, Brett, I'll cover for you. I'll tell him you were asking for directions. Go, quickly.'

Brett touched her hand with his finger; she got the message. He rushed on ahead, not looking back, ignoring David, brazening it out.

David's face was full of thunder. He brushed past Brett, bumping his shoulder, and stormed up to Tiffany.

'Hey!' Brett shouted.

'So that's him,' David said.

'Who?' she replied.

Brett had stopped to watch.

'He's your lover, I take it?'

'No, he was just asking directions—'

'Don't lie, Tiffany. Do you think I don't know?'

Her mind churned frantically. What was he talking about? Was he on to them? Did he know about their plans? The tickets? She still had the DNA results tucked in her coat pocket.

'What are you even doing here?' she asked. 'I thought you were in the office.'

'I'm in town to see the solicitors.'

His tone changed, as if he'd said more than he intended to.

'I want to know what's going on here. Is this serious? Don't think you're leaving me, Tiffany. You'll only leave this marriage when I say so.'

The girls were picking up on the atmosphere; Callie had begun to cry and Jane was about to follow her lead. Rowan was awake too, his eyes open, searching for his mother's face.

'He just asked me for directions, David. I don't understand why you're flying off the handle. I don't even know him. Why are you being like this?'

David leaned in so close to her that the mist from his cold breath blew across her face. How had she ever thought she loved this man, even briefly? There didn't seem to be a single part of him that cared about her. She'd been ill and vulnerable, and it must have affected her judgement; he'd seemed like her saviour for a time. But he was a nasty, hateful man.

'What are you up to?' he seethed at her. 'You're plotting something. If you believe you can get the better of me, you're wrong. We'll always be one step ahead of you, you daft bitch. Besides, you're crazy, and we've got the paper-work to show it. I'd just settle for a life with the kids if I were you and be happy with it. It's all you're getting, you stupid cow.'

Brett had ignored her instruction to walk off. He had moved closer and was watching as the situation developed.

'Are you all right, Tiff?' he asked.

'He knows you well enough to call you Tiff then?' David goaded her. 'Just asking for directions, you reckon?'

For one moment Tiffany thought he might strike her.

'That's enough,' Brett said, springing forward to grab David's hand.

David spun around, a look of hate on his face.

'Don't touch me!'

He spat out the words, his fist clenched. Callie, Jane and Rowan were now crying. Tiffany was about to join them.

'I want to go to the li-bree, Mummy,' Callie pleaded.

'It's okay, Tiff,' Brett said. 'Me and David will talk about this, away from the children. They don't need to see this; they're getting upset.'

He looked at David.

'Okay, David? They're only children, and you're upsetting them. Let's talk about this. Why don't you take them to the library, Tiff? It'll calm them down. Okay?'

Tiffany nodded, concerned about what he might say to David. She was relieved now she hadn't told him about Rowan. Or the plane tickets. The less anybody knew, the safer they would be. David couldn't get inside her head, so she'd save the details of their escape until the very last minute. That way, David wouldn't be able to stop them.

'It's okay, Tiff, honestly.'

She could tell from the look in Brett's eyes that he was

urging her to go. She stroked Callie's cold cheek and turned away from the men.

'Come on gorgeous, let's get some new books from the library.'

She walked past the car park and headed for the library building, praying Brett would smooth it over without giving the game away. The children had settled now, easily distracted by the prospect of some new picture books. But her mind was not so easily turned. She hated David and she would do anything to get rid of him. That man had tormented her for too long. This wasn't just about getting away from him now; it was all about revenge.

CHAPTER TWENTY-NINE

Charlotte and Will were jumpy all the way back to Torrisholme. With every SUV, every dark car, Charlotte checked her mirrors, straining her eyes to see if it was Vinnie. The man was hard to shake off, like a sticky sweet wrapper stuck on the sole of her shoe.

'So, where is Kate?' Will asked. 'You seemed pretty certain about it back there.'

'I'll tell you later,' she replied, checking her wing mirror for what felt like the hundredth time. 'I'm paranoid about Vinnie Mace. Has he bugged the car? Can he listen in via our phones? And if he catches one of us again... you've seen what he had planned for us; I'm not sure how much of that I could endure. Very little, I reckon. You're safer if I don't tell you. But I will, I promise, when it's time to go and get her.'

Will looked like he needed something to do. With Charlotte doing the driving, he was bouncing his right leg furiously and tapping his hand like a metronome on uppers. Charlotte reached out and squeezed his hand.

'I'm so sorry I did this to you again, Will. I don't know what I could have done differently to stop it. One minute I was reporting on humdrum events, the next this news story about the Irwins exploded in my face. And it caught you in the blast. I'm sorry; this is nothing to do with you.'

Will moved his hand and squeezed her leg.

'You know,' he began, 'I'm not cut out for this. I would have been happy investigating the old press cuttings about the Irwins, taking a passing interest in it, then moving on. But we've always been different, Charlotte. You've always pushed a little harder; you were always more extreme than me. I admire you for it. I wish I could be that way, less safe and predictable, but you get the bit between your teeth and there's no stopping you.'

He squeezed her leg again.

'I was terrified in that industrial unit, but I knew that as soon as you arrived, I'd get out of there. There's something about you, Charlotte. I've never seen you like this in all the years we've been married. You have a purpose now, a real drive.'

They continued in silence for another five minutes while Charlotte thought about it. He was right. Of course, she didn't want any of those terrible things to happen to either of them, and especially not to Olli and Lucia. But she'd never felt such a strong sense of purpose. This work made her come alive in a way she'd never experienced before. At a time in their lives when they should be considering potential retirement dates, she felt compelled to explore this new line of work. It consumed her in a way only caring for her children had done so far.

'We're here,' she said, pulling up at the side of the road without warning. 'Callie and Hollie won't be long. Be careful with Hollie; she's still angry with us. Give her the benefit of the doubt, please.'

'You don't think I'm going in there with you, do you?' Will asked.

Charlotte smiled.

'Now you mention it, it doesn't make a lot of sense to go mob-handed. You get to be the getaway driver this time.'

She laughed, forgiving herself for sounding mildly hysterical. After what they'd just been through, who wouldn't be rattled?

'I can't believe you're my getaway driver,' she said. 'In a stolen van that's supposed to be used for moving furniture. Whoever would have imagined it would come to this?'

'Well, let's add being a lookout to my job description too. Like you, I don't trust Vinnie. Switch your mobile phone to vibrate, and I'll text you if I spot anything suspicious.'

A taxi pulled up further along the road, and Hollie and Callie emerged. Charlotte flashed the headlamps at them, and Callie raised her hand in acknowledgement.

'Okay, we're breaking Tiffany out. Have the engine revving and look out for the bad guys.'

Will gave her a look.

'I'm kidding,' she smiled, leaning over to give him a peck on the cheek. 'See you soon.'

She got out of the car and intercepted the two sisters as Will moved round to the driver's side of the van. She was wary of Hollie and Will getting too close, but Will simply greeted the younger women with a raised hand and made himself scarce, settling in the driver's seat.

'Right, Hollie, get ready to meet your birth mother. This is like The Great Escape—'

She noticed the blank look on their faces.

'Sorry, you're too young to know what I'm talking about. But we're busting Tiffany out and then I want you to look after her in your student flat, Hollie. Is that okay? It won't be for long, but we have to keep her safe.'

'Let's do it,' Callie replied. 'The sooner we put an end to all this, the better. What do you want us to do?'

'Follow me,' Charlotte answered, heading off towards the alley which would lead them to the care home.

It was dark now, and Torrisholme was completely quiet, with only the occasional passing car on the main road. Charlotte was delighted to see none of the owners' cars were in the parking lot. At least they wouldn't have to contend with a pompous Quinton Madeley.

She hadn't had time to work through her plan properly. Her best bet was if Fiona was still on shift. She was torn between going through the front door and slipping in unnoticed. In the end she decided to use a combination of both.

'What are your acting skills like, ladies?' she asked.

'I'm studying drama at uni,' Callie answered. 'If I ever get back there after all this.'

Charlotte touched Callie's arm.

'You'll go back, don't worry. Once this has all settled, you'll be able to pick up your life. I want you both to create a distraction at the front desk. Invent a patient's name and make a big deal of wanting to see them. Tell the front desk staff you've travelled miles to get here. Insist they check their records, but don't cause so much of a fuss that they call the police.'

'What about you?' Hollie asked.

'I'll be crawling through a hedge for the umpteenth time and trying to get Tiffany's attention. I'm concerned she might be in bed and we'll confuse her. We'll cross that bridge when we come to it.'

They went their separate ways in the car park, with Charlotte fielding questions from her young companions before the breakout began. This was officially an abduction, and they were taking a big chance. But it wasn't some fallout over the colour of a patient's bed linen or the effectiveness of their medication. This was a life and death matter; every inch of her believed Tiffany would be in danger if Kate Summers finally revealed what she knew.

The gap in the hedge was easier to get through this time, the undergrowth flattened by her previous escapades. She had worried for a moment that the care home staff might have blocked it off since she'd revealed it as a security vulnerability. Sure enough, when she emerged at the other side, a neat pile of wooden posts and fence wire was stacked up against the wall, ready to strengthen the barrier. That was a stroke of luck; one day later and they'd have been scuppered.

Once back on her feet on the other side of the hedge, Charlotte began to work her way along the patio windows, hoping to see some lights on, and – if she was lucky – some open curtains. She counted along to Tiffany's room and cursed to herself; the room was in darkness.

As quickly as she could, she moved past the other windows, hopeful of finding another way in. The building was shut up for the night. As she reached the end of the wall, she found a part of the building she hadn't seen before. It had been obscured from view as she'd approached; now she realised the building was more extensive.

It seemed to be a communal room. Residents were sitting at tables playing games, reading books, doing puzzles and flicking through newspapers. A small group was gathered around the television set, watching the news. The windows were all closed and there appeared to be no way in, other than via the large patio doors at the far side.

As Charlotte moved along the wall, she heard a familiar

voice. Through the window, she could see the rear of the reception desk. Two staff members were attending to Callie and Hollie, who both had indignant looks on their faces. The body language of the staff members suggested impatience and agitation; she probably didn't have much time left.

She waved at the window to attract attention. Callie spotted her first, almost giving the game away by glancing up at her and waving back. Charlotte ducked down for a moment, just in case one of the staff members had noticed.

When she stood up again, Callie was waiting for her. She gave a little nod and shrugged her shoulders. It looked like she and Hollie were running out of steam with their charade. They needed to come up with something quick between them or she'd never get Tiffany out of the building.

Charlotte raised her eyebrows and held up her hands to indicate to Callie that she'd drawn a blank too. At that moment, Hollie noticed Charlotte at the window and instinctively gave her a wave. The male staff member who was trying to resolve their fictional enquiry turned around, and Charlotte heard his muffled voice through the glass.

'What the hell is going on out there?'

Moments later the fire alarms began to sound throughout the building. This was her only chance.

CHAPTER THIRTY

Before Charlotte had figured out what was going on, the residents in the communal lounge started to file out of a fire door at the side of the building, with nurses and support staff guiding them towards the assembly point.

'I did that,' came a voice from behind her. It was Hollie.

'I can't believe you pressed the fire alarm,' Callie scolded her. 'Look what you've done.'

'I'm pleased you did,' said Charlotte, turning around to face her accomplices. 'I was out of options on this side of the glass. Now, we need to find Tiffany and sneak her out in the confusion. Keep your heads down, let's split up and don't get spotted by the staff, whatever you do. If we get separated, meet back at the van.'

Charlotte scanned the crowd of people who were diligently assembling on a patio area at a safe distance away from the main building. She spotted Fiona quickly, her distinctive uniform marking her out as an employee rather than a resident. Charlotte sidled up to her and noted the look of surprise when Fiona realised who she was.

'We're breaking Tiffany out,' Charlotte whispered. 'I

can't tell you how pleased I am that you're working a long shift today.'

'I can't get involved in this; I'll lose my job. But if you want to know where Tiffany is, she's over there.'

She pointed, and Charlotte picked out Tiffany immediately, then caught Callie's attention and gestured in Tiffany's direction.

'Hey, who are you? You're not supposed to be here—'

The voice of a male nurse came from behind her. She turned, instinctively.

'You're that woman who escaped through the hedge—'

Charlotte recognised him immediately as the man who'd been clutching at her ankles as she'd tried to escape the first time she sneaked in the grounds.

Her response was as lame as they come, but put on the spot, it was the best she could do.

'What? No, that wasn't me; it must have been someone else—'

'I recognise your shoes. It is you. Did you set the fire alarm off?'

'Gerry, look,' Fiona intervened, 'Olivia is getting distressed. Go and calm her, I'll deal with this.'

Gerry glanced between Olivia, Charlotte and Fiona. His sense of professionalism seemed to be creating the strongest pull. Olivia looked like she suffered from an extreme form of anxiety and needed rapid reassurance.

'Just get her off the premises,' Gerry urged, clearly agitated that he was unable to resolve this problem. He headed off towards Olivia.

'The Madeleys will be here soon,' Fiona told her. 'They're automatically alerted whenever there's a non-routine fire alarm. I'd move swiftly if I were you. There's a gate on this side of the building too, which the on-duty fire warden will already have unlocked. Once they've confirmed that the side of the building is safe, they'll lead the residents to the front car park until the fire brigade get here and declare the care home safe to re-enter. I'd sneak out that way if I were you.'

'Thanks for your help, Fiona. I know you didn't want to get involved but believe me, you've done more than enough. Thank you.'

Charlotte moved deeper into the assembled group, veering away from Gerry who was doing a remarkable job of calming Olivia. She felt a pang of guilt at the distress and disruption they were causing. These were fragile patients, and Olivia was in such a distressed state that it was upsetting Charlotte to see her. Thank heavens for people like Gerry with their vocation as a carer. She wouldn't have the patience to do the job.

'We've got Mum,' said Callie, appearing from nowhere with Tiffany and Hollie at her side. 'She's a little confused,' she continued in a whisper. 'I haven't told her about Hollie yet. It's not the time.'

'Good thinking,' Charlotte reassured her, giving Hollie's hand a squeeze. It must have been agony for her, finally meeting her birth mother, but finding her dazed and disoriented. She looked close to tears.

'It'll be all right, you'll have all the time you need to get this sorted out,' Charlotte said softly.

There was mayhem as the fire warden tried her best to organise everybody into groupings by room numbers to count them all. Someone was leading the first group towards the open gate at the side of the building and fire engines had arrived at the front, their blue lights sweeping across the foliage in a rhythmic motion.

'Hello Tiffany, remember me? I'm Charlotte from the

newspaper. We've come to get you out of here. Callie's here too. You remember Callie?'

She watched a flash of jealousy cross Hollie's face for a moment.

'Okay, let's go,' she announced, leading the way towards the fence.

'Excuse me! Excuse me!'

Somebody else had spotted them in the crowd.

'That's the woman we were talking to at reception,' Hollie said, looking behind her, panic in her voice.

'You're Jane!' Tiffany said suddenly. 'Oh Jane, you're back too. I'd know you anywhere. You've still got that lovely little freckle under your left eye—'

They'd just got what they needed. The DNA test was now a formality. Tiffany was able to spot her daughter in a crowd twenty years after losing her. Charlotte hadn't even noticed the freckle, but she knew only too well a mother's ability to pinpoint the blemishes and features of a child's body with the accuracy of a Google street map.

'We've got to go,' Charlotte urged. 'Are you up to a bit of running?' she asked Tiffany.

'These drugs keep me slow, but if Callie and Jane help me, I'll be fine.'

The girls took an arm each and moved ahead with Tiffany. The receptionist caught up with Charlotte and grabbed her arm. For a moment, Charlotte froze, believing the game was finally up. Then she decided to play the outrage card. She hated herself for doing it, but there was no time for officialdom and red tape.

'Ouch, you punched me!' she shouted.

The receptionist backed away immediately, releasing her grip.

'I didn't, I just wanted to—'

'Is that how you treat your residents? Manhandling them like this?'

She despised her response more with every word that came out of her mouth. The woman looked horrified.

'No, I... er... look, I'm sorry, I just wanted to—'

'I was just leaving!' Charlotte exclaimed, as if she had every right in the world to be there. She rushed away, towards the gate, hoping the receptionist's defensive response would last long enough for her to escape. She rushed through the gate, ignoring the staff member who was corralling the residents over to the assembly point. Keeping her head down, she followed Tiffany, Callie and Hollie towards the alleyway shortcut which would take them back to Will.

Tiffany was doing well, but it was obvious her senses were impaired, probably by whatever cocktail of drugs she'd been given. For a second, she had another flash of guilt. What if Tiffany needed her medication? What if they were placing her in danger by taking her away from the care home? She'd never forgive herself if Tiffany came to any harm, yet her gut told her they were doing more good than harm by breaking her out.

When they finally reached the van, Will was standing outside it, looking worried.

'What's up?' she asked. 'You look like you've had bad news.'

'Get in the van. You can drive,' was all he said, moving to the passenger side.

He had the engine running already. The van wasn't built for five adult passengers, but Tiffany and her daughters managed to squeeze into the rear section which didn't have any seats.

'Drive, quickly,' Will said, frowning. He looked into the

wing mirror on his side of the car as Charlotte pulled out from the kerb.

'What's wrong?' Charlotte asked again.

'I thought I saw Vinnie's car pass by earlier.'

'How did you know it was Vinnie?'

'I didn't, but it slowed as it approached me, then carried on as if nothing had happened.'

'It could have been anybody.'

'Yes, but ten minutes later, it reappeared behind me and parked up, like the driver had double-backed—'

'Are you sure you're not being paranoid? How can he know where we are?'

Will paused for a moment, checking the mirrors again.

'The car isn't there now. I think we're safe... Whoa, what the hell are you doing?'

'Sorry everybody,' Charlotte said as she pulled the car to the side of the road and braked sharply behind a bus. She got out of the van, opened the back doors and handed Callie all the money she could find in the recesses of her pockets.

'Here, move fast before that bus pulls away. Take Tiffany to the infirmary, get her checked out to make sure we're not putting her in danger.'

'But they'll be on the lookout for me—' Callie began.

'I know, and that's good. I want you all safely in a public place where they can't get to you. You won't have long to wait; I'm going to ask a man called DI Comfort to come to you. I'm as certain as I can be that he's safe. You can talk to him and tell him what we've done.'

'What about you?' Hollie asked. 'What will you do?'

'We need to go,' Callie told her. 'The bus driver looks like he's getting ready to move off.'

Callie helped Tiffany out of the back of the van then the three women rushed out onto the pavement and stepped up to the bus just as the driver was signalling his intent to pull out. Will and Charlotte watched them move safely away.

'So, what about us?' Will asked. 'What happens now?'

'It's time to finish this,' Charlotte began. 'Tiffany is safe now, and we have all the documents Kate asked us to gather. We're going to pick up Kate. It's time to deliver her back to her colleagues at the police station.'

CHAPTER THIRTY-ONE

'Where is DCI Summers?' Will asked.

'It suddenly made sense to me when I spoke to her from the Overton phone box. There was a distinctive noise in the background, and I just remembered the voice mail message from Sam Halford on her house phone. She's in one of the wind turbines. It's an ingenious place to hide out. She's got as much electricity as she needs to keep her phone charged.'

'It goes from the turbines to the National Grid doesn't it?' Will asked.

'Something like that. But there are plugs for tools and equipment up there. There's lighting, it's sheltered, and you can see if anyone is coming. I wondered why Sam Halford had left a message on her answer phone. He may be a professional contact, or they might even be working together. Either way, whether Kate got in legitimately or not, I'll put money on her being there.'

'What now?' Will asked.

'We put her in this van and drive her directly to a safe place where DI Comfort can speak to her.'

'What about this leak at the police station? Isn't it dangerous?'

'I don't know what else we can do. We've got all our ducks in a row; Tiffany is safe and in a public place, and we have all the documents Kate needed. You and I have seen enough to land Vinnie in a lot of trouble. We must move now, and we have to do it fast.'

Will pondered it for a couple of minutes.

'You're right,' he said at last. 'We can't risk Vinnie getting to us again. It's now or never.'

Charlotte took out her mobile phone.

'I'm calling the police. It'll have to be the press number at this time of night, but I'll insist on talking to DI Comfort.'

Charlotte dialled, looking into Will's eyes as she waited for the call to connect. She was greeted with a voicemail message which basically meant *don't bother us on this out of hours number unless it's really important*. She pressed the hash button, and the call was re-routed to whichever poor soul had drawn the short straw of fielding the calls that night. She recognised the voice on the other end immediately.

'Police Press Office, who am I speaking to please?'

'Is that you, Toni?'

'Charlotte? What on earth are you doing calling at this hour?'

'What are you doing answering my call at this hour?'

Toni laughed.

'How well do you think the police are funded, Charlotte? I take my turn on the overnight press enquiries just like everybody else on our fast diminishing press team. At least if it's you, it means I'm spared a confused pensioner demanding I alert all patrols to a missing dog.'

Charlotte laughed. The voice mail message made it

crystal clear the hashtag option should only be deployed if it was an urgent query, yet she could imagine how many members of the public ignored the instruction.

'So, how can I help you, Charlotte? Is it newspaper related?'

'I have to speak to DI Comfort,' she replied.

'You know he's off shift, I take it?'

'Yes, I assumed he went home at some point, even if he is in the middle of a big operation. Though as a taxpayer, I'm not really sure why police officers need to sleep; it doesn't feel like they're giving us the best value for money.'

Both Will and Toni laughed. Charlotte was doing it for her nerves as much as anything, still feeling the crackle of fear sparking through her body.

'Is it a press enquiry or is it related to the case? You'll appreciate I don't want to invade his home life if I can avoid it.'

'It's a bit of both.'

Charlotte recalled how unhelpful Toni had been on their previous call. Maybe she'd caught Toni at a bad time. She liked this woman; they'd clicked ever since they first met in the rest rooms at Morecambe Town Hall, and now she wanted to give her the benefit of the doubt.

'Where are you now?' Toni asked.

'I don't really want to say.'

'I mean, where can I reach you? I'll get DI Comfort to call you back. What's it in connection with?'

'It's a confidential matter,' Charlotte answered, sensing she sounded like a broken record.

'Come on, Charlotte. You know it's the first thing DI Comfort is going to ask me. Give me a clue, at least. You're more likely to get a call back tonight if you do.'

She took a deep breath and decided to give Toni Lawson the benefit of the doubt.

'I've worked out where DCI Summers is located and I'm going to fetch her now.'

'The police should do that, Charlotte, not you as a civilian.'

There it was, the change of tone again.

'I'm aware of the rules, but it's not going to happen that way,' Charlotte snapped. 'I'm only willing to reveal my information to DI Comfort and it has to be in a way of my choosing. Now please, Toni, put the call through to him and tell him to call me straight away. It will be well worth his while switching off Netflix or whatever.'

She could tell she'd raised Toni's hackles; the silence said it all. At last the press officer sighed and acquiesced.

'Okay, Charlotte, have it your way. But this is well out of order. If you hadn't come to my rescue that day handing me the toilet roll underneath the cubicle, I wouldn't be doing this for you right now. One good turn deserves another. But this is the first and last time, okay? I like you a lot, but I can't bend the rules for you.'

'Understood,' Charlotte replied, hoping to give the impression that she'd been suitably chastened. She gave Toni her mobile phone number and Will's too as a back-up. They ended the call, with a promise that Toni would do her best to get DI Comfort to respond to her the same night.

'All sorted?' Will asked.

'Yes, we're good to go. If you spot a phone box on the way, let me know. I want to warn Kate we're coming for her.'

Charlotte started the van and turned it around to head back towards Heysham.

'Text the kids, will you?' Charlotte said as they entered

Morecambe once again. 'Tell them we're fine and everything will be right again by tomorrow.'

'You're sure?' Will asked, turning in his seat to look at her.

'No, but one way or another, it will be in somebody else's hands after tonight. For better or for worse, it ends for us here.'

'Thank God,' Will replied.

'Describe the car you thought was following you earlier.'

'You're kidding me?' Will said, looking back to check who was behind them.

'Three cars behind us, there's an SUV. I think it's black, or navy blue; I can't tell in this light. Can you see it?'

Charlotte's phone rang.

'This must be DI Comfort. Can you take my phone and put it on speaker?'

She passed her phone over to Will, who was turning in an attempt to get a better view of the car he suspected was tailing them.

'DI Comfort, it's Charlotte Grayson from the newspaper, you're on speaker because I'm driving.'

'What is it, Charlotte? Do you really have DCI Summers?'

'Yes, and she's completely innocent in all this. I have all the evidence you need to confirm it and to explain what's going on with Callie Irwin.'

'You need to let the police handle this now.'

'No, that's not happening. I want you to arrange for DCI Summers to be processed at Lancaster Police Station, not by her colleagues in Morecambe.'

'You don't get to say how this works, Charlotte.'

'It's how it works now. I don't want anybody getting to her who knows her professionally, understood? And I want legal representation lined up for her the moment I drop her at the police station.'

'You're not in a position to make demands.'

'DI Comfort, you need to stop talking and start listening. If you want to get a result in this case tonight, then you do it my way. That means Lancaster Police Station, immediate legal representation and you work to my time frame. Got it?'

Will looked at her and raised his eyebrows.

'Okay, have it your way,' DI Comfort replied at last. 'When do you want all this?'

'Within the hour. I can't give you an exact time. I'm sure there's a coffee machine at Lancaster Police Station; you can all keep yourselves occupied until I get there.'

'Anything else?' he asked with a hint of sarcasm.

'That's it. And thank you. If you do this, you'll be helping out a colleague. She'll owe you, big time. And you'll tie up the biggest case Morecambe has seen in a lot of years. See you later, DI Comfort.'

She ended the call. Will touched her hand as it rested on the gear stick.

'You're right, it's the same car I spotted earlier. We've got someone on our tail again.'

'Dammit,' Charlotte cursed. She floored the accelerator, pulled out into the wrong side of the road, and overtook the car in front. The driver she'd overtaken sounded their car horn at the reckless manoeuvre, but she didn't care.

'What the hell are you doing?' Will asked. He looked shocked.

'We're out-running these bastards. I'm going to shake them off. Make sure your seatbelt is fastened.'

CHAPTER THIRTY-TWO

December 1999

'Are we doing the right thing?' Brett asked, balancing the cup from his flask of soup on top of a packing box. 'My sister isn't convinced we are. What if we're making more trouble for ourselves in the long run?'

Tiffany shook her head. 'You don't know David and Fabian like I do. Would you commit your sister to a mental facility like they did?'

'No, but—'

'But nothing, Brett. I was going through a difficult time, but it never occurred to those two jackals that they might actually make things better by taking the kids off my hands occasionally, helping around the house and generally being a bit more supportive. Instead, they find a doctor who says I'm a potential danger to myself and the kids and they coerce me to co-sign a power of attorney which takes away any control I had. Would you do that to Kate?'

Brett took a sip of his soup and offered her the cup. She

took it from him and blew on it to cool it a little before drinking.

'No, I wouldn't,' he replied. 'I would never do that to my sister. We went through everything together when my dad died. Kate was scrupulously fair about it, sitting me down and talking me through all the paperwork. She insisted I understood and agreed on everything she did. I'd do the same for her. We trust each other completely.'

'And that's how normal families behave,' Tiffany replied. 'My family is not normal. When my father died, Fabian acted like a hyena preparing to pick a carcass clean. Dad was barely cold in the ground before he started. He should have been like Kate, dividing it fairly and explaining everything. Instead, he tried to pull the wool over my eyes and secure planning permission on the land for something very different to what we'd agreed.'

'Our lives are going to change drastically after this, Tiff. Who can tell if I'll even get back up to Morecambe to pick up my stuff?'

He looked inside the pristine container which he'd rented to store his belongings. The removal team had dropped off all his furniture, and he was just locking up the final items which he'd cleared from the house.

'We'll get back, Brett; it'll die down eventually. This storage container is great. You can just come and go without some security guard clocking you in and out all the time. Do you mind if I leave a couple of small things here, just to keep them safe?'

Brett had opted to rent a container from a new storage company which had just set up on the industrial estate. At first he'd considered a more conventional storage unit in a warehouse, but he realised after an initial visit to check it out that he had to sign in and out every time he entered the premises. He wanted something more informal and less traceable.

He was one of the first customers at the new site, which was made up of twenty brand new containers arranged in a circle. With the pass code to the main gate and his own padlock for the container, he could come and go as he pleased, at any time of day. Protected by CCTV, it had night-lighting around the circumference. So long as he kept paying the low rental fee via direct debit, his container would be left alone.

It was perfect for what they were planning. The next time he came to this place, it would probably be under cover of night, with a hired van. He'd load his belongings, make his way back to wherever their new home was and disappear again into thin air. He'd end the payments on the unit, and nobody would ever know it had been there; even Kate wasn't aware he'd secured the unit.

'You can have this soup if you want, while I get the last boxes from the car. You can leave whatever you want here. It's all paid for, so you may as well.'

She finished the soup and then walked over to help Brett with the last of the items.

When the final box had been loaded in, they sat on the edge of the container floor, taking a moment to relax.

'How long does Joanne have the kids for?' Brett asked.

'I'll need to be getting back soon. You know, I wish I'd had someone like Joanne when I was working through my post-natal depression. Preferably my husband wouldn't have been sleeping with her, but a bit of support was all I needed. I wasn't crazy, I just needed help.'

Brett turned to face Tiffany and then kissed her.

'I experienced some mild depression when my dad died. Nothing like what happened to you, but I was in a very dark place. I never spoke to Kate about it. I couldn't see a path ahead without my dad; it seemed like my world had collapsed on itself. I owe my sister everything. She's a formidable woman. After dad died, she sorted out all the finances, helped me buy my house, and made sure I was on the right track. I want to be that person to you, Tiffany. I don't want you to feel like you've been abandoned ever again.'

She kissed him on the lips and hugged him, certain she wanted him to be the person her children called their father.

'What happened to your dad, Brett? You never talk about how he died. This is the first time you've mentioned your depression. Was he ill?'

'No. It was horrible. Someone killed him whilst on duty. He got caught up in some mess of a situation and he was murdered.'

'Oh, I'm so sorry, I had no idea.'

'It's okay. I was angry for a while. They got away with it; his killer was never found. I'm sure burying the anger caused my depression. It's a hard thing to deal with. We always knew something like that might happen, him being a copper, but in Morecambe? You expect it in inner cities, not in sleepy seaside towns.'

'I'm sorry about your dad,' Tiffany said again. 'What made Kate join the police force, given what happened to your father?'

'Kate reacted in a more constructive way. She decided joining the police force was the best way to bring his killer to justice. Whereas I channelled my grief into anger, Kate resolved to find out who was responsible for his death—'

'Has she found out?'

'Not yet. But if there's any kind of trail or a shred of

evidence out there, I have no doubt she'll find whoever it was and bring them to justice. She just doesn't stop, my sister. She's exactly the kind of person you want batting on your team. Whatever it takes, whatever the personal sacrifice, if it's the right thing to do, she'll do it.'

Tiffany didn't know Kate very well; they hadn't got off to the best of starts during their altercation at the leisure centre. But sitting there with Brett, shivering from the cold, snuggling as close as their winter clothing would allow, she hoped she would get to know her better one day soon. She sounded like one hell of a sister.

'Oh, I forgot my phone. It's in the front of the car,' Tiffany said. 'You wouldn't get it for me, would you? I'm feeling a bit stiff after moving those boxes.'

'Sure,' Brett replied, standing up to walk towards the vehicle. 'I won't be a moment, then we'd better get you back to Morecambe to collect the children from Joanne.'

Tiffany watched him as he walked over to the car, his back to her. She slipped a folder out of her bag, walked inside the container and surveyed the boxes labelled *Books*, *Office equipment*, *Shoes*, *Kitchen utensils* and so on. A man's life was packed up in here, yet it all fitted into a half-size container.

Checking that Brett was preoccupied in the car, Tiffany looked for a safe place to hide the folder. He wouldn't be coming back to the storage unit after they closed the doors that day, and she didn't need to put anything else in there. She'd got his permission, but he didn't need to know what it was.

She slid the folder under a box marked *Family photographs*. She'd remember that; it was stacked up right at the front and there was only one box like it.

'I can't find it, Tiff,' Brett shouted over to her.

'It's okay, I've found it in my bag. I forgot where I'd put it.'

It was a white lie, but one which would protect them both. The folder held some particularly important information. She hoped it wouldn't be needed. But if it was, it would blow the lives of Fabian and David into shattered fragments.

CHAPTER THIRTY-THREE

'Careful, Charlotte. You'll have the police after us if you carry on pulling stunts like that.'

She'd just careered in front of an oncoming vehicle, darted towards the verge on the wrong side of the road and then screeched across back to the right side of the road again.

'I'd rather have the police on my tail than Vinnie Mace. I don't want either of them coming after me until we've extracted Kate from her hiding place. And I must warn her we're on our way. She may be armed, and I don't want her to shoot us.'

Will lurched sideways in his seat as Charlotte made a sudden turn to the left, taking them down a leafy avenue, but said nothing.

Charlotte was relieved he'd chosen to let her get on with it. If she had to debate every crazy manoeuvre she was making, it would be a long drive.

'Keep checking the mirrors please, Will. I'll make sure I don't hit anything coming towards us if you can be on the lookout at the rear. Are they still there?'

'I can't see... damn it, yes. How is he doing that? No normal driver could stay on your tail the way you've been driving.'

'He has to be tracking us,' Charlotte replied, frustrated and angry. 'How would he do it?'

'Satellite or something?' Will ventured.

'This is Morecambe, not Mission Impossible,' Charlotte snapped at him. 'I'm sorry, I didn't mean to have a go at you. It must be something simpler... The phones. I'll bet it's the phones. When Vinnie grasped my finger and I thought he was about to remove it with the circular saw, that's when he did it. He must have unlocked my phone with my finger-print. I was so relieved he hadn't sawn it off, I didn't think about what he was up to. Check my phone; see if he's put an app on it.'

She tossed her smartphone over to Will, who began searching its contents.

'This looks fishy,' he said after a short time. 'Locatrr is an app on your phone; did you put it there?'

'Nope, it's not mine. Open it and see what it does.'

'Oh hell yes, this is the one. It's like watching ourselves on an Uber delivery app, it shows which road we're on, our speed, direction and route history.'

Will pressed a button at his side so his window glided open. He was about to throw Charlotte's phone into the road.

'Whoa, stop,' she shouted. 'Don't throw it out of the window. It's our only link with the outside world. Just remove the app or disable location settings, but don't get rid of my phone.'

Will said nothing for a moment.

'It's gone,' he said. 'I'll check mine.'

He pulled out his own phone.

'For fu—'

'Same on yours?'

'Yep, he's installed it on mine too. Right, we're clear. Let's see some more of that driving again. You must be able to shake him off now.'

Charlotte floored the accelerator, taking a sharp right turn, then a left, then another left. The tyres screeched on the last sharp turn and Will whistled through his teeth.

'You've got to admit it, that was a little bit Mission Impossible.'

Charlotte needed to be heading over Heysham way, but she'd lost her bearings in the back streets now and was fearful of moving too far away from her destination.

'I can't see him,' Will confirmed after turning to look through the rear window. 'I think you've done it.'

'Will you put your maps app on your phone and set Heysham as the destination? I need you to act as navigator for a bit; we have to get back on track now.'

As Will tapped on his own phone, Charlotte's gave an electronic beep as it sat on his lap. He picked it up and read the message.

'It's DI Comfort. He says it's all set up. He's also cautioning you against going it alone, but I'm guessing you'll ignore that bit. It says he's heading to Lancaster Police station now, and he'll see you there.'

'Great, now get me over to the Heysham Road via the back streets and let's shake Vinnie off our tail.'

'Okay right at the end of this road, then left at the first junction.'

Charlotte was driving much too fast for residential streets and she knew it, but it was late at night, as safe a time to break the law as any. She scanned the road as she drove, looking for movement. She was just about to take a fast-left turn when an elderly man appeared out of nowhere, with a fluorescent vest over his coat and a matching canine equivalent on the two Scottie dogs which were on a lead at his side.

'The fluorescent jacket doesn't act as a force field,' Charlotte cursed. The old man gave a friendly wave as he and the dogs toddled across the road, oblivious to the fact they'd narrowly avoided becoming roadkill.

'People seem to think those jackets make them indestructible. What is it with people in this country? Anything fluorescent seems to assume magical powers.'

'I'm sure you've lost him. There's a phone box over there. Want to risk it?'

Charlotte pulled over abruptly at the side of the road.

'I'll keep the van running. You move into the driver's seat. If you see Vinnie, let me know and I'll come running.'

'What if we damage the van?'

'We've stolen it, Will; it's a bit late for that. Besides, does Tom Cruise check the insurance certificate every time he jumps on a high-powered motorbike?'

'Okay, point taken,' Will replied. 'I guess it's a bit late to be thinking about that anyway.'

Charlotte was searching for loose change in the dashboard compartments of the vehicle. She found a one-pound coin and picked it up.

'You see anything, and you alert me, okay?'

Will nodded.

Charlotte found Kate's number and dialled it. It rang several times before being picked up.

'Kate, it's Charlotte,'

'Oh, thank God. I thought you'd never call. There's been movement outside where I'm located. They may be on to me—'

'You're at the turbines, yes?'

'How did you know?'

'I forgot to tell you about a message Sam Halford left on your answering machine. You know him, I take it?'

'Yes, he's been helping me with my informal investigations, but I suspect he doesn't realise how helpful he's been yet. I stole a key to one of the turbines at our last meeting. I'm not proud of it, but I needed to hide somewhere where they'd never think to look for me.'

'Look, Kate, I'm coming to get you. But we've been followed. I hope I've lost him now, but I'm coming to get you out of there. We have all the paperwork, Tiffany is safe, and DI Comfort is waiting for us at Lancaster Police Station. We just need to get you in safely.'

'There's movement on the wind farm, Charlotte.'

'Have you got a weapon?'

'What weapon? This is the UK, Charlotte. It would be a lot easier if I was issued with a firearm, but that's not how it works in Morecambe.'

'Sorry, silly question, where are—'

Will was flashing the headlamps on full and waving frantically at her through the driver's side window.

'I've got to go, Kate; can I call you on my mobile now?'

'Yes, call me back. This might be nothing or it might be something.'

The phone went dead.

Charlotte left the phone box and ran across to Will, who'd moved the van closer.

'Get in,' he said, 'he's back.'

Charlotte climbed in the passenger side and Will accelerated fast, before she'd even got the door shut.

'You're sure it was him?' Charlotte asked, fastening her seatbelt.

'As sure as I can be in this light,' he replied. 'If only we could change vehicles. We're a sitting target in this rusty old van.'

'Let me call Kate again; she might have some idea what to do. Keep taking turns into side streets, but take us towards the turbines if you can.'

She dialled Kate on her mobile phone. It would have been a lot easier if she could have done that all along. Were they tracking her calls too? She'd keep the conversation non-specific, just in case.

'Kate, it's me again. We think we're being tracked. Any idea how they're doing it? They had trackers on our phones, but we got of rid of them.'

'They could do it via phone masts, but it's not so accurate. Is there a tracker attached to the car? They're pretty easy to come by these days; people get them sent over from China via eBay and the like.'

'That would make sense. It would explain how Vinnie always seems to be one step ahead of me. What do they look like?'

'It'll be fastened to the vehicle somewhere, either on the inside or outside. They use them in the US now for insurance purposes. Big Brother and all that.'

Charlotte's shoulder struck the side of the passenger side door as Will flung the car around a sharp corner.

'Steady,' she said. 'I thought you were nervous about the insurance.'

'Oh hell—'

'What is it, Kate?'

'One moment.'

The silence was unbearable. All Charlotte could hear was the rhythmic sound of the turbine blades turning while she waited for Kate's response.

'I've got trouble,' she said at last. 'I'm not alone.'

'Where are you, Kate? Which turbine?'

'Unit 12,' she replied. 'Come quick. You may need to get DI Comfort out here.'

'What's happening, Kate? Are the turbines clearly marked?'

Kate was speaking in a whisper now.

'Yes, there are lots of numbers on the chassis, but you'll see the Unit 12 wording, it's clear enough. I'm going to lie low and find somewhere to hide in this generator room.'

'You're at the top of the turbine? I thought you were at the base, Kate.'

'I'm at the top, it's safer. It's one hell of a climb. Some-one's started to come up the ladder, Charlotte. If it's not an engineering team, I'm in deep trouble.'

CHAPTER THIRTY-FOUR

'We need to step on it. Is he still tailing us?' Charlotte asked.

'Every time I think I've thrown him off, he pops up in front of me or behind me.' Will answered. 'There can't be a device attached to this old van. The company car, maybe, but not this old thing. He didn't have time, did he?'

'Who knows? Perhaps he just got lucky after I removed the apps from our phones. It's not like we're trying to lose him in the centre of London. This is rural Lancashire. We have to get to Kate now; she's got visitors, and they may not be friendly.'

'What's the plan?' Will asked, taking what felt like the hundredth sharp turn into a back street.

'We're getting nowhere with this. I'm going to take a chance. I want you to drive towards the wind farm. As we're going down the country lanes, you can switch the lights off, stop the car and let me get out. We need to do it fast. Then you can switch your lights back on. I want you to lead Vinnie away from there.'

'What about you? I'm not leaving you on your own.'

'I'll cut across the fields when we get close. Vinnie can't track me with the app off my phone. Drive towards Overton; let him think we're heading back to Sunderland Point, then drive on to Lancaster Police Station. I'll meet you there.'

'How will you get there?'

'Will, I don't have all the answers. We're reasonably competent between the two of us. I'm sure we'll figure something out. In the worst-case scenario, Kate and I will hide in the fields somewhere and DI Comfort can send somebody out to collect us. I still have documents hidden which I'll need to present as evidence, but what we've got in the car is good enough for starters. They're under the carpet in the footwell. Get to the police station and make sure those documents are receipted properly, with a legal witness present, before you hand them over.'

Will's silence told her he was uneasy about the plan, but there was no other way around it. Besides, she owed Kate this.

Will found the main road once again, and they headed towards Heysham, still driving at speed.

'We're going to hit the country lanes soon, so be ready for me to give the word.'

Will nodded his response, flicking the car headlamps on full beam as they left the street lighting behind them.

The lanes were narrow and winding now, often single track, with hedges so high at their sides that they might as well have been walls. Charlotte wasn't sure they were in the right place; it was much easier in the light of day when the wind turbines were visible. Then she remembered there were small red lights at the top of the structures, to warn low aircraft of their presence in the dark. She focused on them in the distance.

'Veer to the right as soon as you can,' she told Will. 'Get ready to lose the lights.'

'I won't be able to see the road—'

'The moon's bright enough and it's only a couple of minutes. We have to do it this way.'

Up ahead, Charlotte noticed an illuminated area in a dark field. It looked like somebody had placed a flood lamp there. After a moment, she realised it was a tractor and a farmer doing some night-time ploughing.

'I can't believe I'm going to do this.'

'What?'

'Stop the car.'

'What about the headlamps?'

'Just stop the car, Will.'

He braked hard, and their seat belts locked.

She leaned over and kissed him before turning to open her door.

'Remember what I said. Meet me at Lancaster. DI Comfort is your man. Make sure Kate has legal representation when she arrives.'

She slammed her door and made a motioning sound with her arm to encourage Will to carry on driving. She'd seen stubborn mules look more willing, but he did as he'd been urged and set off down the country lane.

She walked through the open gate of the field and ducked in behind the hedge. The farmer had stopped the tractor, leaving the engine running. The cab door was open too, but he wasn't visible in the darkness. Then, some way up ahead, she saw the lit screen of his mobile phone. He was answering nature's call at the edge of the field, avoiding the glare of the tractor's headlamps to hide what he was up to in case anyone came along. As Charlotte activated her phone to send a message to Will, a car engine sound came out of nowhere. It was Vinnie, with his headlamps off, following Will in the van.

She randomly pressed the buttons on her phone, desperate to darken her phone screen in case Vinnie spotted it in the darkness. His car passed by, then stopped, and reversed back to the gate. He switched on his car lights. As the beam of his headlamps swept by, she felt exposed in the sudden flare of brightness. He'd spotted her, he had to have spotted her.

She looked at the car, then the gate and over towards the tractor. The farmer's phone screen was still lit up, and he was some distance from his vehicle. She'd already considered taking it when she had asked Will to stop the van, figuring that if she lost her nerve, she would run across the fields over to the wind farm. Now she knew it would have to be the tractor option.

Charlotte put her hand on the edge of the gate, pushed it forward and slammed it against the post opposite, where it latched up with a metal locking mechanism. Without looking back, she started running directly towards the tractor.

The farmer had realised something was up and was shouting at her from the darkness. She imagined him trying to run through the furrows, pulling his trousers up from around his ankles, and almost laughed out loud.

'I'm so sorry,' she shouted, 'but this is really important.'

She'd never been in a tractor cab before, much less driven one, so didn't have a clue where to start. All she saw was a dazzling array of headlamps in an all-terrain vehicle that would get her across those fields fast, providing the best chance of reaching Kate Summers before Vinnie did.

Once in the cab, she looked at the controls. Gear stick, clutch, brake, accelerator. They were caked in mud and there was a prevailing waft of body odour, but it all made sense. She pulled the cab door shut, dipped the clutch, selected a gear and lurched forward.

There was some resistance; the vehicle was moving, but not as fast as she'd expected. The plough was holding it back, still sunk into the mud. Charlotte checked the cluster of levers, and saw one of them was in a different position from the rest. It was her best chance. She pushed it, experiencing more resistance than she'd expected, but it lifted behind her and the tractor began to move freely. The farmer was now running at her side, shouting at her. She looked over towards the gate. Vinnie's car headlamps were on, directed at the field, and he was opening the gate and coming for her.

'Get out of the way; find somewhere to hide!' she shouted at the farmer.

'Get out of the bloody cab!' he shouted back at her, just audible above the roar of the engine. She was still driving slowly enough for the farmer to leap up to the steps at the side of the cab and cling onto the door handle and the large wing mirror, screaming at her to stop.

Charlotte cursed as she realised she was heading in the opposite direction to the turbines. She spun the tractor around, driving over the newly ploughed furrows; the farmer wouldn't be winning any ploughing competitions now she'd messed up his straight lines.

She moved through the gears, not entirely sure what to do next. Vinnie was driving into the field. What was he intending to do, chase her?

She soon knew the answer. He stopped the SUV, leaned out of his window and shot at the tractor. The bullet ricocheted off the top of the cab, startling the farmer so much that he released his grip and dropped to the ground. Charlotte made a frantic arm movement to him.

'Get out of the way,' she urged, 'he's crazy.'

Vinnie was back in his car and ready to pursue her again. She looked around, desperately weighing up her options. There was only one thing for it: to go cross-country. And to start her journey, she needed to find out if the tractor was capable of crashing through the only obstacle in her way: a thorny hedge which bounded the perimeter of the field.

CHAPTER THIRTY-FIVE

Charlotte closed her eyes as the tractor hurtled towards the hedge. She had no idea what the result would be, but it had to be an improvement on continuing the game of cat and mouse with Vinnie or running across muddy fields on foot.

When she opened her eyes once again, she was on the other side of the hedgerow, with clusters of hawthorn bush attached to the front grille and an entire root being pulled along by the blades of the raised plough. Up ahead, the red lights of the turbines punctuated the darkness, like sentinels of the countryside, standing proud in the rural landscape.

She aimed the tractor towards the lights, amazed at its height and power. The cab was set up for a tall farmer, so she couldn't see in the rear-view mirror, and had to turn to confirm that Vinnie was still on her tail. He was driving more cautiously, navigating the uneven ground.

To her side she spotted sheep, alarmed by the glaring lights and uncertain which way to run to avoid the monster in the night. As she veered to the side to avoid the flock, she realised she was only a field away from the turbines now.

Vinnie had no idea Will was safely away with the documents, but he could still abduct her and hold her hostage. She regretted not telling Will to send DI Comfort directly to the wind farm; but she had to deliver Kate into safe hands, away from the rogue police officer at Morecambe station. She would only release the documents once DCI Summers was safe from any possible sabotage or interference.

A bull appeared suddenly from the darkness. Charlotte slammed on the brakes, throwing herself forward and striking her head on the steering wheel. The tractor stopped dead and stalled, and Vinnie's car ran into the raised plough. The bull stayed exactly where it was, as if it had every right to be there.

Charlotte was dazed, but she couldn't hang about. She started up the tractor again, thankful for it firing straight away, and checked either side of the cab doors for Vinnie. He was standing to her right-hand side, his gun pointing at the cab. How the hell had he moved so fast?

Over the engine noise, she heard him shouting at her.

'Get out, Charlotte. It's over. We know where Kate Summers is hiding. If you don't stop running, we'll go for your kids.'

It was all she needed to hear. They'd hit the lowest common denominator. Well, tough guy or not, it was time Vinnie Mace learnt an important life lesson: a mother whose children have just been threatened is more dangerous than an Afghan rebel could ever be. Or a bull, come to that.

She floored the accelerator, spun the steering wheel and made a 180-degree turn, sending Vinnie hurtling to the ground to avoid the blades of the plough which swung over his head. The bull began to trot towards him, and as she straightened up the tractor to resume her original course, she saw Vinnie struggling to find his feet. She didn't know if the bull stereotype was true, but if he chased Vinnie it would give her some time to get to the turbine first. The tractor's speed was impressive. She'd been stuck behind one many times along the country lanes of Lancashire, but this model was bigger and faster than she'd imagined.

Careering through the next hedge, she arrived at the far corner of the field in which the wind turbines stood. The headlamps on the tractor gave off sufficient light for her to make out the steel bases of the structures in the distance.

She'd been told by Kate to look for Unit 12. As she passed the first turbine, she saw a cluster of black lettering at the base. At first it seemed confusing and overwhelming, but as she stared at the letters, she saw what Kate meant. It was Unit 7.

There were no signs of Vinnie behind her, but his car headlamps were still visible in the distance, where she'd left him with the bull. The image of two, angry, macho alphas having to fight it out in the fields below her was oddly satisfying, despite the immense stress she was under. She had to find Unit 12 as fast as possible and get Kate away from the area. With any luck, her visitors were a maintenance team and they would have whisked her away to safety by now.

At last she spotted the twelfth unit. Keen to distract Vinnie away from it and buy extra time, she drove the tractor further up the hill, away from Unit 12, switched off the ignition, turned off the headlamps and stepped out of the cab. She placed the keys in her pocket; the tractor had proved an excellent escape vehicle, despite its cumbersome size. Using the torch on her phone would help to light the way, but it was too risky. Knowing a tough guy like Vinnie

Mace, for all she knew he'd have made best pals with the bull and would arrive riding it like a stallion in a shower of testosterone. Well, screw that. She and Kate would outwit them, using guile and cunning instead. It seemed like a plan, at least.

She ran down towards Unit 12, almost losing her footing on the way, but she recovered her balance fast enough to avoid an ankle sprain. On arriving at the base of the steps leading to the entrance of the turbine, she saw the door was ajar. If it hadn't been for the sound of the turbine's blades punctuating their phone calls, she would never have guessed where Kate was hiding. It was a genius move, hiding on Fabian Armstrong's own doorstep.

Charlotte walked cautiously up the steel steps and opened the door. It creaked on its hinges. The base of the turbine was lit, as it had been when she'd climbed up to report on her experience for the newspaper. She expected to see Kate Summers waiting for her, ready to move at a moment's notice. Instead, Sam Halford was out cold on the concrete floor, his head bloodied where he'd been struck by a blunt instrument.

She rushed up to him, calling his name, checking he was still alive. He was breathing faintly, but his face was ashen and his body limp. Charlotte looked up towards the ladder which led to the top of the turbine. She called out, the echo of her voice seeming to get lost in the vast, circular structure.

'Kate. Kate. Are you up there?'

There was silence for a moment.

An unfamiliar voice came from the top of the turbine, echoing back down its long, tubular frame.

'Charlotte Grayson. At last. Come up and join us. I have Kate Summers with me now.'

Charlotte sensed her body being seized by a sudden, cold frost.

'Who the hell are you?' she called back. 'Is Kate safe?'

'I'm Joanne Taylor, Charlotte. Don't you think it's time you and I met?'

CHAPTER THIRTY-SIX

December 1999

The moment Tiffany felt herself falling to the ground outside the village hall, she knew it was all over. They were one step ahead of her; they were always one step ahead of her.

She'd glanced around the car park for Brett as soon as she walked outside. He was there; she saw his lights. He'd stuck to the plan and was tucked away out of sight at the far end of the car park. She could always rely on Brett.

From nowhere, Joanne appeared. Then David, with another man at his side. As soon as she saw them, she knew things weren't right. Frozen in shock, she stared at them, then... oblivion. What had they done to her? A wall of darkness descended, her legs crumpled beneath her and the gravel scraped against her face as she struck the ground.

She woke sometime later, not knowing for how long she'd been out cold. A crippling fog swirled around in her head and her limbs were numb. She was in a confined space. The distinctive smell of dried formula milk on the blanket underneath her told Tiffany she was lying in the boot of the car. A wave of panic washed over her, but she couldn't make a noise or move. The drug they'd injected into her was too strong.

Tiffany tried to calm herself for a moment to listen. There were voices. Some she recognised, but others were unfamiliar. David was there, and so was Joanne. They sounded more tense than she'd ever heard them before. It was unusual; they were usually cocksure, confident of their power and status.

There were other voices too, strange voices, in an accent she couldn't quite catch. They were some distance away, close enough to get a sense of the conversation, but not so close to hear specific words. They were speaking in English but with a foreign accent, Eastern European, possibly even Russian. She could hear one of the children too. Where were they? It was Callie, babbling, but she couldn't hear the others. They must be in the back of the car, just at the other side of her.

As Tiffany lay listening in the darkness of the car boot, she heard the light tread of a thief's footsteps, of someone fearful of alerting anyone within earshot.

There was a gentle click in front of her; somebody was opening the car door.

'Man!' Callie exclaimed.

Tiffany heard a calm shushing sound, the gentle reassurance of a person who was happy to deal with children.

'Hi, Callie,' came a whisper, 'I need you to be really quiet if you can.'

It was Brett; he'd followed them.

'Brett,' she whispered in a voice so hoarse that she could barely speak.

She tried again; he hadn't heard her.

'Brett—'

'Tiff?'

She heard the cautious crunching of feet on the ground.

'Man gone,' Callie said, like it was a game.

Tiffany heard Brett's nervous breathing before he spoke again.

'I need you to stay really quiet,' Brett said. 'This is dangerous Tiff, stay still and wait for my lead—'

'What's going on?' she whispered. 'Are the kids okay?'

The car boot clicked, and Tiffany jumped. As Brett raised the cover a little, she turned to see his mouth and nose through the narrow gap, lit up by some lights in the distance. She immediately sensed his tension.

'Where man gone?' Callie asked.

'Oh, thank God, Brett, what the hell is going on?'

'They drugged you, Tiff, I watched them do it in the car park. It was David and Joanne and some other man who made himself scarce immediately afterwards. They took you and the kids. So I followed them.'

'Are the children okay?'

'Only if we can get them away from here. I'll call Kate too. She can help.'

'What's going on, Brett? What are they doing?'

'They're Russians, Tiff. I think David's doing some deal over the children.'

Tiffany jumped up, the flow of adrenaline breaking through the debilitating effects of the drug.

'Stay down, Tiff. These people have guns. Whatever shit David's got involved in, it's serious. There's a big bag of money sitting on the ground by this woman's feet. It all sounds a bit tense. This is dangerous, Tiff; I suspect they're trying to sell the children for some illegal adoption racket.

It's crazy. This sort of thing doesn't go on in Morecambe. It doesn't happen to people like us.'

'We have to do something, Brett.'

'I'm trying. My car is parked along the road. I'm going to try to move the kids while they're all talking. If we can get the kids away safely, David and Joanne can look after themselves.'

'Help me out of here, Brett. I'm weak. Whatever they gave me has knocked me for six.'

'It's not safe, Tiff. If they see us, I don't know what they'll do.'

'We can't just sit here.'

Powerless to do anything, all she knew was that she wouldn't let her monster of a husband take her children.

'Look, Rowan is sound asleep, he's the easiest for me to take. He's on the side of the car furthest away from them—'

'We need to speak about Rowan, Brett.'

'Not now, Tiff. Let me take Rowan. If he wakes up, he'll be the most difficult to move. If he starts crying, we're done for. I'll call Kate when I'm back at my car and see if we can get some help. Trouble is, I don't know where we are. It's some woodland; I've never been here before. We're miles from anywhere.'

'Okay, you take Rowan and call Kate. I'm going to try to get my limbs moving properly. If we can transport Callie and Jane between us, we can make a run for it. Screw David and Joanne, they'll get what they deserve. Go.'

She listened as Brett made his way to the side of the car. The back door was open already, and she felt the gentle vibration through the bodywork of the car as he carefully moved it fully open.

'Come on, gorgeous,' Brett whispered.

In the darkness, she imagined Brett carrying their

sleeping baby, all the time whispering to him and cradling him gently. She'd never seen David be so caring, and now she knew her husband was the stuff of nightmares. He and his girlfriend had probably planned this all along. How could she have been so stupid?

She heard Callie speaking again.

'Where's man gone? Man! Man!'

Her daughter was treating it like a game of hide and seek. If she kept up the noise, she'd attract the attention of the Russians.

'Brett? Brett? Are you out there?'

No answer.

'Man! Where are you man?'

'Callie, darling, it's Mummy,' Tiffany whispered. 'Can you be nice and quiet like a good girl?'

'Mummy? Where Mummy?'

'Hush, Callie, nice and quiet now, my darling. Don't wake up Jane.'

Tiffany knew she had to move. She gently pushed up the lid of the boot until it was half open and raised her head, trying to get a sense of what was going on.

They were in a woodland clearing, as Brett had said, and a group of people had gathered some distance away, illuminated by the headlamps from two cars. One was the small run-around car. Joanne must have followed David from the village hall. She didn't recognise the other, a people carrier big enough to carry several passengers. She made out David's silhouetted form; she'd recognise his posture anywhere.

Joanne was next to him, she was taller than he was. She'd often wondered what it felt like for someone so controlling to be with a woman who towered over him.

Perhaps she'd got it all wrong; maybe Joanne was the strong one in their relationship.

There were four of the Russians, or whatever nationality they were: one woman and three men. There was a dispute; something about money. It always seemed to be about money.

Tiffany looked around for Brett but couldn't see or hear him.

'Callie wants Papa Smurf,' came the child's voice once again.

She had to move. Her legs felt like they were made of rag, but she and Brett had to make their escape with Jane and Callie. Then they'd be rid of David and Joanne for good. Her husband would rot in jail for what they were trying to do. She'd seen television programmes about the illegal adoption trade: children being taken in the night and sold to couples desperate to have children. Well, it wasn't happening to her family.

With a force of will, she pulled herself up and climbed out. She had to find the strength, however much the drugs had messed her up. The car was in complete darkness, some distance from where David and the others were standing. At least it gave them a small advantage.

The voices were getting heated, and Joanne seemed to be leading the altercation; David was taking a back seat. Was this her work? Had she come into their house like a cuckoo, determined to throw the babies over the side of the nest? Was she arguing over the price of her children? Tiffany felt nauseous at the thought. She could claw the woman's eyes out for it.

The voices were becoming increasingly tense as Tiffany opened the side door and leaned across Rowan's empty seat to touch Callie's hand. Only his small teddy bear toy remained.

'Mummy!' Callie exclaimed.

'Shh, be quiet, darling. We're going to play a game, sweetheart. We're going to hide somewhere, and we have to be really quiet. Is that okay?'

Jane stirred in the child seat next to Callie. Jane was a grumpy waker; she often heralded her presence with a whine. She would take Callie first and Brett would have to lift Jane. It was a delicate operation at the best of times, but at least the raised voices were offering some degree of cover for Callie's babbling.

Tiffany leaned over and gently unclipped Callie from her child seat, staying low. As she started to lift Callie out, she heard a shriek from Joanne. She froze, waiting to see what happened.

There was shouting, from David this time, and raised voices. Whatever language they were speaking, she could tell they were using expletives. Something had just happened; it had all become suddenly more intense.

Then, in the stillness of the New Year evening, a loud cracking sound filled the cold air. For a moment, Tiffany thought it was a firework, heralding the beginning of a new millennium. But from the panic in Joanne's voice, she knew exactly what it was; a gun had just been fired.

CHAPTER THIRTY-SEVEN

Charlotte looked up into the centre of the turbine. So Joanne Taylor was here. It was hardly surprising, after Callie and Jane's reappearance. Who else was still alive from 2000? It made perfect sense though; she'd suspected another player was involved in recent events, and here she was, one more ghost from the past.

Surely Joanne Taylor wasn't going to make her climb all the way up there, without safety gear?

'Can't you come down and we can sort this out on the ground?'

It was the worst system of communication ever, her words lost in the echoes along the long, hollow body of the structure.

'You know we can't. Vinnie Mace won't be far behind you. This has to be done here.'

Of course it does, Charlotte thought. She had to be mindful of Vinnie; he wouldn't be far behind.

'Do you have a weapon?' Charlotte called out.

'Just a baseball bat, courtesy of a recent visit to Kate Allan's house. You might have locked up her house after you left. That's how I figured out where she was hiding. That message from Sam Halford on the answer machine was all I needed. I know Sam of old—'

Charlotte cursed that she hadn't deleted the phone messages when she was snooping around Kate's house. If Joanne was on the scene twenty years ago, it made sense that she'd have known of Sam from back then.

'I only want to talk,' Joanne continued, 'these weapons are just for self-defence. Trust me, I'm the least of your problems compared to Vinnie Mace.'

Charlotte heard the slam of a car door out in the fields beyond the turbine. It had to be Vinnie. She looked across at the door; she'd pulled it to, so it would hopefully take him a little while to figure out which one they were in. Unless he got lucky the first time.

She looked up at the seemingly endless steel ladder. She only had plimsolls on her feet, and no harness, no gloves, no overalls and no Sam to encourage her along the way. Charlotte didn't know if she could do it.

Sam stirred at her side and she rushed over. He was groaning and rubbing his head, dazed and confused.

'Sam, it's Charlotte Grayson. Are you all right?'

'What the hell happened?' he mumbled, his speech slurred and hesitant.

'You've been hit, probably by a baseball bat. There's a dangerous man heading this way. We need to hide you over there, by the electrical kit.'

She pointed to the large, grey electrical unit into which the cables ran from the top of the turbine. It was out of the way, behind the ladder. If Sam could conceal himself there, he would be safe.

'Be careful, Charlotte,' Sam warned as she offered him her arm and he staggered to his feet. 'She's strong, and I didn't stand a chance. I was only up here to run a routine fault check; she ambushed me. Damn, my head feels sore.'

'Have you got your phone?' Charlotte asked.

'No.'

She paused to think it through. Kate had a mobile phone which could receive a signal at the top of the turbine. Sam was in a bad way; they should call an ambulance. But Joanne Taylor was back on the scene, a twist she hadn't anticipated at this late stage. Nothing about this affair surprised her now.

'Here, take my phone. Wait until the man who's following me has reached the first platform. Then call yourself an ambulance. The police will come, but don't tell them about me, please. I have to get Kate safely out of here—'

'Kate Summers? She took the spare key, didn't she?'

'Yes, it was her. She's been hiding here.'

'I didn't know. I thought I'd misplaced the keys, but I didn't say anything. I hoped they would turn up somewhere—'

'It's okay, Sam, it's not your fault.'

'Are you coming, Charlotte?'

Joanne's voice echoed from the top of the turbine.

'I want you to hear something from Kate. I want you to learn it from her first, not me. Then you can put it in your crappy newspaper and let everybody in Morecambe know the whole truth about what happened.'

Charlotte made sure Sam was as comfortable as possible, then moved round to the other side of the turbine's base to begin the climb, spurred on by the desperate wish to end it all. She knew how high it was and how terrifying it would be. But Kate was up there, and she needed Charlotte's help. She'd done it once, and she could do it again. Besides, if she wasn't at least one platform ahead of Vinnie, he'd get a clear shot at her with his gun. There was no alternative.

She began to climb.

'Don't look down,' Sam called over, his voice weak. 'Keep a firm grip at all times and face forward as you climb. You can do it, Charlotte.'

If only she shared Sam's confidence. However, without the boots, the goggles, the helmet, the harness and the gloves, she felt lighter and more agile. She could feel the narrow rungs through the flimsy soles and the direct touch of her hands gave the sensation of a firmer grip.

She repeated Sam's words in her head, looking ahead constantly, one hand and one foot moving at any one time. She climbed deliberately, pacing herself, aware there was a lot further to go.

'What happens to Vinnie Mace?' she called to Joanne, convinced they must be working together. Vinnie had claimed ignorance about the attempt on her life at Sunderland Point. Was Joanne after some different resolution?

'Let me worry about Vinnie Mace.'

'Did you try to kill me at Sunderland Point?'

'Just climb, Charlotte.'

She was surprised to reach the first platform in a short time. One moment a blur of ladder rungs passed before her eyes, and the next she was raising her head above the solid floor of the first platform.

A clunking sound echoed from below. At first, she wondered if it was Sam, then she realised it had to be Vinnie. He spoke and confirmed it.

'What's the plan, Charlotte? There's nowhere for either of you to go once you reach the top. We've got Will already.'

No, not Will. He got away, didn't he? There was only

one car following them, even Vinnie Mace couldn't be in two places at once. He must be bluffing.

'By the way, the bull is dead. It took four bullets to kill it. Which means I have three bullets remaining. One for you, one for Kate and a spare for whoever's up there with Kate. I don't have to shoot those bullets, Charlotte. I never needed to kill you, and we never wanted to murder you. We just need the documents.'

The undulations of his voice told her that he'd begun to climb. He would be faster and fitter. She had to keep going to stay a safe distance ahead of him.

There was a metallic clanging sound above her and something made her step out onto the platform to check what it was. A tin of something flew past her head, travelling at great speed down the central, open section of the turbine's base. She heard it as it struck the ground. What the hell was Joanne playing at?

'Dammit, Charlotte, you nearly had my head off!'

It was the first time she'd heard Vinnie rattled. What did he expect, that she would just give herself up for dead? Whoever had sent the tin flying down towards the bottom of the tower had done her a favour; it might make Vinnie a little more cautious and slow him down a bit.

She climbed back on the ladder and continued her ascent. This was the section where she'd frozen with fear the first time she'd made the climb. Sam's advice was good; it helped if she moved at a steady rate and didn't look down.

As she climbed, Charlotte continued to move her hands and feet in a well-coordinated sequence, making sure at least two parts of her body were always in contact with the ladder.

She was beginning to tire, aware of her calves burning and her arms aching. Vinnie's movements were so forceful that she could feel the vibration as he climbed the ladder. He wouldn't be far away from her now. As she sensed the second platform closing in above her, she became aware of movement below her, in her peripheral vision. He had reached the first platform and was continuing to the second.

Foolishly, she looked down. Her head began to spin and her legs weakened beneath her. If she wasn't careful, her sweating palms would slide off the rungs.

'I can see you, Charlotte. Stop at the next platform; we can still sort this out. Nobody has to die today.'

'And what about Tiffany?' Charlotte screamed at him. 'What happens to her?'

'Tiffany was a fool to herself. She should have cooperated with Fabian. She got what was coming to her—'

'No Vinnie, she didn't. She got what Fabian Armstrong decided to give her. It's clear she's the victim in all this, she and the children.'

Charlotte started climbing again, fuelled by anger. She forced herself onwards, pulling her body up the ladder with renewed strength. Her throat was dry and her heart pounded in her chest as if it might explode at any moment. She wasn't even sure what the plan was. All she knew was that she had to reach her friend. Tiffany was protected already, and now she had to do whatever it took to get Kate Summers safely away from there.

She was almost at the third and final platform. Joanne had gone quiet. Why? Was she lying in wait for Vinnie Mace? It would make sense.

As she pulled herself up above the third platform, she hesitated, wondering what might greet her there. She swallowed hard before looking.

Joanne Taylor was standing tall, athletic and imposing, blood dripping from her lip and a dark bruise under her left eye. It looked like she and Kate had already been in a fight. She was wearing the wedding ring that had been pictured in the newspaper cuttings. Charlotte now knew for certain she'd been in Callie's room in the ICU. Joanne had set off the smoke alarms. She had left the photographs of Kate and Brett for Callie to find.

'Welcome, Charlotte,' she said with a smile, her eyes focusing on something at the far side of the turbine's summit. Casually, she picked up a tin of soup from a small pile next to a rucksack and a small gas stove. Kate had come well-prepared for her exile in the steel structure. Joanne threw the tin through the hole in the platform where the ladder entered the upper section. Charlotte heard it clanging as it ricocheted off the rungs of the ladder below.

She stood up fully and followed Joanne's gaze. At the rear of the turbine, close to where Sam had opened the doors to allow her to take a look at the view of the bay beyond, Kate Summers was perched on a tool box, her mouth taped shut, and her wrists and ankles bound. She had her back to the dark oblivion beyond. The only thing between her and a fall that would kill her was one loose chain across the open mouth of the doorway. The remaining two chains had been unhooked at one end and discarded onto the steel floor. There was sheer terror in Kate's eyes, knowing all it would take for her to die was a gentle push from Joanne Taylor.

'Now, it's time for you to hear a few home truths from your friend,' Joanne began. 'Did she ever tell you that she and her brother killed David Irwin?'

CHAPTER THIRTY-EIGHT

'Tell me what this is about,' Charlotte said. She looked over at Kate again, not knowing what to do. Kate was clearly petrified, so close to the edge of the open doors that an involuntary leg movement would be enough to send her flying over the edge. Although she was signalling with her eyes, Charlotte didn't understand what she was trying to convey.

'I've waited twenty years for this moment; twenty years to flush these rats out of their sewers and send them all to hell where they belong. And I want the money that was cheated from us all those years ago.'

'What did Kate do?'

Charlotte was mindful Vinnie was still on his way up, if he hadn't been struck by one of the tins already.

'She and that brother of hers killed David Irwin on the night of the new millennium—'

'That's ridiculous. I know Kate, she wouldn't do that.'

Joanne stormed towards Kate.

'No!' Charlotte shouted.

Joanne tore the tape from Kate's mouth. She was so tall that she had to lower her head in the confined maintenance area. It was clear now that she must have set off the fire alarms in the hospital and contacted Callie and Hollie out of the blue to bring them back into the open. But why?

'Tell her!'

Kate looked directly at Charlotte, but she was still unable to figure out what she was trying to tell her.

'I tried to save David Irwin that night. My brother, Brett, risked his life to save him. David was dead well before Brett reached Morecambe. He died because Fabian Armstrong crossed you. You got caught up with some dangerous men, Joanne; you were out of your depth. You and David brought that upon yourselves—'

'Shut up!' Joanne screamed at her. She looked unhinged, her eyes full of fire. Kate would need to keep her calm if there was any chance of getting out of there alive.

'I told Brett not to drive off with David,' Joanne said. 'He wouldn't listen to me. He refused to take me in his car. He went running to his big sister and between the two of you, you killed him and disposed of the body. I saw you in the papers, Kate. First on the scene? You were there before anybody else because you were covering your tracks.'

Charlotte's attention was diverted. Where was Vinnie? Joanne knew he was making his way up. He had a gun too.

'Was it you that emailed Hollie? And Callie too?' she asked. She was desperate to understand how it all slotted together. Perhaps, after all, Joanne was working with Vinnie.

'Of course it was me who contacted the girls,' Joanne answered. 'You're a bit slow on the uptake, Charlotte. It's Jane to me, of course, not Hollie. I also slipped a photo of Hollie into your husband's pocket at the university cash machine too. Weren't you even slightly suspicious about him, Charlotte?'

Charlotte was angry with herself for doubting Will. This woman must have been watching them, waiting for her to lead her to Kate Summers, seeding doubt in her mind to confuse her. So, Vinnie and Fabian hadn't caused all the problems. There were two parties involved here, and they both seemed to be after a different thing. Judging from the contempt in Joanne's eyes, she was here to settle a score or two.

'You're like a cat with nine lives, by the way, and persistent too. Most people would have called it a day after having a brick put through their window and a petrol bomb hurled at their workplace. You should have kept out of the way. I didn't want to harm you, but you kept sticking your nose in, speaking to Evan Farrish and trying to unearth the truth about a case that the police had lost interest in years ago.'

'So it was you who hit me at the causeway? Why?'

Joanne laughed like a maniac on the edge of sanity. It was as if she'd wished for this moment for so many years, and now it had come, she was unable to process it properly.

'Yes, I've been following you for some time. If it hadn't been for that fisherman coming along in his tractor in the nick of time, I'd have got both you and Kate at the same time. Imagine it, both of you found drowned at the causeway; it would have been poetic justice for Kate. As for you, you're like a dog with a bone. I'd have expected you to back off a long time ago. You're a pain in the neck, if truth be told. I just needed you out of the way in case you and your friend on the paper exposed me. It was nothing personal.'

Joanne stopped talking, picked up the baseball bat and walked casually over towards the hole in the floor where the ladder emerged. She concealed herself in the shadow of the turbine's machinery. As Vinnie's head began to emerge, his gun at the ready, Joanne waited at his rear, the baseball bat poised in her hand. Vinnie's eyes were on Charlotte, the gun trained upon her.

'Where is she?' Vinnie asked.

Joanne was completely calm, allowing him to get halfway into the area before she stepped out of the shadows and took one violent swipe at his hand, sending the gun flying across the chamber. The sound of wood against bone made Charlotte flinch.

Vinnie cursed as the gun slid across the steel floor towards Kate's bound feet. The shock of it made her lurch backwards, and for a split-second Charlotte thought she was going to topple out into the darkness. Kate forced her body forwards, changing her centre of gravity, and somehow managed to stabilise herself.

Joanne took a second swipe at Vinnie, this time striking his head. He'd managed to climb high enough up the ladder to land on the floor of the upper chamber as he took the full impact of the blow, his body crumpling.

'We'll get to Vinnie Mace in a moment,' Joanne said, walking confidently over to the gun, picking it up and holding it to Kate's head.

'I don't know much about guns,' she continued, casually waving it about as she spoke.

'For instance, if I pull the trigger now, is the safety even on? Let's give it a try—'

She placed the gun at Kate's temple and her finger tensed on the trigger. Kate's eyes were scrunched tightly shut.

'No!' Charlotte cried.

The gun did not fire.

'The safety must be on,' Joanne said with a laugh. 'Best take it off then.'

She did something to the gun, placing the baseball bat at Kate's side to free up a hand.

Charlotte decided to keep her talking. 'What do you want, Joanne?' she said, 'You realise this is over now, surely?'

'Well, it is for you and your friend here. Now the incriminating documents have been retrieved, you've done what I needed you to do. You two are no longer required.'

'What about Vinnie?'

'Once I've finished with you two, Vinnie and I are going to make a little deal. Were you aware Tiffany Irwin was the sole heir for the land? Her mother cut Fabian out of the picture because she reckoned he was ill. And by ill, I mean mentally ill. And did you know Fabian and David hatched a deal to force Tiffany out of the picture and conceal the truth about the will? Now you've found the crucial documents, it gives me all the leverage I need to take what's rightfully mine... Or what would have been rightfully mine if this bitch and her brother hadn't killed David—'

'I told you, Joanne, Fabian had David killed. You're lucky Brett saved you.'

Kate was using a softer tone now. Charlotte thought she was wise, considering the fanatical look on Joanne's face, which suggested the past twenty years had been building to this moment. Kate's face was ashen with fear and her eyes were fixed on Vinnie Mace.

'We tried to save David. In spite of all he'd done to hurt Tiffany, my brother still tried to save his life. I had blood on my hands that night from trying to stop the bleeding. But Brett was wasting his time. David was dead before my brother even put him in his car.'

'You're a liar!' Joanne shouted. 'And you even denied me a funeral—'

Kate was signalling to Charlotte with her eyes once again, but Charlotte just wasn't getting it. Kate continued to distract Joanne in her calm voice.

'Brett had to get rid of the body. He was covered in David's blood. The babies had disappeared into the night. Fabian had tried to kill his own sister on the sea front, making it look like a suicide attempt. For God's sake, the man is a monster, you must see that. You and Brett were lucky to escape with your lives that night—'

Joanne was moving towards Vinnie now, gun at the ready, and at last Charlotte saw what Kate had been trying to tell her. A small kitchen knife was tucked under Kate's rucksack. She'd brought enough items to survive in the turbine for a couple of days. The thought of having to carry anything on her back up the endless ladder made Charlotte cringe.

She looked at Kate to indicate she'd spotted the knife. Kate had an urgent look in her eyes, watching Vinnie, who had begun to come round from the blow to his head.

Joanne pointed the gun at him.

'I want you to crawl towards Kate over there,' she commanded.

'You don't have to do this, Joanne,' Vinnie urged. 'Fabian will make a deal. Now the initial lease is up on the turbines, he's getting this land re-designated for industrial use. It's going to be worth a fortune. He'll cut you in. We both want the same thing; the original will has to be destroyed along with the psychological reports confirming Tiffany's sanity. Once they're gone, Tiffany loses any power she might have retained.'

'Walk over to the doors and make a video call to Fabian,' Joanne demanded. 'I want him to see where you are.'

Vinnie crawled over to Kate then stood up at her side

and pulled his phone from his pocket. His head was bleeding; he'd received quite a wound.

'Call him!'

Kate caught Charlotte's glance. Joanne and Vinnie were distracted. Swiftly, she knelt and took the knife from underneath the rucksack, tucking it into her back pocket.

Joanne caught the movement in the corner of her eye.

'Stand over there by your friend!' she shouted at Charlotte. 'Get where I can see you.'

There were three bullets in the gun, according to Vinnie. One for each of them. And now the safety catch was off, so the next time anyone pulled the trigger, somebody would be shot.

As Charlotte inched towards the open doors of the turbine, she saw the headlamps of a vehicle below. Was it the police? Had Will come back for her? She couldn't tell. But it was a long way down and she and Kate seemed to have little bargaining power left.

Fabian's voice came over Vinnie's phone, set to the speaker.

'Remember me, Fabian? It's Joanne Taylor, back from the dead.'

'Joanne?' his voice came over the speaker, calm and in control. 'Vinnie?'

'It's her,' he confirmed.

'I've done your work for you. I have Charlotte Grayson here and Kate Allan. We need to talk business. Kate has led Charlotte to the paperwork now. I just need to be certain of my cut.'

Fabian was completely cool on the end of the phone.

'Sure, Joanne, you and David were always part of the arrangement. Until Kate Allan killed David, that is.'

He was lying, Charlotte was certain of it.

'Do you have the paperwork with you?' Fabian asked.

'Charlotte has it. Or more likely her husband does,' Vinnie replied.

'That's fine,' Fabian answered, 'we're good. We have someone watching the son's rented place now, I'll tell him to go in and start roughing them up a bit—'

'No!' Charlotte shouted. 'I'll tell you where everything is. Call Will now, and he can collect the documents. That's if you were bluffing about holding him captive already. Don't hurt the children.'

She prayed Olli and Lucia had taken their advice and gone to the Travelodge for the night. They'd be safe that way.

'Do we need Kate Allan now?' Joanne asked.

'I think we're done with her,' Fabian replied.

'Good, at last. See ya, Kate!'

Joanne strode up to Kate and raised her foot to kick her off the end of the platform. Joanne was so tall, she narrowly missed striking her head on a vent pipe which ran along the ceiling. Charlotte saw her chance. With Joanne on one foot now, Charlotte drew the knife from her pocket and launched herself at her. Joanne tried to compensate but was off balance. She struck her head on the pipework, dropping the gun onto the steel floor. Kate pushed herself forward to fall on her face, away from the edge of the platform. Charlotte sliced the tape around Kate's hands, dropped the knife and reached out for the discarded baseball bat.

Vinnie was fast, letting his phone drop to the ground as he leapt over Kate's crumpled form to make a grab for the gun. In a single move, he took the handle of the gun, rolled over, pointed it at Joanne and shot her twice through the head.

Joanne didn't even see it coming. She lurched backwards towards the open doors at the back of the turbine. Charlotte grabbed the baseball bat and ran at Vinnie, copying Joanne's move to knock the gun out of his hand.

But he was too agile and already up on his feet. He pointed the gun at Charlotte.

'I've had enough of you,' he said coldly. 'But I'm not wasting the last bullet on you.' He raised the gun and shot Kate Summers in the thigh. She gasped with the pain and shock. It was all Charlotte could do not to scream. With Joanne's body bleeding out on the floor and Kate in excruciating pain, she heard Fabian's voice come over the phone.

'Got it all in hand Vinnie?'

'But of course,' he replied, wiping the gun thoroughly on his shirt. He pulled the trigger again, but his bullet count was correct. The weapon was empty. He put his foot on Kate's wounded leg, pressed down hard and grabbed her hand, placing the gun in it and ensuring her fingers gripped it hard enough to leave prints. He then kicked the gun out of the back of the turbine into the air and turned to Charlotte.

She was poised with the baseball bat, waiting for her move. He lunged at her, fearless and confident, and she swiped the bat, but he simply grabbed it in mid-flight and threw it to the ground.

'I'm sick to death of you, Charlotte Grayson. Just so you know, we're going to do whatever we have to do to your kids to get those documents from your husband. We're aware he's heading for Lancaster; we have a tracker on your phones—'

'But we removed those.'

'Silly woman. You removed one of them. You don't think I'm stupid enough to leave them both on the main screen of your phone, do you?'

'Oh,' was all Charlotte could say, feeling wretched at being duped so easily. No wonder they hadn't been able to shake him off.

'Will won't make it to his destination, I'm afraid. We've got everything we need from you now, Charlotte. Cheerio.'

With the sure arrogance of an accomplished killer, Vinnie grasped Charlotte by her neck, lifted her up off the floor and threw her towards the open doors of the turbine, as if she was an old rag doll which was no longer needed.

CHAPTER THIRTY-NINE

December 1999

As soon as Brett heard the gunshot, he ended his call to Kate. His heart pounded like a hammer in a steelworks plant as he made his way back to Tiffany and David's car, keeping his head down all the time.

Tiffany was up ahead, lying still and silent on the ground, and the passenger door was still open. He swallowed hard.

Glancing across at the group of people in the distance who were illuminated by the headlamps in the clearing, he could hear Joanne screaming hysterically. David was on the floor and the other men were shouting. He would have to move fast to get his new family out of there. *His family.* He liked the sound of that.

Checking the coast was clear, he darted across from the undergrowth where he'd been taking cover and moved closer to Tiffany.

'Oh, thank God, Brett, we've got to get the children out of here—'

In among the shouting and confusion, Brett had tuned out Callie's crying. She'd been startled by the gunshot and was looking for her mum. She was leaning forward in the child seat, hovering over the footwell. If she toppled over...

'We need to take him to hospital, you bastards!' Joanne shouted.

The men were laughing and goading her. Whatever the deal was between them, it sounded like the terms had just changed.

'We have to get the kids out now,' Brett urged Tiffany.

Jane had been woken by the sound of the gunfire and the shouting, and was beginning to stir, half attempting to go back to sleep, half moaning that she'd been disturbed.

'Callie, darling, Mummy's got you.'

'Can you take both girls to my car?' Brett asked.

'Why, where are you going?'

'To help David—'

'No, Brett. Whatever Joanne and David did, they made their bed, and they have to lie in it. They've got our runaround car over there; they can drive themselves to hospital.'

Brett looked over to the increasingly tense scene by the other vehicles. Even at that distance, he could tell Joanne was pushing her luck. David was rolling on the ground, screaming in pain.

'We can't leave him like that.'

'The children, Brett, they're the most important—'

'He's your husband, Tiffany. You must have felt something for him at one time?'

'Those feelings are long gone. I don't owe him anything.'

'But Rowan. He's Rowan's father.'

'Haven't you figured it out yet, you fool? You're Rowan's father.'

'But I can't be—'

A rush of confusion swept over Brett. It was too much to deal with at one time.

'Brett, you're his father. If you look under the box of family photographs in your storage unit, you'll find all the proof you need. I left it there to keep it safe. I hid some other documents there too, to pick up before we leave tonight.'

She saw that her handbag was still in the front of the car. She took out the plane tickets and handed them to him.

'These are open tickets to Australia. Kate has the passports already in the envelope I gave you. We have everything we need to get away.'

'But... when? How?'

'I was going to tell you. Tonight. Before we left Morecambe. I had it all planned. I wanted to see your face, knowing we had a new life ahead of us and that you were a father. We can still have it, Brett. But we have to move now.'

Another gunshot sounded out and Joanne screamed again. Brett saw her stagger backwards, holding her leg, shouting out every expletive in the book.

'You lying bastards, we had a deal. We had a fucking deal, you morons—'

One of the men walked over and struck her with the end of his gun.

'Mr Armstrong says screw your deal.'

Joanne dropped to the ground like a brick, out cold. David began to beg for their lives, grovelling while struggling through the pain of his wound.

The woman who was with them picked up the money bag and started to walk back to the Russians' vehicle.

'I want you to take Callie and Jane over to my car,' Brett whispered. 'Strap them into the child seats and have the engine running. Don't put the lights on. If you can pull off the road a little further, do it. I'll come back for you; I promise.'

'Brett, please, don't—'

'I can't leave him to die, Tiffany. I can't leave Joanne here wounded. We can't start our new life together like this. I have to do the right thing, to help David and Joanne.'

One of the Russian men kicked David in the face and he too crumpled on the ground. The woman had returned from the large people carrier with a fuel can. She opened the doors of the runaround and began to douse it with petrol. The men walked over to David, took his arms and legs and began to move him towards the vehicle.

Tiffany had both girls now, carrying a mithering Jane in her arms while Callie walked beside her.

'Get to the car,' Brett urged. 'Stay out of sight; I'll be with you as soon as I can.'

'I love you,' Tiffany said.

'I love you too, Tiff. I can't wait to spend the rest of our lives together.'

Tiffany rushed over to the cover of the bushes. Brett followed her, then moved off towards the cars, using the undergrowth to keep him concealed. He levelled up with the parked vehicles. David had been piled into the runaround and was slumped over the steering wheel. Joanne was being moved to the seat beside him. It was obvious what was being planned. He counted the Russian figures, moving around the car. He'd lost one; only the woman and two of the men remained.

The woman lit a match and set fire to the petrol trail leading to the runaround. It was all Brett could do not to shout out when the flame rushed towards the vehicle. The three of them turned around as if it was an everyday occur-rence, getting into their own car, starting the engine and driving towards the road. Weren't they planning to take the children?

As the Russians' car changed direction and moved towards Tiffany's vehicle, Brett broke cover and ran towards the flames. They were already towering above him, the fierce heat holding him back. He had to reach David and Joanne before the fuel tank went up; it could explode at any moment.

Brett covered his face with his sleeve and ran towards Joanne, pulling her out of the passenger seat. She groaned, blood trickling down her face where she'd been struck. Brett pulled her into the bushes, then returned for David.

The flames were now making their way across the front fascia and his trousers were beginning to smoke. As Brett lunged forward to grab David under the arms, he felt the wetness of the wound where he'd been shot. His side was a mess of torn flesh. Brett panicked. The steel of the car was so hot now, it was creaking from the expansion. He pulled David's dead weight from the car seat, dragging him across the rough ground and into the cover of the undergrowth. As he sat on the earth to catch his breath, the fire hit the fuel tank and the car exploded, sending out a deadly flare so sudden it made him duck.

'I'm going to get help,' he said to Joanne, who was now semi-conscious. 'If I take David to my sister, Kate, she'll know exactly what to do.'

'You bastard. If it wasn't for you, none of this would have happened.'

'What?' Brett said, incredulous. 'I just saved your lives.'

'You wasted your time, Rambo. You and Tiffany are

over, whether you like it or not. Fabian has taken care of it. You don't get to see in the new year, whatever happens. You've screwed this up big time. Fabian is going to be really fed up with you now.'

'It was Fabian who wanted you killed,' Brett protested. 'Even I could see that from where I was hiding.'

Brett ducked and instinctively pushed Joanne to the ground as the beams of a car's headlamps swept over their heads. Tiffany's car was in motion too, being spun around in the clearing. In the rush to save David and Joanne, he'd forgotten to check the whereabouts of the Russians. As the first car completed its turn and the second passed in front of them, he screamed out as he saw Tiffany's lifeless form slumped in the back seat. The third man, who Brett had lost track of, was driving Tiffany's car. Callie and Jane were in their car seats in the back.

'I've got to follow them. They've got Tiffany.'

'They're gone, you idiot. This is not the sort of job Fabian gets some local knuckle-dragger in a Morecambe pub to carry out. These Russians are professionals. They'll get you sooner or later. You're a dead man, Brett. You should never have got involved in Fabian's business.'

'I have to follow them.'

Brett ran towards where he'd parked his car. The headlamps were still off, just as he'd left it. Had Tiffany even made it as far as the car? He rushed up to the rear window; Rowan was gone. They'd got Rowan, his son.

Then, in the silence of the night, he heard a gurgle from the boot of the car. He rushed to open it up. Rowan was there, wriggling out from underneath a blanket that he kept there for emergencies. Tiffany must have hidden him. She'd chosen to save one of her children, the son he had fathered.

They were all his children, as far as he was concerned.

When he met Tiffany, they came as a package, and he loved them all.

He had to follow them, to alert Kate and get the police involved. There was no way out of it. He secured Rowan in the baby seat they'd bought for their escape, climbed into his car, started the engine, then moved around to where David and Tiffany's second car was swiftly becoming a burnt-out metal carcass.

'Help me with David,' he cried to Joanne.

'You're not taking him. Fabian will kill him now. He's useless to them.'

'I have to get him to a hospital—'

'They'll kill him, you fool.'

Brett looked at Joanne's wound. She was hurt and bleeding, but in nowhere near as much danger as David. He moved to lift David, but Joanne tried to pull him away, screaming hysterically that Fabian would finish him and she was his best hope. Brett's only chance of helping Tiffany was to follow the Russians along the country lane before he lost them. At this time of night, he could follow their head-lamps in the darkness. Once they hit the main roads, they'd be gone.

Even as he moved his hand towards Joanne, he despised himself for what he was doing. But they were out of options, so he had to go; he couldn't stand there arguing with her. He pushed her, and she fell to the ground. Returning to David, whose clothing was now drenched in blood, Brett lifted him by the armpits and bundled him into the passenger seat, resting him on the blanket Rowan had been concealed in, to absorb the blood.

He drove off, his mind a confusion of a million ques-tions without answers. Would Joanne survive out there? Could he save David and get to Tiffany and the children in time? He floored the accelerator, aware there was so little time left now, throwing the car around the corners of the winding lanes as if he were auditioning on a rally track.

Soon enough, he picked up two headlamp beams way up ahead. He switched to sidelights, not wanting to alert them to his presence. If they'd missed Rowan, they couldn't have found his car. Maybe they'd decided to settle for the two children, bearing in mind the car was burning in the middle of nowhere and it might be spotted. Tiffany must have sacrificed herself and the girls to save Rowan. There was no other explanation. She'd saved his son.

Brett kept at a safe distance until they joined a main road, then tucked himself behind them at a safe distance. The roads were deserted; everyone was getting ready to celebrate the new millennium. As he drove, he used one hand to dial Kate on his mobile phone. She answered immediately.

'Brett?'

'They've shot David, Kate. They've taken Tiff and the girls. What do I do? What do I do, Kate?'

'Where are you Brett?'

'Just coming into Morecambe now.'

'I'm on the promenade, Brett. Near Woolworths. I'll wait in the arcade next to the Winter Gardens. Come to me.'

As Brett tailed the cars along the promenade, he watched as they turned off at the abandoned Midland Hotel. What were they going to do there? Torn for a moment, he hesitated. They had a gun. He was out of his depth. Kate would help. Kate would know what to do. Kate always knew what to do for the best.

With every sinew in his body wanting to follow Tiffany,

he drove on past the decaying hotel and pulled up opposite the dark arcade at the side of the Winter Gardens.

Kate rushed out to him, dressed in her civilian clothes. Brett looked at his watch; this was the time they were supposed to meet. Only it was meant to be different.

His sister rushed around to the passenger side of the car, her hands checking the lifeless body of Tiffany's husband.

'Oh my God, he's dead, Brett. He's already dead. What happened? Where are the children? Where is Tiffany?'

'Joanne said they want to kill us and sell the children for adoption. There were Russians there. I didn't know what to do, Kate—'

He broke down in tears, out of answers, not knowing what to do for the best. As he sobbed, he sensed a calmness coming over his sister; he'd witnessed it once before, when the police officers came around to the house to tell them their father was dead. She was taking control.

'Brett, I want you to take the baby and David's body, and hide—'

'But... Tiffany and the girls... they were taking them to the promenade, Kate. I don't know what's going to happen.'

'I'll handle it, Brett. I'll get Tiffany and the children. David is dead; you can't help him now. We must do our best for Tiffany and the girls. Trust me, Brett. I'll get to Tiffany and call my colleagues. I'll get them to safety where Fabian can't touch them. But you must hide, Brett, in case they come to you. I'll work it out, Brett. I'll figure something out. Now go!'

'But where shall I hide?'

'Somewhere out of the way where nobody will see you. Remember the place we discovered in the summer? Sunderland Point? Nobody lives out there. Find a place to hide the car and lie low. I'll get to you. Take the envelope from my mailbox, like we discussed. You'll need your documents. Keep your mobile phone on. Now go! Go, Brett.'

Brett drove off, watching his sister in his wing mirror as he did so. As she grew smaller in the distance, he watched as she calmly returned to the darkness of the arcade, carefully wiping the blood from her hands.

A cascade of coloured streamers shot out across the table as the gathered friends let out a cheer and a spontaneous round of applause to celebrate Charlotte and Kate's arrival. The two women smiled, and Charlotte hugged her family members, but it was overwhelming and, on consideration, a little too soon.

Charlotte lifted a glass of bubbly with her still-bandaged hand and made a toast.

'To good friends and lucky escapes!'

Laughter and cheering filled the room as glasses were raised.

Charlotte and Kate were late for a reason. It was the first chance they'd had to talk properly since the events which had rocked their lives. They'd met up at a nearby pub prior to joining the group, keen to set things straight before getting caught up in the celebrations.

'You got away with just a bandage then,' Kate remarked as the two women embraced at the entrance to the pub. This was only the second time they'd hugged like this; the first time had been at the edge of the wind turbine as they'd sobbed together, relieved at having escaped with their lives.

'The chain burned my skin as I tried to get hold of it. It's still incredibly sore, but it'll heal. Cream and bandages aren't a bad price to pay considering what happened.'

Kate wiped a tear from her eye, and they ordered soft drinks. They exchanged small talk until they'd found a quiet corner away from anybody else where they could speak freely.

'So, where are you up to with your job?' Charlotte asked. 'Do you still have one?'

Kate sighed, more weary than Charlotte had ever seen her.

'Yes, just about, after the misconduct panel. I was saved by mitigating circumstances and the overall outcome of the case. I'm going to get a written warning that will stay on my record. The Chief Constable called me in. This is off the record, by the way—'

'Of course, Kate. This is between you and me now. There was nothing else you could do. You did your best.'

'He basically said I did a superb job in exposing what Fabian and Vinnie were up to. But the historical error I made over concealing David Irwin's death had to be noted on my record. He acknowledged I was a rookie copper at the time and that I was disciplined back in 2000 for disappearing for three days, but that my career has been exemplary since then. He's made it go away, but he let me know how difficult it was for him to pull it off. It'll always be there lurking on my personnel file, but I can go back to my desk at the beginning of next month. The suspension on full pay will continue until then.'

'I'm so pleased, Kate; it was the right decision. You saved my life up there. It's been constantly on my mind, and

I'm still not sure how we made it out alive. I thought I was a goner after Vinnie threw me out towards the rear of the wind turbine. I've never felt a scarier sensation in my life; when I did the tandem skydive, at least I was strapped onto something.'

They sat in silence, replaying the events in their minds.

'Oh,' Charlotte said, remembering something else she had to thank Kate for, 'the digital forensics people confirmed that the pornography Vinnie placed on our computers won't be a problem for us. They've taken away our devices as evidence, but we're not under any suspicion. That was a nasty trick. So was the haul taken from the doctor's house to frame the kids. Doctor Henderson isn't pressing any charges, he backed away completely. I'm not sure what will happen to him now.'

Kate looked down at her drink.

'Can I trust you with a secret, Charlotte?' she asked. 'This must stay between you and me. But I have to tell someone, after all the secrets I've been concealing.'

'It's safe with me, Kate. You saved my life; I owe you everything.'

'Vinnie didn't fall. I pushed him off the edge—'

Charlotte gasped.

'I haven't admitted it in my official report. But the man was too damn strong, and he'd shot me. I told them he tripped over Joanne's body. I was too sore and weak to fight him. Besides, we were right on the edge of the turbine. I was watching your grip loosen on the chain, and it was Vinnie or us; I chose Vinnie. The man wouldn't have stopped until he'd finished us off.'

'I heard the thud as he hit the concrete at the bottom of the turbine,' Charlotte began, 'it wasn't a nice way to go.'

She paused, the image of Vinnie's final moments still vivid in her mind.

'I have a secret too,' Charlotte continued.

'Charlotte, I know. I figured it out on my own a year ago. Why do you think I'm telling you this now? I realised you and Will were involved in Bruce Craven's final hours much more than you ever admitted. It's fine; he got what was coming to him, just like Vinnie did. Sometimes we have to make decisions that most people will never have to confront in their lives. I'm comfortable with mine. I suspect you and Will know you didn't really have any other choice with Bruce. We're all honest people; the guilt we'll carry with us is punishment enough.'

'I won't say a thing,' Charlotte said, after replaying the events in her head. Kate was right; it must have been a split-second decision. When Vinnie had pushed her out of the top of the turbine, she'd heard the swish of the blades outside. He'd not quite hurled her far enough, so she was able to grasp for something to hold on to. One of the chains that had protected her at the top of the turbine on her first climb with Sam Halford had saved her from Vinnie Mace. It had all happened so quickly.

'Is there any way an investigations team can tell exactly what happened up there?' Charlotte asked. 'They have specialist crime scene people who can figure these things out, don't they?'

'You and I are the only witnesses left, Charlotte. Joanne's body was still in the position where Vinnie had shot her. You saw how he got my prints on the gun and was trying to set it up as a triangle between the three of us. As for his fall... well, he probably died as soon as he hit the ground. It's fine, Charlotte; he's dead and we're safe. Fabian Armstrong has been charged with a list as long as your arm:

fraud, unlawful imprisonment, intimidation, murder, illegal weapons use... you name it, it's probably on the list somewhere.'

'Will he end up in prison?' Charlotte asked. She already knew enough about men like Fabian Armstrong. They got thugs like Vinnie Mace to do their dirty work and expensive lawyers to take care of anybody who dared to challenge them.

'I'm certain he will, eventually. He's not a well-liked man. They'll need to build a case against him and make sure it's watertight, but his head will roll, I'm certain of it. So, what news do you have for me? How are Tiffany and the kids?'

Charlotte didn't know where to start. So much had happened since that night.

'Well, Tiffany can't join us at the meal this evening; she's still in a bad way. But she's getting the treatment she needs now. It'll be a long haul for her to recover; you don't spend your life tranquilised and get to walk away like it never happened. She's addicted, I think. The poor woman lost so many years.'

'What about the girls?' Kate asked.

'They seem good now. Joanne Taylor had set Hollie up. She'd spent years and years tracking the kids down. She probably couldn't believe her luck that Hollie had gone to university in Lancaster. She created a connection between Hollie and Will, to get to me and you. Hollie's a good kid. She's confused by it all, but Joanne had convinced her you were to blame for all the secrets in her life. She was trying to do the same to Callie too, but she fell into police hands before Joanne could get her claws into her. It's lucky Callie came to me when she fled from the hospital. Joanne was completely screwed up by what had happened in the past. I'm not sure we'll ever know the full truth.'

'It was a mess then, and it's still a mess,' said Kate, shaking her head again. 'Joanne was confirmed as Evan Farrish's killer, by the way. She'd planted evidence from my house at the scene to make them suspect me. I'm not sure why she killed Evan. I suspect he may have recognised her and threatened to inform the police. We can't tell for sure though, not with both of them dead. You saw the look in her eyes; she was crazy for revenge. Poor Evan. I hope I don't end up that way when I retire.'

'He was a good guy; he didn't deserve it,' Charlotte agreed.

Kate sighed. 'It's those kids I feel sorry for. What a terrible start to life.'

'Well, we managed to save the original will and testament covering Tiffany's inheritance of the land, thanks to you and your information about Brett's container,' Charlotte said, smiling. 'At least Tiffany can prove it's all hers now. Fabian got their father to make a new will. He knew about the original but kept quiet about it once they'd had Tiffany committed. What a brother. I wouldn't fancy having to unpick that legal knot.'

'Neither would I,' Kate agreed. 'It's going to take some sorting by the sound of it. But with Hollie's DNA test confirming her identity as Jane, it's only a matter of time until the kids and Tiffany get what's due to them. There'll be an investigation into the adoption of the children twenty years ago. From the parents' point of view, it seems they believed it to be a legal and legitimate arrangement. The paperwork was forged. They paid a lot of money to a private agency to adopt those children. I hope there are no charges pressed; it would destroy the children.'

'So, what of Brett?' Charlotte asked, after mulling over Kate's words. 'What happened to him? It's the only part of the story that seems unresolved.'

Kate smiled, looking as if she'd been bursting to share the news.

'I've been in contact with him, but I couldn't tell anybody. As far as the authorities are concerned, he died at Sunderland Point, though as his only next of kin, I'd never asked them to declare him dead.'

Her eyes brimmed with tears.

'He's alive, Charlotte. He reached out to me when he read about Callie being found. He saw it on the internet. That's when he told me about the documents in the container. He's been living in Australia for twenty years, raising Rowan on his own. He still feels like a fugitive and won't dare show his face while Fabian Armstrong is still alive. I'm travelling to Australia next month for a reunion with him. I'm not telling anybody until I can be certain he won't get into trouble with the UK justice system. I still don't know who the bad apple is among my police colleagues, so I'm playing my cards close to my chest for now.'

'Will he come back to the UK? What about Tiffany?'

'There's too much water under the bridge to say,' Kate answered. 'But Rowan was their child, so he'll possibly come back to the UK when she's well enough. Only if it's safe for him, though. I guess they might pick it up from there. Until then, Brett and I are getting to know each other again over Skype. I feel so angry about the time we lost. I thought he was dead, Charlotte.'

The two women hugged again, reluctant to leave for the celebration meal until they'd worked through everything.

'What happened during the three days you went AWOL from the police, Kate? Were you protecting Brett?'

'He was hiding out at Sunderland Point with Rowan. I took food to him, as well as nappies and milk for the baby. We were young and scared, Charlotte; we didn't know what to do. Then, one day, I woke to the news that they'd found the car on the slipway. Like everybody else, I assumed Brett was dead. David's body had vanished, Joanne had disappeared into the night, and Brett and Rowan were gone too. When I spoke to Brett on Skype, he told me he'd put David's body in his car so it would be washed out to sea. He hoped it would clean the blood off the car, so the police wouldn't think he'd killed David. He was so scared, Charlotte. But he protected me. He knew he had to disappear to keep Rowan and me safe. The whole thing was just a big mess.'

Charlotte reached out and squeezed Kate's arm.

'We'd best get to this party,' Charlotte said, standing up and checking the time on her phone. 'I've been promising the staff a night out for weeks. It's the least I can do after all the shifts they've been covering for me. Shall we go?'

Kate stood up and picked up her bag.

'Let's do this.'

Although the get-together was a little overwhelming for Charlotte, it was long overdue. As she pulled the streamers out of her hair and looked around the table at all the smiling faces, she reflected on the people who'd come into their lives since returning to Morecambe.

There were several copies of The Bay View Weekly on the table, the biggest selling edition ever printed. She and Nigel had shared the front page byline and Teddy had been ecstatic at the national attention their reporting had received. Any issues around police complaints, stolen jetskis and damaged company vehicles swiftly faded away after that.

George and Isla were there, getting on well with everybody, but looking much older now. It was unfair to ask Isla to keep working at the guest house; she deserved to retire.

Olli, Lucia and Willow had formed a little gang, and they'd gravitated to Callie and Hollie by virtue of their ages, along with Piper and Agnieszka.

Will and Nigel were chatting away about some funny news story or other. She wouldn't have wanted it any other way, knowing she owed all these people a debt; they'd been through so much together. She'd put her husband through quite enough to last one lifetime already.

As Charlotte sat there, watching and enjoying everybody's happiness, she noticed Kate was similarly quiet and reflective. It was impossible to go through what they'd been through without it affecting their lives.

Kate smiled at her as if she knew what Charlotte was thinking. Change was coming. For all of them.

The third and final Morecambe Bay Trilogy is available now in paperback and e-book formats. Start reading First To Die today.

AUTHOR NOTES

Phew, what a close call for Charlotte once again. I reckon she deserves a break after all that action.

I hope you enjoyed reading the conclusion of this second Morecambe Bay Trilogy as much as I enjoyed writing it. The good news is that there is one final trilogy remaining for Charlotte and her friends. The last three books of the series will bring together all the characters you've met across the series and you'll find out what happens to them.

I came up with a massive shock plot twist for the third and final trilogy in the middle of writing this set of books, so I can't wait to get to work on this new story and weave that big surprise into a new plot. I can tease ahead a little though, to give you a hint that DCI Kate Summers and Charlotte will be working closely together in this new adventure.

You'd think they'd have had enough of each other after their recent exploits. But in the next book, the two friends will stumble across a clue as to who was responsible for the death of Kate's father all those years ago.

That's all I'm saying for now, but as you'd expect, it'll be non-stop suspense, twists and turns plus the usual array of deadly situations for Charlotte.

So, Bound By Blood finally tied together all the loose ends set up in Trust Me Once and Fall From Grace. Many people write to me saying they knew so-and-so did it early on in a trilogy, but the truth is, I usually don't commit to the final plot outcome until I'm writing the third book, so even I'm not sure who it is until I'm forced to choose a particular character by the plot. I like to set up all sorts of possibilities and then choose a final course of action as late as possible in my writing.

For instance, David Irwin was going to be alive, until I wrote the scene in Bound By Blood where Kate has blood on her hands in one of the scenes set in 1999. I decided then that David dying would give Joanne Taylor her motivation for revenge. There was also a possibility of Rowan's role being very different, making him one of the baddies alongside Joanne, but I liked the idea of him and Brett making a life together in Australia and giving Kate Summers a happy ending. I believe she deserves it.

The legal situation Tiffany is caught up in is not unlike that of Britney Spears, whose father secured control over her estate after her own highly publicised breakdown. Despite her efforts to regain control, she has been unable to at the time of writing. Tiffany's dilemma is not too dissimilar, though in her case, her evil brother does not have her best interests at heart.

The final scene at the top of the wind turbine was always going to form the ending of the last book in this trilogy. Having been to the top of one of those structures and looked out of the open doors at the top across the open landscape whilst working for the BBC, it was simply too good a dramatic opportunity to miss.

As I was writing the scenes where Brett is packing his items into container storage, and Will and Charlotte are breaking into it twenty years later, I was packing my own belongings away too. We moved to Spain for the winter of 2020, so it was useful for me to gain first-hand knowledge of how it all works. I was packing my own gear away one day, then writing all about it the next. I won't be leaving my container abandoned for two decades, but many storage units do get left for years.

Sunderland Point has served as a rich environment for this trilogy and I'm so pleased my wife and I spent a day scouting locations and re-familiarising ourselves with the area.

By the way, did you spot a baddie from another book making a fleeting guest appearance? Vinnie mentions his friend Kyle who helps with the unpleasant end of the business from time-to-time. Kyle is a central figure in my stand-alone thriller *So Many Lies*. If you want to find out what bespoke services Kyle supplies to the local criminal fraternity, give it a read. And if you've read the book already, you'll never look at a meat pie the same way again!

I'll tease you for the final trilogy by saying we spent a day in and around Morecambe prior to departing for Spain, where I came across a couple of superb locations to use in the final story. I lived in Lancaster for many years and had never heard of these places before, let alone visited them, but once again, the seaside landscape will provide me with some excellent material for my psychological thrillers.

If you haven't read it already, do check out my Don't Tell Meg trilogy, which is set in the same geographical area of the UK and which introduces Steven Terry and DCI Kate Summers for the first time.

The best place to find out about my writing is at https://paulteague.net.

A final word about the fictional nature of these trilogies.

Although I do set in them in real-life locations and make the settings as accurate as possible, I do sometimes have to bend the facts a little to fit the story.

So if you find yourself thinking that something is not quite right about one of the locations used, remember that I'm writing fiction and not local history books, an occasional flexing of the truth is required as an author to make the story work better.

Oh, and just for complete clarity, absolutely everything in these stories is made up, it bears no resemblance to real people or situations.

Paul Teague

FREE GIFT

Are you enjoying the second Morecambe Bay Trilogy?
You can now access an exclusive gift showing you many of
the locations used in the book, with many amazing
photographs of Sunderland Point.

Grab your FREE copy of Charlotte's Sunderland Point
Scrapbook ...

This downloadable scrapbook will show you all the key
locations used in the second trilogy.
You'll get to see what Sunderland Point looks like as well as
several other key locations, such as Happy Mount Park,
Hest Bank, Lancaster University and the stone graves at
Heysham.

**To grab your copy head for
https://paulteague.net/SB2 on your PC.**

ALSO BY PAUL J. TEAGUE

Morecambe Bay Trilogy 1

Book 1 - Left For Dead

Book 2 - Circle of Lies

Book 3 - Truth Be Told

Morecambe Bay Trilogy 2

Book 4 - Trust Me Once

Book 5 - Fall From Grace

Book 6 - Bound By Blood

Morecambe Bay Trilogy 3

Book 7 - First To Die

Book 8 - Nothing To Lose

Book 9 - Last To Tell

Note: The Morecambe Bay trilogies are best read in the order shown above.

Don't Tell Meg Trilogy

Features DCI Kate Summers and Steven Terry.

Book 1 - Don't Tell Meg

Book 2 - The Murder Place

Book 3 - The Forgotten Children

Standalone Thrillers

Dead of Night

One Last Chance

No More Secrets

So Many Lies

Two Years After

Friends Who Lie

Now You See Her

ABOUT THE AUTHOR

Hi, I'm Paul Teague, the author of the Morecambe Bay series and the Don't Tell Meg trilogy, as well as several other standalone psychological thrillers such as One Last Chance, Dead of Night and No More Secrets.

I'm a former broadcaster and journalist with the BBC, but I have also worked as a primary school teacher, a disc jockey, a shopkeeper, a waiter and a sales rep.

I've read thrillers all my life, starting with Enid Blyton's Famous Five series as a child, then graduating to James Hadley Chase, Harlan Coben, Linwood Barclay and Mark Edwards.

Let's get connected!
https://paulteague.net

www.ingramcontent.com/pod-product-compliance
Lightning Source LLC
Chambersburg PA
CBHW021135110726
47900CB00002B/366